Academy Days: Compilation

Dasha Tryon Wallace

Dasha Writes
LLC

Contents

Year One

I wondered if I would ever become the spy my mother was, because in the beginning, all I ever seemed to do was fail.

Arabella Cooper "Cinders"
Report 3 Paragraph 1

Chapter One

London, England

May 1826

Ella looked one last time at the image of her mother before leaving the Hall of Legacies to the training room. After the quiet of the portrait room, it was odd to hear the clash of metal and thump of someone being thrown to a mat, all accompanied by the chime of teacups and chatter. Ella watched in awe as excitement and nervousness filled her. It was overwhelming. It had only been a few minutes before when she had been told that the academy doubled as a secret society and that her mother had been a part of it. She had been left alone with the portrait of her mother, and now she had no clue what to do.

She looked to the mats and saw that two different girls were sparring but were in no mood to speak to her. Though Ella itched to go talk to them and ask them to show her some moves, she knew not to interrupt them. The others on the opposite side from where the girls were sparring were all talking amongst themselves and didn't notice her. Feeling very much her fourteen years, she shuffled from side to side.

Just when she was going to walk over to the ladies at the tables, a girl popped up next to her. She beamed, "Hello, are you the new girl?

Ella instantly took a step backward, biting her tongue to keep from squeaking in surprise. She hadn't heard her come up beside her.

The girl with honey-brown hair giggled at her reaction. She had been one of the girls who appeared as a servant one moment, then was with the nobles the next. Now that she was closer, Ella could see that they were about the same age. Her familiar green eyes were bright. And she had a perpetual smile on her round face, adding to the glint in her eyes.

"I'm Eleanor Taylor, but you can just call me Eleanor since we will be working together," she continued, holding her hand out in greeting. Ella didn't know what to make of this overly perky girl.

"I—" Ella started to answer Eleanor but was interrupted by a different girl speaking nearby.

"I've seen her around the servants' quarters. How could she be trained to be a Guardian when she doesn't have any noble blood?"

The girl that had just spoken was instantly recognizable. She stood off to the side, arms folded. Her dark hair was smoothed back into a high bun, completely different from Ella's frizzy brown hair that had already fallen out of the bun that Clementine had put it in this morning. Her sharp features held a very recognizable expression: a penetrating glare. The girl with the glare was who had started her on the oddities around the academy. And already, she was getting on her nerves. This was just like being back with her stepmother, always talking about bloodlines. Ella had not been invited to join this secret society only to turn around and be bullied in the same breath as she used to be. This would be different.

"I believe I also saw you washing windows in the mornings. Who are you, anyway?"

The girl's cheeks flushed red as she said, "My name is Luella Jones, and I was cleaning for class to get used to being undercover."

"Well, you did a poor job of it. Anyone could tell that you didn't know your duties. Looks like you need to go to class again."

"That is enough, Lady Cooper." During the exchange, Madame Briar had come up behind them, and with a few words, stopped the argument before it began. "Lady Taylor and Lady Jones, please go to class. I need to speak with Lady Cooper."

The snooty girl was instantly cowed and turned on her heel to head to where the others were having tea. Eleanor smiled at her, then followed.

Madame Briar looked down at Ella and raised her eyebrow. "Making friends already?"

Ella blushed. How this woman could make her feel like an errant child was beyond her. The headmistress motioned for her to follow. And Ella did while sneaking glances at the fighters; this time, instead of a fan and a dagger, they were dueling with a chain and a parasol. Ella had to tear her eyes away as she trailed Madam Briar down another corridor. Unlike the dark hallway that led into the walls, this one was well illuminated by the golden glow of sconces.

There were only a few turns until they arrived at a door at the end of the corridor. Madame Briar opened the door and led Ella into the hidden office, her green day dress swooshing. It should have looked out of place down here in a secret chamber, but for some reason, it didn't.

Compared to the immaculate office of the headmistress, this was simple, with a solid desk and no decorations. The only ornamentation was a symbol carved into the wall. It was a circle of eyes with an open fan in the center and a crown on top.

The headmistress explained, "That is the symbol of the fan society." Ella turned to Madame Briar, who had moved to sit at the desk and motioned for her to sit.

Ella hurried to comply as she asked, "What does it mean?"

"The eyes represent observation. We watch and set observers in the nobility to hunt for signs of danger. But should the need arise, the fan is to remind us that we have weapons of our own. The crown on top is to remind us who we are doing this for. To protect the royal line and save England."

This is what my mother did, Ella thought proudly, but then a question crossed her mind that she couldn't help but ask aloud, "Was my father a part of the Fan Society?"

She shook her head with a smile. "No, we are a society of ladies, though we do have some supporters who are men. Your father was your mother's mission."

"What?"

"We have observers set among nobility called Guardians who are set to get close to someone important in society."

Ella furrowed her brows. "But my father wasn't important. He didn't even have noble blood. My mother did."

"Times have been changing due to the Industrial Revolution. The nobility are no longer the only ones with power. With the Industrial Revolution, more opportunities had arisen. Your father became a rather successful businessman at a young age due to this. And since the balance of power was changing due to nobility, to those with money, we needed someone to help keep an eye on the new power coming up. Your mother was one of those."

A sickening feeling landed in the pit of her stomach. "Did my mother really love him?"

Madame Briar raised her brow. "So your real question comes to light. Yes, your mother did love him." The confusion must have been readable since Madame Briar laughed. "We said to keep them close; we don't always mean marriage."

A blush suffused Ella's cheeks. She had known that most marriages in nobility were business ventures, but what little she remembered from her parents was a loving relationship. And after her mother's disappearance, the sorrow that her father had endured broke her heart. If her mother had been lying to him, it would have devastated her.

"But you have time to think about it," Madame Briar said, interrupting her thoughts. "For now, you should be worried about what you are learning here. The girls here are the best of the best. You will have to learn many different things ranging from how to distract while still being undercover, to picking locks and defense."

Anticipation made Ella want to bounce in her seat as her thoughts drifted to the girls who had been sparing. "As part of the Fan Society, do we do a lot of fighting?"

Letting out a small chuckle, Madame Briar answered, "It depends on where you are placed and where your talents lie. Though, you aren't a member yet."

Her excitement deflated a little at her confusion. "Then why am I here?"

"You are here to learn. Every year, there is a test you must pass for you to continue your training here, as well as a mission. They are trials to prepare you before you get thrown out to the savages of society where one wrong move could be devastating."

Ella nodded in understanding, her mind turning to images of her stepmother and her ruthlessness.

With a twitch of her lips, Madame Briar pulled a ring from her finger and showed it to Ella. It was a signet ring, and the insignia bore a striking resemblance to the Fan Society's symbol.

"After you have completed your first mission, provided you have passed all of your school years, you will be officially recognized as a member of the Fan Society," Madame Briar said as Ella handed the ring back to her.

"Did my mother have one of them?"

"Of course, dear."

Pride filled her at the thought of her mother being a part of this. The golden signet ring resting back on Madame Briar's hand pulled at her. She would receive a ring of her own, just like her mother. "What do I need to do?"

Another smile graced Madame Briar's lips as Ella hung on to every word Madame Briar said.

Chapter Two

Thoughts swirled in Ella's mind as she walked back to her room. Madam Briar had told her many things, but one of the biggest was to keep everything a secret. That meant lying to the one person she had always promised she wouldn't lie to: Clementine. And considering they shared the same room, it would be difficult to avoid her, even if she wanted to. The turmoil of her thoughts did little to help her decide on what to do, and the walk back to their room felt far too short.

Hesitating before her door, she took a deep breath and opened it. Almost instantly, a blur came toward her before squeezing her in a hug.

Ella gasped, "I need to breathe, Clementine."

Her friend held her for a few more seconds before finally releasing her. Then she proceeded to look her up and down to see if anything was wrong. Ella sighed and let her. Clementine was a few years older than her and was the closest thing to family she had left, and she knew that Clementine was only worrying about the punishment she should have received. Not that she could tell her that Madame Briar had taken her in to be part of a secret society instead of punishing her.

"Alright, enough, Clementine. I'm fine," Ella said, sitting on her bed.

With a sniff, Clementine sat on hers. "Those vicious women had you been punished for that brat of a girl. I ought to . . ."

Ella listened to her friend ramble about Ella's stepsisters, the initial cause of the ruckus. As she sat on the bed and badmouthed Audrey and Effie, people would be surprised by the words coming out of her mouth. With her innocent looks and perfect acting skills and her name meaning mild and merciful, it was hard to believe Clementine was anything but.

Ella couldn't help but laugh at her words, "What were you going to do?"

"I was going to talk to Mary, who knows a guy who's a server who would be willing to put in dirty water in their wine, and put in this thing in their meal which would make them spend the day in the bathroom," Clementine said with a satisfied smile on her face as she pulled a container of herbs from her skirts.

"I am not going to ask where you got that, and remind me to never get on your bad side. For now, we need to just leave them be. It would do me no good to get into trouble right after that fiasco at lunch." Ella made a face.

"Did you get a punishment? It was Effie's fault for tying the tablecloth to your apron," Clementine insisted with a sniff, anger still burning in her eyes.

"Yes. I am to be sent to the stables to muck stalls, and then I have an hour of the headmistress personally taking care of me," the first lie spilled from Ella's lips, and a dark feeling began growing in the pit of her stomach. Though, it wasn't really a lie; Madame Briar *was* going to send her to the stables. Only, it wouldn't be for stable work.

"How can they make you do stable work? You haven't even trained in that." The pain and anger Clementine showed on her behalf made Ella feel even more guilty for lying to her. Since Clementine was not part of the Fan Society yet, she could not know about what she was doing. And what Ella had said was what others would know about. Hopefully, soon she could be part of them, but for now, she was not allowed to speak to her about such matters.

She could feel the words she wanted to say sitting on the tip of her tongue, but she swallowed them. Instead, she put on a forced smile and said, "The academy has that much power and history. It can do what it wants within these walls. Not even the king can say much about how the academy is run. But I will do what I've always done and do my best. What else can I do?"

"Of course. We will get through this like we always have. Together." Clementine nudged Ella's shoulder for encouragement, then stood to get ready for bed.

"Yes, of course. Together." Guilt weighed on Ella's mind as she realized that this would only be the first lie she would have to tell her friend. And it would not be the last.

Making her way to the headmistress's office, excitement buzzed at Ella's fingertips. The dark feeling she had felt last night was diminished by the thought of her first class of spy training. As she passed by various servants, she couldn't help but wonder if any of them were a part of the Fan Society as well.

As she stepped up the headmistress's door, she knocked. The door opened to reveal a servant. Curiosity burned within her as she entered.

"Close the door, Mary," Madame Briar called, and the servant complied.

The office still reminded her of subdued elegance, what with its beautiful cherry oak desk and two massive paintings that dominated either side of the room. One of King George the IV and the other who Ella now knew was the founder of the academy and the secret society, Queen Jane. The young queen was dressed in the typical wide skirts and hair covering of the 16th century. Her eyes seemed to hold mysteries untold and on her hand was a gold ring.

Sitting, framed by two windows with her grey hair lit by the morning light, Madame Briar waited until the door was firmly shut. She raised her hand, motioning for her to sit, and nodded to the servant who let her in. In the moments it took to get to the desk, the servant had ghosted out of the room, and *not* through the painting that she had gone through previously to enter the walls.

"You have much to learn and not a lot of time to learn it. The other girls have had many more years of training than you."

"How can they have many more years than me? You can't get into the academy until you are fourteen years old. I'm only a couple of months late," Ella said, confusion bleeding into her voice. The academy was still one of the top schools for training young ladies of society, as well as the best servants. But they only accepted certain ladies at the age of fourteen.

Raising her eyebrow at the interruption, Madame Briar replied, "Don't interrupt, dear. And yes, you are correct about entering the academy, but all of the girls were also trained from a young age to be proper ladies, and due to your unfortunate circumstances, you did not. If you want to be a part of society, you must be able to play the part or at least understand the rules. I would not have any graduates from my school be seen as regular riffraff."

"But what about the . . ." Hesitating, Ella didn't know if she was allowed to mention the Fan Society in this room. Madame Briar waited for her, her expression never changing, but Ella could feel the weight of it. Clamping her mouth shut, Ella stopped her question before it could be finished.

With a twitch of her lips and a tilt of her head, Madame Briar showed her approval when Ella stopped. "Now, we have a lot to get done. First, we need to start with proper greetings. The gentlemen must always greet first. If it is between ladies, the one of lower status gives her greeting first. When you do, you must . . ."

For the next hour, Ella sat in silence as her excitement of learning spy stuff drained and was replaced by the drone of Madame Briar lecturing her on proper greetings. The only interjections were when she spit out rapid-fire questions to make sure she was listening. That hour drained her more than laundry day ever could, and it was still morning.

"And that will be all from me for today." At Madame Briar's words, relief spread through Ella until she added, "Now, head off to the stables. They are expecting you. I told you yesterday where to go."

She was about to open her mouth to comment but thought better of it. "Yes, Madame."

Leaving the office, Ella headed to the stables. As she walked, Ella could only feel disheartened at what she was supposed to learn. But it was not going to get to her. She would eventually have to learn about spycraft; this was just a beginner class. And since she was being sent to the stables, it had to have something to do with learning how to be a spy. She wasn't just sending her there to muck stalls, was she?

Stepping out into the chilly morning air, she hurried out of the shadows of the massive academy and into the warm sun. Ella looked back at the old building, at its weathered stones turned gray with age. The stately structure sat there with its many windows reflecting the late morning light. If only people knew what was hidden inside those walls.

With a quick turn, Ella moved at a brisk pace to reach the stables. The cold winter still kept its grip as she moved to pass the large carriage house. Then she stood shifting from foot to foot.

Nervousness caused mere seconds to feel like years as she waited for the person who was to tell her what to do. A young stable boy soon came up to her; with polish on his cheek and straw in his hair, he waved over to her. His hair was pulled up in random spikes and was damp for some reason, and his face made him look like he was perpetually sleepy.

"Sorry I took so long; had to finish polishing the leather. Well, come on then," the boy said, rubbing his finger across his cheek, making the black smudge darker.

Ella followed behind him, curious about what she would be doing. She had never had much interaction with horses, as her stepmother never really enjoyed horse riding. Said it made her smell too much. Ella wondered if she needed to change into riding skirts as she brushed the apron of her servant's uniform.

The boy took her down the cobblestone walkway that was wide enough to drive a carriage through. He began pointing at each of the horses and started rattling off names. Ella barely had time to look at the horses' heads that popped up over the half-doors as she had to trot to keep up with him.

Then he came to a sudden stop in front of a stall near the end of the aisle. "This is Lady Gray. She ain't got no other name, but you will help me take care of her," he said, patting her mane with a gentle touch.

The horse leaned over and nibbled on his hair, causing yet another spike to be made in his already messy locks.

He then turned, noticing that she hadn't moved. "Well, come on. She ain't going to bite," he said as Ella stared at the horse lipping at his hair like it was brown grass.

The horses were much bigger than she expected, not that she was scared of heights. It was more that it was a living, breathing creature that could easily run you over if it wanted to. And there would be nothing you could do about it.

"You can touch her." When Ella didn't move, the boy grabbed her hand and placed it on the horse's neck. It shifted beneath her hand, snorting. With a jerk, she pulled back. The boy laughed. "Come on, today you will be helping me with gear. We have a lot to go through."

She followed behind him, and soon they entered the tack room. He kicked at the scattered straw on the floor as he took his place on one of the wooden benches. "Now, you sit over there. I want you to look at all the pieces of leather and check for tears or places where the leather is cracking. If there is anything amiss, show it to me, alright?"

Ella looked around at the mass of harnesses and halters dangling from hooks that covered the wall. She got that sinking feeling in the pit of her stomach. "And are we supposed to do *all* of this?"

The boy laughed, handing her a bridle and getting to work on polishing a saddle.

The girl is great at coming up with solutions on the fly and is capable of coming up with an response that sounds educated even if she doesn't know the answer. She will have to get over her fear of horses, though. There is much that she must catch up on. It will be hard work. We shall see if she can handle it. And we need to keep an eye on Clementine. It seems that she might be coming on sooner than expected.

Madame Briar
Progress Report 3, Year 1825-1826

Chapter Three

After spending an hour in the tack room, Ella had finally learned that the stable boy's name was William. That was after she had learned what each strap of leather was for and what each horse's habits where and which horse was his favorite. But she was not allowed to tell the horse that or she would get too prideful. By the time she had made it back, it was time to get ready for lunch. When she entered, the cook took one look at her and said she was not allowed to step one foot into his kitchen.

Ella couldn't blame him. Her fingers were blackened from the polish William was using, and her hair had managed to catch every piece of straw that was everywhere. Her shoes smelled of manure, and she was covered in dirt. She had to rush since she would get points taken off if she was late to lunch duty. Plucking the straw from her hair, she hurried to get a bucket of water to wash her hands. In her haste, she went down the wrong hallway and straight into someone she didn't want to see.

"What is that smell?" It was the beautiful Audrey, fanning her face to blow away the stench. Her floral day dress and pristine features always made Ella look haggard in comparison. Her light blue eyes and baby doll face gave her an innocent look, which Ella knew was a farce. The way she glowered at Ella she was a muddy dog who had crossed her path.

"It is just like Ella to get in the way. I'm surprised she was even allowed in with such a stench," Effie chimed in, face hidden behind a fan. Like a shadow for her sister with her dark brown hair and broader features which were much more plain and homely. It made her seem like everything good was heaped upon Audrey while Effie had to take whatever was left over. And though she didn't get the looks, Ella knew that she had intelligence behind those icy eyes.

Dropping to a curtsy, she said, "Hello, stepsisters. I apologize for my appearance. I was doing my punishment in the stables."

"Oh? I didn't realize that you looked any different. I always thought that you were always rolling around in the dirt. Anyways, begone. You don't belong here. Mother is coming soon; it would make her ill if she had to see you so soon after the incident. I still have stains on that dress from the food you dropped," Audrey said, then with a wrinkle to her nose, asked, "What is that smell? Is that from rolling around in the stables? Jenny, go bring me my perfume. I must get something to remove this stench."

The shadow that was totting along behind them moved forward. It was Jenny their housemaid who didn't even react to the debacle before her. Her dark hazel eyes and long flat nose were not pretty, but she always did her job without a fuss. Every noble had a maid, and her stepmother must have sent her because of her daughters' personalities.

Ella bit her tongue to keep back a retort. Already late, she didn't want to get into an argument that would only lead to getting herself punished. Jenny would always be on her stepsisters' side.

Keeping her head bowed, she replied, "As you wish."

As she walked down the hallway, she could still feel Effie's cold glare on the back of her neck. She was going to cause problems. With a sigh, Ella trudged outside to the water pump by the stables to get a bucket of water to scrub her hands to remove as much of the black grease from her fingers as she could. Then she headed to her room to change out of her uniform into a new one. She was going to be late.

And late she was. The clamor of the kitchen could be heard before she entered. She tried to head to get the plates ready without anyone noticing in the lunchtime hustle, but it was going to be one of *those* days.

One of the servants who was working as a scullery maid chimed to the girl next to her, "Who does she think she is arriving late? I can't believe that they are allowing her to stay here after all the messes that she has caused. Isn't that right, Clementine?"

"Of course. I am surprised that they haven't done more to her."

Ella ignored the comment. It allowed her to get information. Because of the previous circumstances of her home life, Clementine acted like she hated Ella. This had been agreed upon between them years ago back at the manor. She knew that Clementine didn't mean any of it, but it still hurt to hear.

With a sigh, Ella got the dishes ready for plating as the girls continued to gossip behind her back. And after getting everything ready, the girls all made sure that there was not enough time for Ella to eat lunch.

Stomach growling, she finished out the long day and made her way back to the room she shared with Clementine. Clementine was already there pulling out some finger food she had managed to flinch from lunch.

Clementine had learned not to apologize for what she needed to do and instead helped take off Ella's shoes while Ella ate.

"You look exhausted. What did they make you do in the stables?" Clementine asked, wrinkling her nose and sticking Ella's shoes into the far corner.

Slowly chewing to give herself some time to come up with something to tell her, Ella shrugged. She swallowed. "I was lectured for an hour, then asked questions about how bad I was at things. Then in the stables, I was taking care of the bridals for the horses."

A frown formed on Clementine's face. She knew that Ella wasn't telling her everything, but Ella couldn't do anything about it.

"It was worse than that, wasn't it?" Clementine questioned.

"No. It's not like that."

"Are they bullying you?"

Ella sighed. "No."

"Are you sure? Then why are you lying to me?"

"I'm not." She was, and she hated it.

"Didn't we agree that we would be honest with each other? I can't help you if you keep things from me," Clementine said. Guilt rose within Ella again. She *was* keeping a secret. A very big secret. After promising never to keep things from her, she had to do it so soon after making that promise. It made her sick. "Why won't you tell me anything?"

"Because it's not for me to tell!" Ella snapped, then turned around and got ready for bed.

It was difficult to ignore Clementine, but it was the only thing she could do. Already, her classes involved stable work, she ran into her stepsisters, and she had to keep things from her friend.

It was a horrible end to an already horrible day. And the week was just getting started.

The week continued with lessons on etiquette and, in the stables, how to interact with a horse. On three separate occasions, her stepsisters had found her in between her getting cleaned up. And none of that was compared to how her relationship with Clementine was going. They didn't talk to each other, Clementine played her part of hating Ella and gave her food for lunch, but after that, they didn't talk. When they got to their rooms in the evenings, they each just went to bed. It was stifling.

And things did not get better from there.

After the first week of lessons on etiquette, Madame Briar gave Ella a paper with information on a person and told her to memorize it. "What is this for?"

"That is for your next lesson. I think you are capable of starting some of the *extra* classes."

Ella understood. This would be her first time beginning spy work. Finally, something good after the last week.

You will be the adopted daughter of Baron Smith. You were born a commoner, but most suspect that you are the illegitimate daughter of the baron. They do have an heir to the family, so most people are confused as to why he would adopt a girl. You know little about society. The secret that you are to keep on you is . . .

Character Sheet for Arabella Cooper "Ella"
Paragraph 3

Chapter Four

T he next day, when Ella entered the headmistress's office, Madame Briar moved towards the portrait of Queen Jane. "Right here," she said, showing Ella a flower on the side of the ornate frame. She pressed it, and it clicked, releasing its hold from the wall and swinging open.

The headmistress motioned for her to go through, but Ella hesitated.

She asked, "Are you not coming with me?"

"Not, this time."

Ella swallowed her nerves and stepped into the dark passage. As soon as she walked over the threshold, the door shut behind her, leaving her in darkness.

It had only been a week, but living in the shadows of a secret society was something she had to get used to.

She took a deep breath and pressed her fingers to the smooth stone wall, following it forward. The passage felt far longer without Madame Briar, and Ella worried that she might have missed a secret passage that she had to take. Then she saw the light of the room ahead. Relief swept over her as she picked up her pace, and excitement replaced some of her nervousness.

This was going to be the day she started doing spycraft. And after this past week, this was sure to be worth it.

The light revealed a large open room with training pads on one side and a tea party set up on the other, one that she had been to before. Walking down the stairs to the floor of the room, Ella looked around, trying to figure out what she needed to do. Eleanor, the bubbly girl from the week before, came over.

An easy smile grew on Ella's face. At least someone would be on her side. After the discord between her and Clementine, it was nice to see a friendly face.

"Over here. We need to get you changed," Eleanor said, guiding her behind the screens that separated the tea area and the space behind it. Behind were racks of various clothes and several vanity tables that held makeup and other assortments of jewelry and hairpins. "I will help you for the time being until you get used to it, but you will eventually have to do this on your own or with your servant's help. I guess you don't have a servant yet, but Madame Briar knows what she is doing. What is your character?"

The girl had started rambling and Ella was flooded with information. "Huh? Oh, um." Ella tried to remember her answer. "I am a newly adopted daughter of a baron."

Eleanor nodded, humming to herself as she went to the rack of clothes, picking out a dress and then going to work helping her into it.

"I can do it myself," Ella insisted, her cheeks flushing as she tried to pull away. She had always gotten dressed alone since her stepmother sentenced her to life as a servant.

Sighing, she started helping again. "No, you can't. Unlike servants' dresses, dresses of nobility need some help getting on. And besides, you don't have a lot of time to get ready, and it's faster with help. And you will have to pose as a noblewoman someday, so you are going to have to get used to it. Normally, we would have to do more elaborate hair, but we do not have time, and with your character, you should be fine. Just one last thing."

Eleanor walked over to the vanity and shifted through hat boxes that had been stacked in front of the vanity that Ella hadn't noticed before, then placed a flowery bonnet on her head, tying its silky ribbon in a neat bow beneath her chin.

Ella felt like she was playing dress-up. The dress was of much nicer fabric than the normal cotton she wore, but it was still a simple design. A white- and red-striped dress with long sleeves and a small puff on her shoulders. It was an empire-waisted dress tied with a thick red ribbon that was ruffled at the bottom. Her frizzy hair was still a mess; a few tendrils had escaped and amassed about her face like a cotton ball beneath the hat. It didn't quite fit her, the dress was just a little too big, her hair was out of control, and her skin too tan to fit with a dress like this. All in all, it looked like she was a younger sister trying on her older sister's dress.

Turning to Eleanor, Ella asked, "Are you sure I look fine?"

Raising an eyebrow, she gave a critical eye over her work. "For your character, yes. Oh, I almost forgot. Here. You cannot be part of the Fan Society without a fan."

She handed her a white lacey fan, which was just a normal fan, not like the ones Ella had seen the week before that they were fighting with. "Alright. Thank you for helping me."

With a broad grin, Eleanor gave her a gentle push towards the table. "Now, welcome to the war zone."

"Wait, what?" Ella asked, but she was already heading towards the tables and greeting the other members. Nerves were starting to get the better of her, and a longing for Clementine to be a part of this tugged at her heart. But now was not the time to be thinking about this. The test started now.

She took a deep breath and tried to recall everything from her character sheet as she ambled towards the circle of tables. There were only a few round tables with about twelve ladies sitting. A few she recognized from when she first arrived at the academy,

25

such as Luella. Seeing all the looks that made her feel like she had just flashed her ankles, she naturally headed toward the one person who had been nice to her.

Eleanor was seated with a petite blonde-haired girl and an older woman who had grey sprinkled throughout her hair. They were chatting until she came to the table. Then the rosy-cheeked blonde turned to Eleanor, "What is she doing near here? I can't believe they allowed a backwater country girl like her in."

A shock of betrayal ran through her as Eleanor replied, "She is rather new. We shouldn't expect too much out of her."

Ella felt betrayed by Eleanor. Was her kindness just a farce? Eleanor gave her a smile behind her fan as she leaned conspiratorially towards the girl to her right, "I heard that she was adopted. The baron was desperate for a girl, and no one knows why."

Then it came to her. She had forgotten what her character was. Ella was playing the part of a lowly adopted daughter. Looking closer at their dresses, Ella could tell that they fit perfectly and in dresses that were more up to date than what she wore. A few had broaches that had gems on them, while she had no jewelry. Now looking at it from that, Eleanor was acting just like a noble of higher rank would.

Ella sighed, learning that being in the academy was a sink or swim mentality. Letting her nerves show in her smile, she headed to the table. "Hello, it is a pleasure to meet you all. My name is. . ."

Rolling her eyes, the blonde-haired girl turned her petite nose at her. "It is not a pleasure to meet someone as rude as you."

"I agree," Eleanor said, turning to look at her. "I would never want to talk to someone who hasn't even greeted the host yet. It's like she never learned her manners."

Ella flushed a real flush, like the feelings of the character she was playing had collided with her real feelings. Stuttering, she took a step back, "I-I'm sorry. But could you tell me who the host is?"

The older woman had sat with her fan covering her face as she watched the proceedings. When she finally decided to talk, her words were measured. They balanced between condescending and being polite. Just like her stepmother would speak when she believed herself to be above the person she was talking to. "Now girls, she doesn't seem to know what she is doing. Let's help this poor thing. Dear, that is the host of the party. Now, move along," she said, waving her fan in front of her face as if shooing a bug away.

"Thank you, Madame," Ella said, remembering her etiquette lessons, then turning to the lady she was pointing to. Any excitement that she still had disappeared. The lady that was the host of the party was Luella.

Already, Ella knew how this conversation was going to go down. With a sigh, she headed towards her. It was better to get this over now.

Ella strode over to Luella. She was dressed in a ruffled dress that was white and had pink flowers on it. Her dark brown hair was tucked up into a bonnet that was covered in flowers. It looked like garden fairies came and placed her as their queen. She was talking to a few other ladies at her table until she saw Ella walk up to her.

Ella already disliked her. The expression that Luella wore looked exactly like her stepmother's. But her position was still one where she couldn't do much about it.

"My name is Lady Smith. It is an honor to be here." This time, Ella remembered her "character" name as she gave her greeting.

The look of complete superiority was still there as she said, "Yes. Now, be seated. The tea is about to be poured."

Anger built within her as yet again she was snubbed. And all she could do was smile and go to where she was seated. After learning about her mother and the Fan Society, she had thought things might change, and yet, though her clothes had changed, her situation hadn't. And now Clementine didn't even talk to her.

In her anger, Ella didn't see that the rug had been flipped up. Her foot caught on the rug, sending her crashing down onto the table, spilling porcelain cups into shattered fragments onto the floor.

Ella felt her face flush red as people dressed in servants' outfits rushed to pick up the pieces. Those who were at the party looked down at her and sniffed in disgust as they whispered amongst themselves while giving her looks. Ella could only sit on the floor surrounded by shards of porcelain, unable to leave because of the sharp pieces and servants who encircled her. By the time they helped her up and the mess was taken care of, she had to hurry and get ready for her work at the stables.

The debacle of the tea party weighed on Ella's mind as she made her way to the stables. She was so lost in thought that she hadn't even realized when she had arrived. William was waiting, and as soon as he caught sight of her, he dragged her to the stables, whistling.

"Can you please let go?" Ella asked, trying not to stumble.

He looked back at her, then quickly let go. "Oh, sorry. I'm just excited."

"What are you excited about?"

"You shall see." He smiled, then returned to whistling as they headed to the tack room.

Ella sighed, back to taking care of tack. At least she couldn't screw this up as she did at the tea party. As she headed to her seat, she was stopped, and instead, he checked to see if anyone was looking. Then he went to the back of the room and pressed down one of the hooks, which opened a door in the wall.

She didn't even have time to understand what was going on as he hurried her through the door. As he shut it behind them, she beheld a small field with a stable only meant for two horses on the far side. A secretive place, perfect for showing a servant who was supposed to be doing punishment how to ride. How this place got here without anyone knowing was beyond Ella.

After William shut the door, he returned to the stalls and opened the stall for the already tackled Lady Gray and guided her towards Ella. William beamed, "Today, you are going to learn how to ride a horse."

Limping back to the academy, Ella just wanted to go to bed, but there were still things that needed to be done. After falling a few times trying to get into the saddle and falling on her way off of the saddle, her ankle was feeling it as she washed up and got ready to prepare lunch. Thankfully, nothing else happened out of the ordinary. Though as she walked around, Ella could feel Clementine's heavy gaze on her.

It continued until it was time for bed. As Ella got ready for bed, Clementine stopped her, "Where did you get this?"

"What? Oh. That." Clementine must have found a bruise from her recent tumble. Ella scrambled for a lie to tell her. "I just fell. It is nothing to worry about."

And it wasn't a lie that she had fallen. She did fall off the horse. Clementine only stared at her, nose flaring, arms crossed.

"If that is the way you want to do it, fine." Clementine turned away, whispering, "I thought we had gotten over this."

"Clementine," Ella called, but for the rest of the night, she refused to answer.

As Ella went to sleep, she could only wonder why she was still doing this. The Fan Society seemed so exciting, a way to get out of her life and find a connection to her mother. But the only thing she found was that she was a failure, and she might never live up to her mother, who was a legend. And would she ever find out what happened to her?

Ella always held out hope that her mother was still alive out there, a blind hope. And the futility of it was breaking down her hope. A tear leaked out of her eyes as she tried desperately to cling to the last vestiges of hope that her mother might still be found alive.

I am so happy to be part of this society and do something for my country. I know that the things I do and learn will be important for what I need to do. And when I get my chance to wear the gold ring of the full membership of the society, I will do everything I can.

Nora "Cinders"
Report 23, page 1 paragraph 1

Chapter Five

The next day started with the usual task of cleaning the many hallways in the academy. Ella almost preferred it, but she couldn't put off her "punishment" of visiting Madame Briar. So, with heavy steps, she made her way up to the headmistress's office. With every step, her heart hung lower in her chest as she walked towards her teacher and a further reminder of her failure.

She arrived at the door much sooner than she had expected. Ella had assumed that the weight she felt in her feet would make it take that much longer to get to the office. Hesitating, Ella held her hand up, ready to knock but not wanting to do it. The turmoil that had rumbled around in her mind last night felt like the aftereffects of a massive storm, leaving her numb. With a sigh, she finally knocked on the door. The one thing she did remember from her mother was to keep your promises.

A servant opened the door. Ella didn't know what reaction she had expected Madame Briar to have on her face, but a smile was not it. Motioning the servant away, Madame Briar stepped out from behind the desk and headed towards the king's portrait. Ella stepped forward, confused.

Just as Queen Jane's portrait opened, so did this one, leading down a new path. This path was the same as the other one. After the door closed, they were shrouded in darkness. Ella trotted behind Madame Briar at her heels, feeling ever the wayward child. This corridor led them directly into the headmistress's secret office. Its plain stone walls, with only the symbol of the Fan Society visible, were starting to become familiar.

Ella avoided looking at the fan symbol on the wall as she took her seat.

"A lady must wait to be seated until the host is ready. Keep that in mind," Madame Briar said, sitting across from her. "Now, on to what we need to discuss. To be eligible to move higher in the Fan Society, you must accomplish these tasks during this school year. Next school year, we will be focusing on the physical aspects of the Fan Society."

Passing her a paper, Madame Briar added, "I do believe you told me you learned how to lock pick, yes?"

Nodding, Ella grabbed the paper. She had learned how to pick locks as a means of survival in her household. Too often she had been locked in her room, and Clementine couldn't get to her. She would have starved if she hadn't been able to get out. Glad that at least something that she learned was going to be useful, she took a look at the paper in front of her.

1. Be able to act as a servant

2. Be able to act as a noble character

3. Ride a horse

4. Perform in a tea party in character

5. Copy a page from a noble's journal

Despair welled up within her as she read. The first task was easy enough, but the rest? Ella counted down the months left of the school year; they had started late, and now there were only a few months left.

"How am I supposed to do this?" Ella gasped, looking to her mentor.

The madame only smiled in return. "I think you are more than capable of doing this, and you will be getting your Assistant soon."

"An Assistant?" Ella's mind instantly went to Clementine, but that thought was pushed aside since Clementine wasn't allowed to know about the society.

The headmistress nodded. "I will tell you more about what a person in the Assistant position does when she comes. But for now, focus on your studies with me. While we are here, we will also practice writing a report. Your first report is one of self-reflection. Write down your thoughts and feelings on how your mission at the tea party went and what could have gone better. I will leave you to it."

With that, she bid her farewell to draft a report. Ell's thoughts churned within her as everything that she had been expecting to happen didn't. Now she didn't know what to think. So instead, she started writing her report as she was asked, pushing away her thoughts. Ella was glad that her mother was insistent on her learning how to read and write at an early age. After her mother went missing, she self-studied to defy her stepmother, who refused to teach her. She had gotten rather good at it.

After completing the report, Ella left and finished her time with Madame Briar with tea etiquette. Then she headed to the stables. During the walk, Ella's thoughts were on the list. Taking a deep breath and pushing away her emotions, she focused on a task that she could accomplish now, and that was riding a horse.

Lessons went better because this time she managed to not fall off the horse when she was getting on. Though she did still fall when getting off of it. By the end of the lesson, she had wanted to kick William just once, as he cooed over the horse. The grey horse that had just dumped her off. She swore the horse did it on purpose. With a sigh, she refrained and instead brushed herself off and headed to do her chores as a servant. The one task that she actually excelled at.

As she was heading to the kitchens after cleaning up, Ella heard a familiar irritating voice.

"Just leave it alone, Effie. Mother's not here now. I can do what I want," Audrey said with a sniff.

At those words, Ella pressed her back against the wall, eager to avoid her stepsisters and their shadow Jenny as they continued down the hall. She ducked her head down, hoping they would just see her as just another servant as she tried to make her way down the corridor.

"Mother would be disappointed in you if she knew you kept skipping classes," Effie replied, keeping her voice calm and collected.

"Mother this, mother that. She has kept me in line with her plans for too long. I will go about it my own way. The teachers already like me, and as long as I am passing, they don't care. I will get the prestige of graduating from the academy, and the connections I am making will make me a strong candidate for marriage when we have our debut. As long as you don't give her a reason to come back, that is."

"We should at least return Mother's things she left behind. If we keep them, she will come back," Effie retorted with a sigh. Ella heard their steps coming closer as she wished that she could run down the corridor. She hoped her sedate pace would make them ignore her and pass her by.

"Of course, that is how it should be," Audrey said with a laugh, passing by Ella without a glance, Jenny and Effie trotting at her heels.

Ella held back her sigh of relief.

Effie still had to pass her, and she was the most observant.

Now Effie passed by. Ella could see Effie's look of annoyance at her sister, hidden behind her fan. Then her eyes shifted towards Ella. The irritation turned to joy as she laughed, "It seems we have an eavesdropping rat."

"What? Oh, I see," Audrey said as her eyes caught Ella. Her plan had failed, and Effie had caught her.

Ella could see the grin on Audrey's face before she flicked her fan open. Then she turned to Effie. "And what do we do to eavesdropping rats?"

Effie's smile rose above the fan's edges as she answered, "We punish them."

In an instant, Ella felt pain blossom across her face, reminiscent of the slap her stepmother gave her a few weeks ago. Tears welled in her eyes, but she refused to allow them to fall. As she looked up, a broad grin stretched across Audrey's face, and satisfaction gleamed within her eyes. Effie's only reaction was her shoulders relaxing. Jenny ignored the whole exchange as she held back a yawn. Fury burned within her; she would not allow them to see her cry.

Instead, she gave a bow. "I apologize for hearing your conversation, ladies. This servant should not have heard a conversation come from such precious lips such as yours without your knowledge of it."

Effie opened her mouth to speak, but Audrey spoke first; only a small furrow of the brow could show her annoyance at her sister. "Oh, stepsister, it is alright. We are generous. I am happy to discipline you while Mother is at home. This will be such a wonderful teaching experience. I am always happy to discipline a wayward servant."

Gritting her teeth, Ella resisted the urge to slap her sister back. It would only cause more trouble than it was worth. Those eyes gleaming with excitement and superiority were begging her to cause more trouble so her stepsister could dole out more punishment. Now that Effie was no longer in her mother's sight, she seemed to thrive on the freedom that had given her.

"Yes, dear stepsister," Ella replied, keeping her head down, gripping her hands in front of her to hold herself in check.

Seeing that she wasn't reacting, Audrey sniffed, then turned back the way she had been going. "Well, begone. I have more important matters to attend to."

"Yes, stepsister." Ella bowed then, turning down the nearest corridor.

After all the stress from the last few weeks, that encounter only made her anger boil. The fifth task of copying a journal entry would be perfect, and if she found something in the journal that she could use against them, all the better. Finally, something good to think about rather than classes that she was failing at and her discomfort at keeping things from Clementine.

And on that happy note, she hurried to do her duties as a servant.

Lockpicking is a pivotal skill. Any information that is worth anything is going to be kept behind locked doors. The best lockpickers can unlock a door within seconds, some even are capable of doing so in front of another person without them finding out. But those are few and far between. To be considered acceptable, no more than the time it takes for tea to steep is permitted when lockpicking. Any more than that is unseemly.

Book with fan on cover
Chapter 2 author unknown

Chapter Six

When Ella arrived at the kitchen, she instantly knew something was amiss. Several scullery maids were sweeping what appeared to be shattered remains of plates. The cook's face was a vibrant red as he shouted, "Find more plates, and wash the dishes as fast as possible!"

Ella was afraid he would shoot out flames from his mouth if he couldn't find more plates. Not wanting to be on the receiving end of his ire, she hurried in and got to work.

A few of the maids had the courage to whisper to each other, "I can't believe she did that! Do you think she will get into trouble? I would miss her here."

Though, they stopped with a squeak as the cook walloped them with a wooden spoon and called for them to get back to work. The lack of dishes and the sharp remains of the plates caused chaos during lunch, and extra work was piled upon the servants. Ella was so busy that only a passing thought of not seeing Clementine was all the curiosity the work would allow. They ended up heading back to their rooms late, leaving them to bemoan the lack of sleep they would be getting the next morning.

Even when she headed to bed, she couldn't see her. Ella did rush. Clementine could still be mad at her from the day before, plus it wasn't time for lights out. Sorrow and concern started to weave their way toward her, but she quickly shoved them away. She had a task to do for the Fan Society, and she couldn't have all her emotions crowding around her. Ella had made her decisions, and she would have to accept them.

Tucking her pillows under her blankets, she made a human-like mound on her bed. It wouldn't deceive Clementine, but she would know what to do if someone popped their head in to check on them. Making sure she had the charcoal she had pilfered from a fireplace and two fruit knives she had taken during the craziness of lunch that had continued in the kitchen throughout the day, she was ready as she would ever be. All she would need to find was a piece of paper which she should be able to find in the nobles' quarters.

Leaving the candle on for Clementine, she headed out of the servants' quarters, listening for every sound. Though most of the servants had headed to bed, exhausted from the day's work, others still had jobs to do. She wouldn't want to run into one of them.

Taking a deep breath, Ella strode through the halls like she had something to do, so they would ignore her in the dark. This had always worked back at home. Her stepmother had always had her run odd jobs at random hours to keep her on her toes. She never thought it would come in handy at a time like this.

Ella easily left the servants' quarters. Now was for the challenge to go through the nobles' quarters find a piece of paper, enter a room, and find a journal to copy an entire page in the dark without anyone knowing. She knew she shouldn't have let her stepsisters get the better of her, but she couldn't back out now. This was her chance.

Slowing her steps, Ella entered the second floor where her stepsisters were situated. Still listening for anyone, she made her way down the hallway to their door. The window at the end of the hallway cast faint moonlight, giving the empty hallway an eerie look. Her steps were muffled by the carpet as she crept up to her stepsisters' door. Pressing her ear to the wood, she listened to see if she could hear anything. She did not, and she took that as a sign that they were in bed asleep.

Taking one last look around her, Ella pulled out the knives from her skirts and slid them into the lock until she felt a click, allowing her inside. Grateful for the well-oiled hinges, she ducked into the room, closing the door quietly behind her.

The room was completely dark. Since the quarters for the nobility were all designed the same way, she knew the room that she was in would be the sitting room and that it would connect to the bedrooms. Taking a deep breath, she tried to remember how the rooms were situated from when she gathered sheets for laundry day and made her way to the other side. She froze when she kicked something that was on the floor, but not even a rustle could be heard through the thick wooden doors. With a sigh, she continued forward, reaching to feel for the curtains she knew were on this side.

Her hands touched the thick brocade fabric, the rough curtains soothing any nerves she had left. Needing light to be able to read, she hoped that the soft moonlight would be better than the smell of a burning candle. With a smooth motion, Ella opened the curtain partway, revealing a moonlit room.

Already, she could see signs of her stepsisters. The object that she had kicked was a heavily embroidered pillow that had been thrown to the floor. Other evidence of a fight included a few books scattered and even a lamp that had been knocked over. Papers had been thrown to the floor, and even an inkwell with its pool of black had leaked onto a desk. Ella could only roll her eyes at the familiar scene. Often, she had been told to clean up her stepsisters' mess after they had a scuffle, which mostly involved Audrey throwing everything she could get her hands on. Usually,

Effie was trying to help out Audrey, who would rather do what she wanted. In the end, Audrey would get what she wanted because their mother would wish it that way.

The only thing keeping Ella from feeling a twinge of pity for her was that her cheek was still stinging from the slap she had received earlier that day. Jenny would get in trouble for not cleaning the mess up right away. But remembering the bored look on her face when Effie smacked her, Ella felt no pity.

But misfortune was another's blessing. Ella snatched one of the papers that had been under the pool of ink, grabbing the bottom one, hoping it would not be noticed in the mess. Then she looked down at a novel that was at her feet. This was a leatherbound book without a title printed on it. Flipping it open, she could see that it was a journal. Her stepmother's journal. Opening it to a random page, she used the charcoal to write the words.

I can't believe that my daughter had to look like him. If only my second daughter took after me, things would have been perfect. I hate looking at that face. The face so similar to my late husband who took so long to die. At least she is helpful and will make sure that Audrey will move up in society.

What Ella read made her hate her stepmother even more and made her understand her stepsister, which gave her an uneasy feeling. She had always disliked her stepsisters, but this journal painted them in a new light. With one swift move, she closed the book. Ella shut out whatever emotions she had and shoved them back down. Folding the page, she tucked it in her skirts and placed the book back on the floor. She hurried once more to the window, closing the curtains and picking her way across the floor. Then, as if she was never there, she headed down the hallway.

Ella couldn't help but feel a sense of relief when she left her stepsisters' room. It was too soon to feel relief, however; she still had to make it back to her room without getting caught. Now it was past lights out. She listened for any sound other than the thrumming of her own heart, her invigorated steps taking her closer to her room. The servants' corridor was just ahead, just a few more steps. Then in the corner of her eye, she saw white fabric in an alcove.

"What are you doing out of bed?" Effie demanded, standing with her arms folded.

Ella froze. She had thought that her stepsister was in bed asleep. She turned toward the sound of the voice. In the faint light, it was difficult to see her, but Ella could pick out red-rimmed eyes and black specks at the hem of her dress. The accusing eyes made her feel as if the note was burning in her skirts and that at any moment she would suspect that Ella had been sneaking into her room.

"I was trying to get my chores done, stepsister," Ella bluffed. She couldn't get caught, not now in the nobles' quarters.

"Its lights out for servants like you. What is a sneaky thing like you wandering around at this time of night, unless you were up to something?" she retorted. The faint moonlight from the window showed a flush on her face.

Ella couldn't help but remember what she read about Effie in the journal. They were about the same age. And she was just doing what she had to in her own way. But Ella knew that she didn't care to bother her when her family couldn't see. Though, she was stubborn enough to not let something like this go.

Ella sighed, furiously thinking about how to get out of this.

Then she remembered, "It is lights out for you, as well. And if you want to get me in trouble, you would have to tell someone in the state you're in."

Her icy-blue eyes grew cold. Effie looked down at her dress, then frowned. "I will let you off for now, but don't think I don't know that you are up to something. I will find out."

"Yes, stepsister. Now I need to get to bed. It's getting rather late."

Ella hurried back to the servants' quarters, breathing a sigh of relief. For now, she wouldn't do anything. The only reason why she didn't want to start anything was that she was a proper lady and didn't want anyone to see her in such disarray. But tomorrow was another story. She had to warn Clementine. If only she would talk to her.

Thankfully, no more incidents happened on the way back to her room. The only problem was the candle was still lit, and Clementine was not there. Ella couldn't remember if she had seen her at all since morning chores. Fear pierced her through like a lightning bolt. Where was Clementine? Worry over her dear friend pushed any fear of being caught out of her mind as she made her way to the headmistress's office.

She was lucky that few people were in those particular hallways as she tore down them heedless of her flapping skirts. Though, for the next couple of days, whispers would circle of a ghost running in the hallways. Heedless of the mess she left in her wake, Ella panted, her heavy breathing echoing the pounding of her heart. Realizing that running through the hallways was a bad idea, she slowed to think more calmly about the situation.

As she hesitated in front of the door, it opened to reveal a familiar face. It was the older lady from the tea party, now dressed as a servant.

"A lady should never run through hallways and should never show her fear."

Madame Briar called, "Come in, dear, we have much to talk about. You are lucky that I had sent everyone away from these halls."

The door opened completely, revealing Madame Briar sitting at her desk, and seated on the other side was Clementine.

There are many types of people who help with the Fan Society, the key one being Guardians. The other is their counterpart, the Assistants. Guardians are placed in front of society and are known, making it difficult to get to some places due to that fact. Assistants are the ones who help the Guardian keep up their façade. They should be capable of many things because they are the main people who are pivotal in helping maintain the cover of the Guardian. They also . . .

Book with fan on cover
Unknown author, chapter 1

Chapter Seven

"Clementine!" Ella called, hurrying over to her friend but stopping upon seeing her expression. Her lips were in a pout and her arms were crossed, her face turned away. "Clementine, I'm sorry, what happened? Why are you here?"

Raising her brow, she said, "Shouldn't I be asking why I didn't know what you've been up to these last few weeks?"

Ella turned to Madame Briar to confirm that she did know that Ell was now training to be a spy. A small tilt of her head was all she needed. Relief instantly filled her that Clementine finally knew, and she no longer had to lie to her. Worry melting away and giving a smile that she hadn't felt for a long time, Ella said, "I'm glad that I don't have to lie to you."

Clementine didn't smile back. Worry began to build again as Ella worried about how she could get her friend to forgive her.

The moment was interrupted by Madame Briar, who, though it was late at night, looked wide awake. "Lady Cooper, it seems that your new Assistant and you will get along quite well. Now, we have things to discuss, ladies."

Ella worried at what Clementine would say about their current relationship, but all she said was, "Thank you, Headmistress."

At that, Madame Briar led them to her secret office, and the paper in her pocket was left forgotten. Once they were seated,

Madame Briar nodded to Clementine. "Should you decide to be part of the Fan Society, your position would be Assistant to Ella. Your job would be to help Ella with her missions and keep her identity as a spy a secret. You will also help maintain her wardrobe since we want the hidden pockets and weapons to remain out of sight."

Taking this in rather calmly, Clementine asked, "How will I be helping her on these missions?"

Madame Briar continued, "You will help in a variety of ways such as being a lookout, passing messages, and gathering information from sources that Ella could not. There may be more ways you could help, but it all depends on where your talents lay."

"No matter what, I will make it my duty to protect Ella," Clementine promised, staring down Madame Briar. Even Ella didn't have the courage to do that.

Warmth fill Ella at the thought that Clementine was planning on joining her, even though she may not be happy with Ella at the moment.

A smile graced the headmistress's face, as she looked pleased by Clementine's answer.

"Wait, why did I have to keep this from Clementine if you were just going to tell her?" Ella said, as the circumstances changed faster than she was keeping up. Just this morning, Ella had to keep everything from Clementine, and now she was a part of it.

"Do you not want me to know?" Instead of the playful pout Clementine would have normally displayed, her expression was painfully blank as she asked her question.

"No, I do. I just thought that . . . I mean . . . I wasn't supposed to tell you anything. And now—" Ella stopped herself before she dug herself into an even bigger hole. She turned to Madame Briar for help. Madame Briar only watched the conversation; Ella would have to deal with this trial on her own.

Clementine held her sorrowful expression for a few more moments until she turned to Madam Briar and nodded. She didn't reply to Ella as Madame Briar returned her nod and motioned for them to leave. Clementine left on her own, leaving Ella behind without a glance.

After Ella watched her go, she asked, "Why did you make me unable to talk about the Fan Society to her when you had planned to let her know anyway?"

"My dear, as a spy you will have to lie to the people you care about for various reasons. But even though you have to lie to them, you must still be able to keep a trusting relationship between them or you will fail in what you need to do." Madame Briar gestured to the door. "You need your rest, dear. I'm sure you will find a way to fix your relationship. I trust your bond."

Ella nodded and made her way back to her room. She was only stopped once by Matron Sophia, who motioned for her to continue on down the hallway. Clementine refused to talk to her that night, and Ella was left to her own dark thoughts.

Ella felt like her eyes only just shut when the call for morning chores was rung. Of course, she probably only had a few minutes of sleep. With the tension from the previous weeks of conflict with Clementine, to her now being a part of the Fan Society, she was unable to relax. Due to her chaotic emotions, what little time she had to sleep was out of reach. Then before that, it was the tension of sneaking into her stepsisters' room.

Sitting up in an instant, Ella felt in her skirts for the sheet of paper. It was still there. Ella breathed a sigh of relief and pulled herself out of bed to do her chores. She would have to give it to

Madame Briar during her "punishment session", which Clementine was now going to join.

For the first time, she couldn't help but smile at the thought of going to class. Before, it had been tinged with regret that she couldn't tell Clementine, but now they were together. The cleaning of the academy went in a daze, partially due to lack of sleep and the other due to excitement.

She made her way to the headmistress's office, at a different time than Clementine, and knocked. When she entered, Ella was surprised to see that Clementine wasn't there. She was sure that Clementine had left earlier than her. Madame Briar, looking as she always did despite having been kept up until late hours, was writing something at her desk. The madame looked up and waved her through the door behind Queen Jane's portrait.

Ella hesitated, then asked, "Where's Clementine?"

Her heart sank at Madame Briar's words. "She has her own things she needs to take care of before she can be of help to you."

Not moving, her heart felt as if it had been dropped down a staircase. Yet again she would have to face the other ladies on her own. At a look from Madame Briar, her cemented feet began to move, and Ella did as was asked. Making her way through the dark passageway, she headed to the main floor. This time, the setup was different. There was only one larger table instead of several smaller tables. From what she remembered of her lessons, this meant that the setting was a more intimate gathering.

Bubbly Eleanor met her again at the bottom of the stairs and helped her once more to get dressed. Ella, now knowing what was more fashionable, asked to wear something different than the one Eleanor chose. This would not go the same way it did last time. Frowning at the suggestion, Eleanor did as she asked. "I don't think you want to wear this, but it is your choice. Remember what we are supposed to do."

"I know, I know. I will do better this time," Ella replied.

Eleanor hmphed at Ella's determined expression and went on accessorizing. But Ella ignored her and focused on all the etiquette that she knew, running it over and over in her mind. This let her practice and ignore the still uncomfortable feeling of having someone dress her. But having seen the complicated laces in the back last time, she decided that it would be better to not complain.

After getting dressed, Eleanor handed her a normal fan and she made her way to the tables. This time, she managed to greet the proper people at the proper time and didn't trip over any rugs. Ella only half understood what was going on. Still in the basics of her noble education, it was hard to tell what was a snub and what was an actual compliment. She also didn't know any of the girls and didn't know what was acting and what they were really like. The only good thing was that fumbling through society was exactly what the character she was playing would do, but it wasn't as though she was playing a part. It was just Ella with a pretty dress playing dress-up.

The party was boring and tedious as it was nothing more than conversations going over her head. That was frustrating enough, but the worst part was throughout the entire party, Luella gave her glares, and it was getting annoying. What did she ever do to that girl to have her give the evil eye every time she saw Ella walk into a room? And this time, she wasn't playing the host.

Still feeling like she was missing something, Ella finished the party and headed to the stables to another class she fumbled through.

While she was walking, she felt a tingling on the back of her neck, as if someone was watching her. Turning around, she couldn't see who it was, but the cold gaze reminded her of someone. She doubted that her stepsister would think that there was a secret room in the stables and follow her in there.

Either way, now wasn't the time to worry about it. She had an evil horse who wanted to drop her on the ground to worry about. She rubbed her back in memory of all the times she had been dumped on the ground

"Relax your hands on the reins. You are pulling to tightly," William scolded as Ella was deposited on the ground again, bruising her tailbone.

The lesson turned out the be the worst one yet. Ella had fallen off the horse no less than five times. And she swore that the horse was laughing at her as she did. She gave the horse a glare. "How am I supposed to relax when that *thing* tries to dump me every chance it gets?"

"That's because the rest of your body was telling the horse the wrong thing. Isn't that right, Lady Grey?" he cooed. Ignoring Ella who was still on the ground, he patted the horse, crooning over her.

"Some lady she is." Ella rolled her eyes. How could she relax her hands on the reins and still tell the horse where to go?

What is the point of having reins when your body is somehow supposed to magically tell the horse where to go? Ella thought. She kept her thoughts to herself knowing that if she said them out loud, William would only pour praises to the horse so she wouldn't have hurt feelings.

The rest of the lesson continued in much the same manner, with her spending her time on the ground. It was a relief as the afternoon light rose, and she had to head off to her servants' duties. At least with them it was easier to avoid the times they tried to trip her.

Then she limped off to meal preparation, classes, and other servants' duties. From the late night and the physically exhausting morning to the mind-numbing evening, she was ready for bed. But her steps to her room lagged as her thoughts lingered on Clementine. Even though she knew about the Fan Society and knew why she had to keep it a secret, Clementine still refused to talk to her. She relaxed when she arrived to her room and found it empty. Then nerves started to build as she paced until Clementine arrived.

"Clementine, I was hoping we could talk—" Ella said but stopped as she was brushed aside. Clementine sat down and began getting ready for bed. The futility of talking to Clementine made Ella prepare to rest as well, an aching silence filling the room.

She had hoped that things would be different the next day, but alas, things failed to be so. This cycle continued for the rest of the week. The only difference was Jenny. After getting caught by Effie, she sent Jenny to keep an eye on her. Ella could always catch a glimpse of her dark hair when she went down the hallways. The one good thing about her was that she wouldn't go into any restricted area.

The one thing that she had wished was to change was her conversations with Clementine. Any conversation with Clementine was short. With the hard work they were doing throughout the day, it was exhausting by night, and it wasn't like they could talk about being in a secret society unless they were in a place where they couldn't be heard. It was almost like being back to her not speaking to Ella.

The pressure started to build until everything fell apart. It was laundry day. Ella was lucky enough to have been chosen to be part of the group gathering laundry. The days had started to hit summer and sitting by hot burners and boiling water did not appeal to her. After making her way up to the second floor, she could hear voices coming from her stepsisters' door.

"I thought you wrote to Mother saying she didn't need to come here. So why is she coming here?"

"I did write a letter. Several times. But I never received one in return."

"Mother always writes back to me! Fine, I will just need to go to classes for the weeks she is here. Don't you dare tell Mother that I haven't been going to classes."

"Yes, Audrey."

Ella hurriedly backed down the hallway as the door clicked open and Audrey stepped out. She sniffed, then went down the opposite direction. Relaxing, Ella went back to gathering laundry. Hopefully, when she got the laundry from her stepsisters' room, they wouldn't suspect that she had heard their conversation. With a quick rap, she waited for Jenny to open the door.

When Jenny opened the door, she made sure to keep it as much closed as she could. "Yes?"

"I am here to pick up the laundry," Ella said, gesturing to the basket in front of her.

She just nodded, grabbed the basket, and shut the door. Within a few minutes, she opened it again, handing her the basket. Jenny was about to close the door when a voice called out, "Just a minute, Jenny."

Opening the door, Jenny revealed Effie. "Eavesdropping again, stepsister?"

"Eavesdropping? On what? I'm just doing my duties, dear step-sister. May I continue to do so? Or do you have another accusa-tion?" Ella challenged, bluffing.

Effie's eyes narrowed, and she flicked her ever-present fan in front of her face. "Yes. Well, then be on your way."

Bowing with the basket, she headed down the hall, still feeling Effie's cold stare as she walked away.

Dear Mother,

I hope you are doing well. I also hope that preparations for the season are well underway. Audrey is doing well in her classes and is well-liked by everyone. She has made some high connections. All of the things that you have left here are being taken care of. You need not worry. I wonder if you want to come to visit us during the break? Don't worry, I've been keeping an eye on Ella. She has been getting into things, but I have made sure to put her in her place. I haven't heard anything back from you. Audrey has been receiving your letters, but mine could have gotten lost. I will have words with the delivery boy.

Sincerely,
Your daughter
Euphemia

Chapter Eight

E lla was cleaning a window when servant came up to her. Crinkling her brow, she looked at the girl and asked, "Yes?"

"Madame Briar wants to speak to you," the servant said, giving away nothing about what the headmistress wanted.

Dropping her rag in the bucket and passing it off to a fellow servant, Ella made her way to the headmistress's office.

Ella was confused; it wasn't time for her lessons. Every step she took toward the office brought her fears forward in her mind. It reminded her of when she had been called to see her stepmother. Every time she had been called in only brought more misery, and she feared that it would be the same with Madame Briar.

Her mind ran through how she still couldn't keep up with the conversations being tossed about during the tea parties, the bruises she received from horse riding lessons, and how she still couldn't get Clementine to talk to her. Did the headmistress not think she was good enough and wanted her removed from the Fan Society? Was she not learning fast enough? Were her stepsisters complaining about her? Did the headmistress want to throw her out so she wouldn't have to deal with her stepsisters? What if they were comparing her to her mother and she couldn't compete?

This was her one connection to her mother, and she didn't want to lose it. Doubts plagued her as she knocked on the office door.

After being allowed in, Madame Briar took her to her secret office. Nervousness about being kicked out of the Fan Society flooded her mind as she shifted from foot to foot, waiting for what Madame Briar wanted to speak to her about.

"Sit down, Lady Cooper, I have something that needs to be discussed." With stiff limbs, Ella sat, awaiting her doom. Madame Briar continued, "I believe you will feel better if I was candid with you, lady Cooper. For you to move farther in this society, you need to be able to show your face, but due to your family situation, that will be difficult."

Already, Ella could feel mounting pressure with each word spoken. She was ready to hear the words that would dismiss her from the Fan Society.

She was so nervous that Ella nearly missed what Madame Briar said, "And so it would be best if you did something so bad that would make it so we have a reason to banish you from this school and do it to a place where your stepfamily would not look for you. After that, you will hide yourself within these walls and continue your training."

Ella could only blink. Madame Briar always said things that kept her off-kilter. Having enough restraint not to just blurt out anything, Ella sorted through what was just said.

"You need me to . . . cause problems? All so that I can be punished so horribly that my family doesn't look for me?"

The madame nodded. "Correct."

"But why now?" Ella asked.

Madame Briar intertwined her fingers, "You are in a very special position. So far, most of your duties as a servant has been relegated to the servants' quarters, and so very few have seen you, and those who have wouldn't have paid you any mind. Your family would be happy to be rid of you and forget you even existed. And when you arrive in society several years later as a noble, they will not connect the servant girl to the noble that will be before them."

"But won't some still suspect?" Ella was thinking of Effie.

With a smile, Madame Briar said, "Then your skills must be up to par. If they suspect, they can't do anything without evidence, and so you must make sure there is no evidence and play the part to perfection."

Worry about her current acting skills and her knowledge of being a noble filled Ella, but she held back her fears. A spy would never show her fear like that.

"How bad does it need to be?" It wasn't particularly difficult to get kicked out of the school, but from what she was talking about, the headmistress was asking for something dire.

Nodding her head at Ella's train of thoughts, Madame Briar smiled. The headmistress folded her hands in her lap. "You need to make it so I will be sent away for hard labor in repayment for the damage you have caused."

Ella could only sit and blink, stunned at what was asked of her. Another question popped into her head. "When do you need this done by?"

"By the end of this school year."

The rest of the day was spent in a stupor. Ella could feel the crushing weight of all the missions she had to achieve, and she only had a few weeks to somehow accomplish the list, Spring had almost turned to summer, and the days had grown warm. Now when she returned from the stables, trickles of sweat mixed with the smell of horses and dirt. And the copied journal entry burned in her mind. Ella had shown it to Madame Briar, who merely nodded and gave it back to her. Ella assumed that it was a good thing, but it was difficult to read the madame.

As she worked through the day, questions flooded her mind as she did her work by memory. Why was she doing this? Was it worth it? Did any of this matter? And the final question: How much longer could she last?

Those thoughts haunted her into the night and the next morning. As she did her morning cleaning, she almost didn't hear quiet Jenny come up beside her. With lack of sleep and the tension and loneliness she had been feeling, she startled, tipping over the bucket of dirty water. Feet now drenched, Jenny's brown eyes still didn't react. Instead, she passed Ella a sheet of paper, then grabbed a towel, wiped off her feet, and headed back the way she came.

Sighing at the mess that was made, Ella looked at the sheet of paper with a date and time. Confusion filled her; she had only been thinking of the worries of accomplishing her missions that had been steadily growing instead of getting achieved and had almost forgotten her stepsister.

Her stepsister would not let an opportunity slide. Now Ella just had one more thing to add to her list of growing worries. Effie would make sure that Ella would pay if she didn't show. Ella scrubbed harder as if she could scrub away her worries.

After rushing to get things cleaned in time, Ella had to hurry to the headmistress. When in her office, she spent her hour learning about how to drink different types of tea. By the end, she had smelled so many different types of tea that she was light-headed as she went to the stables. She could only hope that some of what she had learned stuck.

William came up blathering on about what Lady Grey and some other horse did. It was something about rolling in the grass, but Ella was too busy trying to remember to relax her body while keeping her posture as she went to her riding lesson. This time, she had managed to stay on. Until he put some logs on the ground and had the horse walk over them. Then it was a mouthful of grass for her, and another bruise to add to her growing collection. Her mission of being able to act like a lady and properly ride a horse was still far away from being achieved, making Ella ever aware of the approaching deadline with each fall off the horse.

By the end of class, Ella desperately wished for a glass of water to rinse out the taste of grass that was lingering in her mouth as she finished washing. It was as she was walking to the kitchens that she remembered the note that was given to her. It was easy to remember due to an icy glare from Effie as she strode towards her down the corridor. One extra thing that needed to be taken care of that she had no clue how to accomplish.

Jenny trotted placidly behind her, and Audrey was nowhere to be seen. As she passed by Ella, she whispered, "You better not be late, or I will place all of my attention on you."

Then she continued on her way. After that, the note was in the forefront of her mind as thoughts whirled around like a chaotic dance that she didn't know the steps to. The thoughts haunted her until it was time for bed. Clementine came in and was ready to plop down on her bed when she saw Ella.

"What's wrong?" It was the first time she had spoken since the meeting with Madame Briar.

Ella was unsure of how to treat Clementine and didn't want to say anything else that might strain their relationship. She didn't know if Clementine was still her friend, considering her reactions.

Turning her face so her features were deeper in the shadows, hiding her face so Clementine wouldn't see, Ella pretended like she was about to go to bed. "Nothing. Just get some sleep."

"You are hiding something from me, again. Haven't you learned your lesson yet?" Clementine said as she gave her a look very reminiscent of Madame Briar when she was throwing out questions.

It was then that the wall of emotions that she had pushed back erupted from her, and tears trickled down her face. The annoyed look on Clementine's face immediately changed to one of concern as she sat next to Ella and held her shoulders.

Tilting her chin towards her, Clementine said, "I'm sorry I didn't talk to you for so long. I thought that things would be less stressful now that you were away from your stepmother. I should have known that you would take everything upon yourself."

They just sat there for a few minutes with Clementine chatting about her day and brushing out Ella's hair until she calmed down.

Even though she wished to talk more, they didn't have any time for that. "Clementine."

She stopped as Ella passed her the note. Her eyes flicked across the page, then she passed it back. "What do you want me to do?"

It felt like she was whole again. That loneliness and isolation that she had felt the whole time she was here had changed the moment Clementine said she had her back. The immense weight of everything she needed to do was no longer crushing. And that relief let her finally think about what she needed to do.

Effie could help with one of the tasks Madame Briar had told her to do. If Effie wanted to get Ella into trouble, then she just needed to make sure that it was as spectacular as needed.

Ella sighed, "I just need to you watch my back. I plan on getting into trouble, and I need you to be my eyes and ears."

"Trouble? Are you sure this isn't just another day for you?" Clementine teased.

Ella smiled and explained what Madame Briar had asked of her.

Clementine's expression turned thoughtful. "That shouldn't be too difficult. I mean, you did manage to get into the academy after serving tea. How hard could it be to get you thrown out?"

A sense of rightness calmed the chaotic swirl of thoughts that had been running rampant, and Ella organized the thoughts in her head. "Who knows? Effie might be able to help me." Ella turned to Clementine's questioning glance. "Effie wants a late-night meeting. Do you mind keeping a lookout for me?

Giving her a mock salute, Clementine replied, "Yes, ma'am."

Ella was smiling as she headed to the meeting in the dark corridors of the academy.

I have learned that depending on what you want, what others would consider a failure may be considered a win in your book. And sometimes looking like you have lost is the best way to make sure that you have won.

Nora "Cinders"
Report 3, page 1 paragraph 1

Chapter Nine

The meeting was to take place outside of the hallway of her stepsisters' rooms. It was odd that Effie would ask for a meeting here, where they would be lucky to not get caught.

Plans swirled about Ella's mind as she tried to anticipate what Effie was planning on doing at this meeting to get back at Ella. She must not get caught in Effie's trap. But as she came up the servants' stairs to her stepsisters' hallway, she could hear their voices echo off the stone walls. Ella stayed in the stairwell, listening to their reverberating words.

"Calm down, Audrey. It would be improper if the whole school heard you acting so unladylike."

"Why did you write a note like that? I saw it! You said that you wanted Mother to come here," Audrey's voice rang through the hall with a whine. "You should follow as ordered. I was finally free to do things my way."

Creeping closer, Ella could hear a heavy sigh, "Yes, sister, but if you don't start participating in classes, you will squander all of your opportunities."

Audrey gasped, "Don't tell me what to do. I am older than you."

Hearing steps back toward the stairway, Ella backed away and hid where the staircase curved. Any ideas that Ella had had about Effie's plans disappeared as she heard them stop at the top of the stairs. *Why are they talking where people can hear them?* Ella thought as she struggled to figure out the twist in Effie's plan.

"Let's at least go to the room or in the stairwell so that no one can hear this conversation." Effie's calming words only enraged Audrey more.

"Don't touch me. You should be on my side. Mother is not here and won't be for the next few years. Who do you think is going to look after you for all this time? I'm the one who is connected, not you." Audrey's voice echoed as they now stood in front of the stairwell that Ella was hiding in.

"Audrey, you know that I'm—" Effie started but was halted by Audrey's outburst.

"No. No more." Then it all came tumbling down as Effie tumbled down the stairs to Ella's feet. Blood leaked down her lips as she lay sprawled out on the ground. Horror filled Ella as she looked up the stairs at Audrey's face lit by candlelight. Her eyes met Ella's, and fear turned to hope as Audrey found someone to blame. Before Ella could say anything, Audrey yelled, "A servant pushed my sister down the stairs. Come help!"

It was too late to run. It was already past lights-out, and Audrey's shout would have caused people to stir. They were in an area that her yell could easily be heard. There would be a heavy punishment for this. Ella wouldn't escape from this, but then again, this was exactly the sort of thing that she needed for Madame Briar's latest request.

Feeling a tug of guilt, Ella looked down at Effie to see if she could help. No longer was she sprawled out on the ground. She was already sitting up and had pulled out a handkerchief and was dabbing at a bloody lip. Grunting, she pulled a pillow out from under her with her other hand. The pillow had been hidden in the thick skirts, which in a dark corridor no one would notice.

She started rubbing her ankle, then tsked at it. Looking up at Ella, she exclaimed, "Well? Are you going to help me up?"

This had all been planned. Effie was unfazed by falling down the stairs. This was a dangerous stunt and one that could easily sentence Ella to death if something went wrong. Did she truly hate Ella that much that she was willing to put herself in danger and make it so Ella would be thrown in prison or worse, executed?

Angry at that thought, Ella folded her arms. "And why should I? You set this up. Now I have been deemed as someone who has tried to kill another noble. In a few minutes, guards and other servants will be here to throw me in some prison. Why should I help you?" Then another thought crossed her mind. One that could turn this situation to Ella's advantage and force Effie to co-operate. "Though suppose I kicked up a fuss and woke everyone in the academy. You may have placed me where others could see evidence that I was here, but it makes it just as easy for them to hear everything I say. Yes, I will still get punished, but that won't stop the rumors from running. It would ruin any chance your sister has of gaining influence in high society."

With a sigh, Effie grunted and moved so she was sitting on the stairs, then adjusted her skirts. Focusing on Ella, she said, "What if we make a deal? I can't stop you from getting punished, but I can make sure that you are sent to be a servant for a good person instead of death or imprisonment. Someone who had nothing to do with high society. All you have to do is say that you did it and don't cause a fuss. Then as long as you keep out of my way and never mention it again, I will never bother you. You get out of the academy, and Audrey stays out of trouble. Do we have a deal?"

Ella wanted to spout out no, but she had to accomplish the task, and this was the best way to do it. She sighed. But she was not just going to take it as is. And there were a few questions that she had always wanted to ask. "What if I don't?"

"Pardon?" Her face that had been so smug furrowed, and her mouth opened in shock.

"What if I would rather bring you down with me? I would rather cause a fuss and create horrible rumors about you two. You have always been horrible to me. You hate me. How do I know that you will keep your promise?"

A laugh burst from Effie. "Hate you? I don't hate you. It's just business."

"How is tormenting me just business?"

Sighing like a nanny being exasperated by the incessant questions of a child, she answered in a patronizing tone, "Of course, if I focused my attention against you, then Mother would see my skills. She was very appreciative of it every time I bullied you. But only you."

That made sense, Ella had never really felt any hatred from Effie, merely cold calculation. And other things started clicking into place. Effie had always wanted her mother's attention, and her stepmother always found enjoyment in seeing Ella in pain. Another question rolled around in her mind, and since Effie was in a talking mood . ∴. "Why do you allow Audrey to push you around, let alone allow her to push you down the stairs? Is it because you want your mother to love you?"

At Ella's words, her eyebrow twitched upwards, flinching, her hand frozen. After a moment, Effie continued dabbing at her lip, her calm expression now hiding well-restrained anger. "I thought you were smarter than that. If you make the deal with me, I will also tell you why. Tick tock, stepsister. I hear people coming."

Hearing footsteps nearing them, Ella had to make her choice—and fast. Even though she didn't know if Effie would keep the deal or not, since she was already planning on taking the deal, she nodded. This would be her chance to get her answers.

Effie's lips twitched upwards. Folding her arms, she answered differently than how Ella had expected. "Everything is as planned. I believe you know Audrey hasn't been going to classes? The freedom had gotten to her head. And Mother . . . she hasn't been receiving my letters."

Effie's brow raised as if begging Ella to disagree. The page she had read from her stepmother's journal locked her mouth from saying anything. Instead, she merely nodded for her to continue.

"With this one incident, Audrey would be seen as a hero for protecting me from you and all the blame would be on you. Audrey, stupid as she is, will keep her mouth shut about the incident, especially since she truly thinks she pushed me down the stairs. She also knows that I will back her up on blaming you, since I always have. But since this incident occurred, Mother will be called in to be informed of the incident and we will get to talk to her. Because of the incident, Mother will want to keep a closer watch on Audrey, which means she will be in closer communication with me. Mother contacts me more, Audrey will be under my control, and you will be out of the way."

That was far more than Ella had ever expected. By pretending to lose, she had gained everything she wanted. Ella had thought that Effie was powerless, yet she played the part and gained control of the situation. Her thoughts were interrupted by guards flooding the stairwell from Audrey's cry.

Giving Ella a look that said *you better keep your end of the bargain*, Effie did a beautiful faint; Clementine would have been impressed. A few of the academy guards came checking hovering over Effie and shouting, "Call for a doctor, and someone send for the girl's mother."

As Effie's muttered words in the guard's ear, he motioned for the others, and hands grabbed at Ella, dragging her away. Bits of metal pinched her arm as they yanked her down the hall.

Playing her part, Ella cried, tears falling from her eyes from a bruise that would sure to form on her elbow tomorrow. "It was an accident."

The guards ignored her pleading words, not even slowing to listen.

"It was just an accident!" Real fear filled Ella's words, as she didn't know what was going to happen. She didn't know who was part of the Fan Society and who wasn't. They had every right to kill her on the spot for attempting to murder a noble.

Servants began poking their heads out from the corridors they passed, trying to catch a glimpse of the commotion. One very familiar blonde head came into view. Warmth filled her at the sight of Clementine. Ella locked eyes with her and with a nod, Clementine hurried off. Matron Sophia, head of the servants' quarters, had come and was shooing the onlookers back to their rooms with difficulty.

Keeping to her part, Ella kept mumbling that it was an accident and was dragged away to the basement, glad that Clementine would be there to help her.

That child Ella is nothing but torment for me. My only wish is to torment her. If only it wasn't for her, my life would have been different. Death is too good for her. She needs to suffer.

Journal of Lady Victoria
March 1827

Chapter Ten

The academy wasn't built as a dungeon, but one of the empty coal rooms had been *repurposed* as a makeshift dungeon. After nothing happened for a while, Ella wondered if she had pushed too far. She was only supposed to make it so she would be forced to leave the school. The attempted murder of a noble was a death sentence.

Ella sighed. At least for the moment, no one was going to kill her if they were imprisoning her. Now abandoned in a dark, dusty room, she was left to her thoughts. A lot had happened the last few hours, and she hadn't had time to process it all. But now her brain was no longer in survival mode, and she was allowed to think about other things.

Such as, did she make the right choice? Now that she was locked away, her deal with Effie didn't seem like such a great idea. But what about Effie? Ella had been failing at everything, especially during the tea party, where she acted like a clumsy fool in front of the nobles. A weak, foolish girl. Yet Effie, who was very subservient to her sister, still managed to control the situation while still being a daughter who only wanted her mother's attention. And she achieved her goal.

It made her think of the tea party. Was she really failing? The point of the task was to play the part given to her. And her part was to be a country girl who was adopted into nobility. Just like Ella, this character would have never had any education on nobility, nor would she have been well received. She probably shouldn't have tripped over the rug, but it wasn't so inconceivable that a naïve country girl wouldn't do the same. The only thing she was failing at was that her mindset was wrong, Ella would naturally act the part of a naive country girl because she was one, but if she focused on what she could accomplish while playing the part, she could achieve her goals. Or maybe she had already achieved them.

And the horseback riding. She had never done horseback riding, and with everything going on, did she truly relax? These thoughts rattled around her mind, filling the monotony of not doing anything.

After what felt like a week, being trapped in the cramped room was wearing on her. Still not knowing what was happening, Ella hoped that anything would do. She was answered by the wall opening up behind her.

Eleanor appeared with a bright smile. She was going to hug Ella when, seeing the state of her clothes, she thought better of it and merely gave her a pat on the shoulder. "That was rather epic. Come on, you have gotten even further behind on your lessons. You need to go horseback riding in the hidden pasture. Oh, and you can no longer be outside the hidden passageways until Madame Briar says it's time. And you will have someone show you around the passageways. Then, after you do your horseback lessons, you will need to speak to Madame Briar. She would have seen you now, but some things popped up that needed her attention. Now here we are."

Ella had to blink as the afternoon light burned her eyes. The endless days in the basement and the short journey through the dark passageway made the sudden bright light stab at her. Blinking the tears out of her watering eyes until they adjusted, Ella glanced at where she was. They had somehow arrived at the small stables in the hidden pasture. William was already ready there crooning over that evil horse.

Giving her a push into the pasture, Eleanor called out one last thing, "Oh, and we will make sure to get a bath ready for you after you're done. I'll have someone pick you up later. Ta-ta."

Ella stood there blinking until William came over with Lady Grey. He was beaming, which was not surprising since he was next to a horse. When his eyes settled on her shaking hands that she unsuccessfully tried to hide, he said, "You can relax. Lady Grey is in a good mood today."

She gave the horse a sideways glance. As if that horse could ever be in a bad mood when it enjoyed tormenting Ella so. It snorted and shook its head, as if in answer to her unsaid thoughts. With a sigh, she let him help her into the saddle.

It started all wrong. The horse began wandering off and eating grass. But not today; this horse would do what she instructed it to. "Just move," she said while giving the horse a firm tap of the riding crop.

And to her amazement, the horse did as was asked. William nodded from his observation point, his lips curled up into a pleased grin. "That is how you ride a horse. You've got to relax; being stressed and iffy about where you are going is only going to confuse her."

Understanding hit her like a ton of bricks. Her fear of the horse and falling showed and made all of her actions timid. And all the stress was stiffening her body, which sent differing instructions to the horse. Letting out a deep breath, she released the tension that had been building since she had started that year. She would no longer be pushed around by the horse. She was the one in charge. Just as she was not going to be pushed around by her own insecurities. Sitting up taller in her saddle, Ella pulled her reins to the left and tapped the horse's shoulder. The horse followed instructions and allowed itself to be ridden around the small pasture.

As she rode, the stress eased; everything changed when she had confidence in her actions. No longer having the stress of being alone, it was much easier to do as William had been trying to tell her and just relax. It was a much more enjoyable ride.

But she still didn't like being on the horse.

It was much easier to keep her seat now that the horse did as she was asked. After that realization, Ella felt much more comfortable with riding. At least, enough that if she had to go for a short horse ride, she could keep her seat.

And as she was getting off, this time without a mouthful of grass, her face beamed. Feeling pleased with herself, Ella was hoping that her teacher would have some words of encouragement. And he was smiling . . . at the horse. He cooed over the horse, telling it what a wonderful job it had done with training Ella to not fall off. Then he turned to her. "You did a great job getting off. You will have to get used to having two people help you off, but if you can get off with just my help, you are going to be fine."

"What do you mean two people?"

William started leading the horse back to the stables and answered her, "Well, usually to be lady-like on a double-horned saddle, you need two people to help you off. With just me, it was hard to do that and I kept dropping you. Sorry about that, by the way."

He went back to crooning over the horse and leading it away as Ella stood there in stunned silence. Ella was about to spout some angry words at him, but as she looked at him, she thought better of it. She doubted that he would even care about something other than horses.

Following him, she didn't wait long for Clementine to appear. With a wrinkle of her nose, she hugged her friend, though she wiped off the dirt that had gotten on her apron. Clementine looked her for any signs of injury and tutted at the bruise that had formed on her wrist from the guard's strong grip. Then she headed off towards the academy. "Well, come on."

A smile blossomed on Ella's face as she trotted behind her friend. "What is happening?"

"Hold on, I'm thinking. There are a lot more corridors than you think," Clementine said, her face furrowed in concentration. They had entered from the secret entrance that Eleanor had brought her out, but now they were at a crossroads. Muttering to herself for a few seconds, Clementine's face relaxed as she chose the right-hand path. "There has been a lot happening. You really caused such a ruckus. You were lucky that they haven't executed you by now. I got to Madame Briar just in time. I managed to slow them down enough until Effie could arrive."

Ella swallowed at the thought of her near death. Clearing her throat, she asked, "Since they obviously aren't going to kill me anymore, what's going to happen to me?"

"To be honest. I don't know. You will have to talk to the head-mistress about that. Oh drat, wrong turn." They had opened a room that had Luella standing in it. "Sorry, Luella." Hurriedly, Clementine closed the door behind her. "Seriously, what is wrong with that girl? All I have heard from her is complaints about you. What did you do to her?"

"Nothing!" Ella exclaimed. The corridors were now lit, and she could see Clementine's expression of disbelief. "I swear she has been after me since before I knew about the Fan Society."

"If you say so," Clementine said with a shrug. She led them down a different corridor to another room. Clementine opened it to reveal a room exactly like the one Luella was in. It was very like her previous room in the servants' quarters except it was longer and had a shorter ceiling. The only difference was hers had a copper bath in it. "Now, hurry and wash up. We have to go see Madame Briar."

Ella nodded gratefully, pleased at the chance to get clean, she washed off the stink of her cell and got dressed in new clothes that were set on the bed. Then, as soon as she was ready, Clementine led her off to the secret office.

Knocking lightly on the door, Clementine let Ella in. It was time to find out her fate.

One must have an open mind. If you close it, you will not be able to see opportunities until they have passed you by. Often, the only thing that stops you from accomplishing a task is yourself.

Nora "Cinders"
Report 100

Chapter Eleven

Ella met Madame Briar in her secret office. As soon as she came in, she was given a piece of paper and asked to write a report on how she thought she had done. The madame reminded her that her tasks were to be able to act as a servant, act like her character and perform a tea party as that character, ride a horse, and copy a page from a noble's room. And the extra task she was given to get herself in enough trouble to be forced to leave the school.

After giving her that task, she continued going through the papers on her desk as Ella was left to her thoughts. This was the first time that she had to organize the revelations she had had during her incarceration. After everything had happened, Effie had done her a favor. Her words had changed how Ella viewed the tea parties. She had always felt as though she was doing a poor job, but that was the wrong way to think about it. Every accident, every mistake, could be used to her advantage, as long as she thought of it that way.

With that in mind, she wrote her report.

After she finished, she gave it to Madame Briar and waited as she read it. Ella was on pins and needles, biting her lip as she gauged the madame's expression. The headmistress gave nothing away, which only made it worse for Ella. But by now she had learned that Madame Briar would say nothing until she was ready to.

When she finally set the page down, Ella had just won against herself in a battle of wills; she would not doubt her right to be here. Thankfully, her doubts had been brushed aside for the moment, and her knowledge that she did her best won out.

"I have had many young girls come through my door, all of them bright with promise. Your mother being one of them. I have shown you the Fan Society, and now I want to know: Why do you want to stay here?"

Ella pondered that question. Her answer had changed over the past few months. It had changed the past few days, even. At first, she felt like being a part of the Fan Society was an opportunity, but then the only thing that made her wasn't to stay was her stubbornness to not fail at it. Now, with a fresh perspective, the opportunity that Ella had first glimpsed felt more real to her. This was truly an opportunity. She didn't know what to make of it yet, but it was something she needed to see through to the end.

"I don't know about saving our country or anything like that. But if it means that I can find out about my mother, then I will do it. This is my chance to change my life."

Sweat built on her hands as she hid them under the table, but she kept her gaze on Madame Briar. After pondering this for a few moments, the headmistress replied, "That is a good answer. You are almost fifteen years old and don't yet understand the implications of what we do here. But you will. For now, your answer will suffice. Though I do have something that may change some of your motivations, or at least give you more of a nudge in the right direction."

She handed Ella a stack of papers.

Ella fought the urge to furrow her brows. "What's this?"

Madame Briar didn't answer, only waiting until Ella came to her conclusion. A little annoyed that everything she did had to be a teaching moment, she looked at the papers in her hands. They were various reports all signed by Nora.

"Are these my mother's?"

A smile graced Madame Briar's face as she nodded. "Yes, these are her reports. As her daughter, you have a right to see them."

"Why didn't you show them to me earlier?"

"Why do you think, Lady Cooper?"

Ella paused, mulling it over. "To test me?"

The madame nodded. "Now, your cover story is thus: As a punishment for attempting to kill a noble lady, you were sentenced to slavery in the Americas. Your stepmother was vehemently opposed to your death, saying it was too light of a sentence. We stated instead that you would be sent to the Americas as a slave. That seemed to satisfy her anger against you. And since you made the deal with Euphemia, she will help keep your stepmother's thoughts away from you."

Knowing that Madame Briar had a wide information network, a question burned within her. "Do you know why my stepmother hates me so?"

Sighing, Madame Briar pinched the bridge of her nose, then tsked, "Your stepmother is an ambitious woman, but she was born a commoner. Your mother was born a noble and was well-known in society. She possessed the power and title that your stepmother coveted. Though she now has a title through marriage to your father, she never had the power your mother did. Even now, your mother's name carries greatness far more than hers. Since the object of her jealousy has disappeared, the next easiest target was her daughter. Though it was because of this fact that it was easy to make your existence disappear. As long as you are being tormented, she doesn't care about you."

The words Madame Briar said left Ella with a hollow feeling. All of the torment her stepmother had done to her was because of jealousy. Not even to Ella, but to Nora, Ella's mother. There would have been nothing she could have done to stop her stepmother's hatred of her.

Madame Briar continued, pulling her out of her dark thoughts, "On a happy note, you have passed your qualifications for this year. Though you will need to work more on being a proper noble, and your horseback riding skill needs some work. We will have someone show you around so you can start memorizing the secret paths in the school."

"I passed?" Relief passed through Ella in an instant.

"Yes, your change in perspective is what helped you pass. Some-one who has no confidence would not be able to do the things that need to be done. Now, I will leave you for today so you can get acquainted with your mother's reports."

With clear dismissal, Ella headed out the door. As Ella was about to open the door, she turned back and asked one last question, "Did Effie request anything for me?"

The headmistress nodded. "She asked that instead of sending you to the Americas that you be sent to Baron Smith."

So, she did keep her promise. As Clementine led her through the corridors, Ella thought about how in such little time she had learned how to get back all the confidence she had lost over the years due to being treated like a worthless servant. But she wasn't that anymore. She was a part of a secret society with an important mission to protect the throne. She could have confidence that she was a part of something greater. Ella was meant to be part of this, just as her mother was. Madame Briar had already acknowledged her and believed that she had the capability to be a part of this. All she had to do was not dwell on her dark thoughts.

This time, as she was being guided through the corridors, Ella was led past the training room. As Ella passed, she caught a glare from Luella. The same glare that she'd had since they first met. And Ella was struck with the thought that even if Madame Briar accepted her, that didn't mean the others would so easily.

Year Two

In the second year, I found my talent. In my pursuit to be the best, there will always be others who are there to ensure that doesn't happen.

Arabella Cooper "Cinders"
Report 15

Chapter Twelve

"Well, don't you look like a bundle of joy," Clementine commented as she placed another pin in Ella's hair. She had been practicing during the past few months to better assist Ella in her endeavors as a member of the Fan Society.

Unable to keep the grin from her face, she replied, "Yes, because today I get to see Luella again."

"The one who is always glaring at you? Ready to show her what you got? If you need help, I'm always ready to put some nettle powder in her skirts."

And she would do it, too. Ella smiled at her friend. Even though she was nineteen, and four years older than her, they were as close as sisters. After everything that had happened with her stepfamily and last school year, how could they not?

Ella grinned imagining what Luella would look like if her friend had put nettle powder in her stepsisters' skirts. Maybe then she would stop looking down on Ella with contempt. She had always had that glare on her face as if she couldn't believe that someone as pathetic as Ella had come near her. And it was personal, though Ella had no idea why. As far as Ella was aware, her only reason for despising her was simply because she didn't believe Ella to be worthy of belonging in the Fan Society.

"I wish we could dump the powder in her skirts, but that would only prove her thoughts that I don't belong here," Ella said with a sigh. If she was going to prove that she belonged in the society, she ought to think about how she was going to survive this school year. "This year's task, I will show her that I belong as a member of the Fan Society. And she can glare at me all she wants; it won't matter. Let's get to class. I don't want to be late."

Clementine smiled, put the last pin in, and opened the door. As they wandered the well-lit portion of the hidden passageways, Ella thought back to what had brought her here.

The last few months were strange for Ella. After her final mission of the previous year, she had since lived her life within the walls of the academy. Thankfully, not long after the supposed punishment of her being forced to leave the academy, there was a break for several months for the ladies to go home, allowing her to have more free reign. Most families were on break from the season and were back at their family homes instead of housing in London. During this time, there were very few people in the halls, and Ella spent that time familiarizing herself with the many hidden passageways throughout the academy, as well as allowing Madame Briar to give her more lessons to get her up to speed with the other noble ladies.

But those few months of respite had come to an end now that October had arrived. A few ladies would arrive in November after helping siblings get ready for their debut into society, though the girls who were a part of the Fan Society would be arriving sooner. It was time for the first class back together. Ella's understanding was that this year they would be practicing the physical aspects of the Fan Society. That included the usage of various weaponry.

She might be bad at horseback riding, but she was very good at other physical matters. This time, she wouldn't fail. She couldn't.

Ella tsked at herself. She would not fall back into her previous mindset. The thoughts that she was a failure and that she could never catch up. She could do this, she was capable, indomitable, and had Clementine by her side. Taking a deep breath, Ella made her way into the large training room.

This space was a massive rectangular room that was longer than it was wide. It had mats and mirrors on one side and tables and dresses on the other. There were stairs to one side that led up to Madam Briar's official office. Most of her training previously had been nobility training. But now it was time to learn weapons. Something that was actually interesting. At that thought, she crossed the room with an extra bounce in her step.

Ella was one of the first to arrive, making it difficult to keep from fidgeting as she waited for the others to make their way to class. One of the last students to appear was Luella. Her dark hair pulled up into a bun did little to soften her sharp features. When her blue eyes met Ella's, her lips curled back in disgust.

Distracted by Luella, she didn't notice Eleanor until a bubbly voice rang in her ear, "How are you doing, Ella? Still not getting along with Luella?"

"When have I ever?" Ella retorted, then turned and gave Eleanor a smile. The cheerful girl was one of the first who had become friends with Ella.

"True." Eleanor returned her exuberance, then turn to look behind Ella. "Oh, Madame Briar is here."

And she was. She appeared at the front of the training room. Without even a sound, all the girls turned and waited for her to speak. She was wearing a modest day dress, yet everyone knew she was the one who had the most authority in the room. Her silver hair laced with white spoke of her age, but her face made it difficult to tell how old she truly was.

"The society has three main parts. Miss Flora, could you tell us what those three parts are?"

Ella turned to look at a girl who had a round face and brilliant green eyes. Ella didn't remember seeing her at the tea party before, the horrible day that ended with shattered dishes and avoiding looking at anyone. A black mark that she would rather forget.

Speaking in a quiet voice, the girl answered, "The three groups are Members, Supporters, and Informants."

"Very good. What are the different groups referred to as, Lady Taylor?"

"Guardians, Friends of the Society, or just Friends and Ghosts," Eleanor beamed.

It was like polar opposites. Her pleasant attitude that attracted people contrasted with Flora's pale presence.

"Correct. We will learn about both of them in the next school year. This year, we are focusing on the different branches within the Fan Society. Lady Cooper, can you tell us what they are?" the headmistress asked with a raise of her brow.

With great effort to keep from shuffling her feet with all eyes on her, Ella thought furiously about what they could be. There was a lot that she had to learn, and she had a hard time remembering all the specifics. "There are several different groups. The ones that are nurses and midwives. Those who spread gossip and rumors. And the Assistants who are their supporters."

"That is correct. You have the Medics. They are where sensitive information and high emotions happen. They gain access to information that you would not get otherwise. And the Whispers. They help control information by spreading information and rumors, as you suggested. They also have the ability to change fashion to suit our needs. And finally, as you mentioned, Assistants, who are the partners of the other members of the society who do the things they can't due to the constraints of society. But you missed a very important group. Lady Jones, can you tell us what that group is?"

"Only the Elites, Madame," Luella stated, rolling her eyes pointedly at Ella. "They are the group that has to be able to do everything. They are the one who gets assigned to marry into an influential family. Only the best of the best gets to be a part of the Elites."

She spat the final remark as if to say Ella would never be part of the Elites, and Ella wanted to smack that snooty girl across the face. Yet again, she was looked down upon, and for what? They were supposed to be on the same side. What was wrong with that girl? Why did she have to prove that she was better in everything? And what did she have against her? She had done nothing to Luella. Why did she think that Ella didn't belong here so fiercely?

Her thoughts were interrupted by Madam Briar. "You are correct in many ways. The Elites are also the ones called the Guardians. The Guardians must be a jack-of-all-trades and have a talent for picking up things. But the other branches are specialized and have far more knowledge in their specific field. Everyone has talents, and it is my job to make them shine. That is what this year's task is going to be. You all will be given five emblems. Your goal is to try to take them from each other."

She motioned with her hand, and a girl dressed as a servant came in carrying a tray. On the tray were various broaches, pins, bracelets, and other accessories. They looked like what many of the nobility would wear on a daily basis.

A girl with a perky voice chirped, "But how will you know that the accessary is one of the emblems?"

"Lady Parker, that is a good question. Please come closer."

With a wave, the girls moved forward and formed a half-circle around Madame Briar. She picked up one of the rings and slowly showed it in the light.

When she moved it closer to her, Ella could see a small, barely perceptible Fan Society emblem hidden within the gem.

After showing all of them, the madame placed it back on the tray. "All of these have the Fan Society emblem somewhere on them. You also must have one on you at all times. After class, you will pick your emblems and then it will be time for the task to begin.

"This will be a test of your ingenuity, as well as a chance to show you what life is like for a spy. It is a game of give and take. How much you are willing to give, and how much you can take for yourself. Here is where you will find your strengths and weaknesses in yourself, and also in others. This will test you in ways you never knew you would be tested. These girls are your allies and as of the end of this class, also your enemies."

Madame Briar walked down the row of girls, looking each of them in the eyes. Ella could feel the excitement rise around her as all the girls got swept up in her speech.

As she got to the end of the row, she stopped. "The girl who is last in the test will not be able to become a member of the Guardians. But the girl who has the highest points will be helping on a mission." She eyed Ella and Luella before slowly continuing her steps, and the girls around her eagerly glanced around, ready to be chosen for a real mission. "Any other questions? . . . No? Time for running. Hop to it."

The girls exchanged curious glances, dressed as they were in day dresses, not the sort of thing you went running in. Madame Briar snapped her fan once to show she wasn't joking, and the girls sprung into action, running around the room with fancy shoes and thick skirts flapping at their legs.

During the second year, I had learned much more about my mother, who had always seemed so distant from me. This woman who had disappeared when I was young now felt much more tangible to me. And after reading her stories, I wanted to make her proud. I would be one of the best Legacies and show them what the daughter of Nora could do. I just had to figure out how to do it.

Arabella Cooper "Cinders"
Report 100

Chapter Thirteen

E lla collapsed into bed after the long day. Due to the lack of students at school, they were able to do classes all day. And she was feeling it.

Clementine came in to help her out of her sweaty garments. "Long day?"

"You can say that again." After an exhausting hour of running, Madame Briar had them move on to another exercise. They were forced to do it all over again, only this time in a ballgown. Madame Briar said it was to get used to moving around in different dresses, but with all the heavy petticoats, and after an already exhausting morning, it felt like it weighed more.

Lunch had been a tea party, but with cups made of iron. They were supposed to pretend that they were normal teacups. Trying to drink delicately out of a heavy cup was not easy. Her wrists were still feeling it.

"What about you?" Ella asked, massaging her wrists as Clementine got her ready for a bath.

"We had a long, in-depth discussion on sewing in secret compartments, how to fix blade cuts, and the best ways to remove blood stains out of silk. Speaking of which, you are now supposed to wear gloves at all times."

"What? Why?" Ella hated wearing them for etiquette classes, and now she had to wear them even longer?

"Oh, don't you start with me. I agree with the decision. You have spent the last few years as a servant, and your hands show it. If you want to be able to pretend that you are a noblewoman, you must look the part. At least the one good thing about never being able to leave the hidden passageways is that you will lighten your skin tone," Clementine said as she began pulling pins from Ella's hair.

Ella rolled her eyes. Being stuck inside was a pain, but at least it gave her time to memorize the hallways. No more getting lost, and there were still more pathways that she hadn't been shown that she wished she had time to explore.

"Ouch." Ella winced as her frizzy hair caught on a pin.

"What did you do to yourself?" she asked while her fingers gently brushed the bump that had been growing on her head. It was already painful to manage her curly hair, and now with all the intricate designs that her hair needed to be wrangled into, Ella wanted to chop it all off.

Snorting, Ella replied, "Not my fault. We were practicing how to faint properly, and Luella was my partner. You can guess what happened next." Ella's mind drifted to the final lesson of the day: Fainting. Ella had practice with Clementine, but it was much harder with wearied legs. . . and a partner she couldn't trust.

"Ahh. She missed catching you not-on-purpose-but-total-ly-was?" Ella nodded her head. Clementine tutted and continued, "You need to work on your fainting skills then, and it shouldn't matter who your partner is."

"As if you could do better," Ella snapped.

It had been a long day.

Clementine stopped her work, then gave a dramatic sigh and fell to the floor with a whimper. She laid beautifully on the floor, just waiting for a dashing man to come and save her. If Ella didn't know any better, she would have thought she actually had fainted.

Cracking a smile and finally releasing the tension that she hadn't realized she had, Ella said, "Fine. I won't make a bet against your acting skill anymore."

Opening her eyes, Clementine sat up. "Good. I thought you knew better. Now you just need to show her how fantastic you truly are by making sure you are the one going on the mission. You should steal all of her emblems right out from under her. That would show her."

As she finished getting ready for the night, Ella planned just that.

The next few weeks started in much the same manner: running around the training room in every type of clothing that might be needed, and then on to other exercises. Many of the girls wore the emblems, and due to the exhausting nature of the classes and how long they went, it made it difficult to get any of the other emblems. And Luella didn't help matters.

After pushing her away instead of allowing her to practice how to spill water on someone for the fifth time, Ella burst out, "What is your problem with me?"

Looking down on her, Luella gave her that signature infuriating glare. "You do not belong here. You are going to tarnish the Fan Society name. You shouldn't even try to win the right to go on the mission."

Yet again not explaining why she thought that Ella didn't belong. Standing up and brushing the water from her skirts, Ella remarked, "Well, that isn't your choice, now is it?"

"Right you are, Lady Cooper. It is mine." Madame Briar had moved closer to them during their spat. Feeling the weight of the headmistress's gaze, Ella knew that this was another test.

Ella was going to prove to everyone that she deserved to be here. That meant becoming a Guardian, just like her mother had been.

A smile graced Madame Briar's face at Ella's expression. "It seems like we are going too slow in the training. I need to move forward to weapons. Lady Parker, can you please go fetch an iron fan and a practice fencing sword?"

The lively blonde-haired girl hurried to do as ordered and returned with them. Madame Briar picked up the iron fan, then motioned for Ella to pick up the sword. Ella had never held a sword before, and this one was long and thin; the edge had been blunted and had a rubber tip attached at the end. Giving it a few test lunges, she then looked to Madame Briar.

Seeing that she was done, the madame said, "The goal is for you to score a touch with your blade. Now begin."

At those words, her teacher flicked the fan open.

Testing, Ella lunged towards her teacher.

With a quick snap, the tip of the sword was knocked away. Madame Briar tutted, "You can do better than that. Remember the lady with the lowest score will not be allowed to become a Guardian."

Madame Briar hadn't even moved, not that Ella could discern. Desire to win sparked within hers as, in an instant, she lunged again, stabbing forward three times in quick succession. And each time Madame Briar did nothing more than tap the end away, unconcerned that Ella was stabbing a sword at her. Throughout the exchange, she still hadn't moved more than a mere flick of her wrist.

A couple a of snickers scattered through the room, led by Luella. Growling in frustration, Ella struggled to control her emotions. Anger flashed through her as she readied her next action. She was going to make Madame Briar move. Instead of lunging towards her torso, Ella lashed out towards her feet. Madame Briar only pivoted, like she was doing a turn for a dance, causing the sword to completely miss her.

Yet again, a scattering of snickers was heard, the loudest being from Luella. Ignoring the amused onlookers, Ella concentrated on Madame Briar. The dance continued as Ella slashed and lunged, trying to get her mentor to move. And nothing worked. Every strike was avoided or batted away without looking like she put any effort into it.

Breathing heavily, Ella tried not to brush the trickle of sweat that had started crawling down her forehead as she looked for a way to get past Madame Briar's defenses. This was the head of the Fan Society, a master of her craft. She was the one who had taught Ella's mother. A sense of pride that this was where she would be learning warmed her, but she was still mildly annoyed at her predicament.

Luella spoke up, her voice snide, "Madame Briar, you are so talented. Or maybe Ella just isn't good enough."

Ignoring the snarky remark, Madame Briar addressed the group, "With your partners, you will be doing this exercise. One will be attacking while the other is defending. When the attacker gets a 'touch', then it will be their turn to defend. Remember, you do not need to do wide movements. A lady must show restraint when needed. Do not move more than needed, as this will help conserve your energy, especially against larger opponents."

While she was talking, weapons had been brought out to each pair. Ella looked to Luella, finding that instead of the usual glare, she had on a smile. With a glint in her eye, Luella asked Ella, "Since you attacked, do you want to try defending now?"

She held out the fan like it was a death sentence.

Grabbing it, Ella took up the challenge. "I would be happy to." She passed Luella her sword and without warning, Luella struck.

Only reflex made Ella able to knock the blade away in time. The fan was heavier than she expected and made it difficult to block her next attack. Luella tsked, and her next move came with more force. Flicking her blade toward Ella again, Ella twisted her wrist so the fan swung down, knocking it away. Irritation flickered across Luella's features, and she flicked her blade out again and again like a vindictive seamstress. By the grace of her reflexes, Ella was able to continue to block. The quick, heavy attacks came faster and less refined as each attempt to land a blow on Ella failed to meet its mark.

As this went on, Ella's wrists began to tremble, and her arm fell lower. Seeing her chance, Luella thrusted forward, stabbing Ella hard in the gut. With a grunt, Ella dropped her fan and bent over, clutching her stomach.

Standing over her, Luella grinned in triumph. "I win. Guess you are still the loser. With those skills, you should just give up on the chance to go on the mission."

Wanting to snap back at her, Ella restrained herself. Wiggling her fingers to get feeling back in them, she calmed her breathing. Now was not the time for this. Ella reached down to pick up her fan, but as she did, she noticed something sparkle. Peeking out from beneath Luella's skirts was a broach that had been clipped to her shoe. One that had an emblem hidden in its gem. Hiding her hands with her body as she crouched, Ella slipped the broach off Luella's shoe and grabbed the fan with her other hand. As she stood up, the broach dropped from her lifeless fingers. The vibration from the previous clash of metal on metal had caused her fingers to go numb, and she couldn't grip it properly. Luella noticed, picking up her broach.

"So close," she chided with a laugh, holding it just out of reach. "Seems you still aren't good enough to be here. You should quit now, before making an even bigger fool of yourself. There is no way you can fill Lady Cooper's shoes."

Anger grew with every word that was spouted from Luella's mouth as she continued to look down on Ella. Ella wanted to snatch the broach from her snobby fingers but was interrupted by Madame Briar, saving her from another disgrace that would have truly proven Luella's words correct.

"Ladies, tomorrow will be the return of classes. This will be a good time to try to relieve the other girls of their emblems. I have just received word of a mission that must take place at the end of the school year. An undercover agent needs a young girl to play the part of a daughter on an easy mission. Because of this, whomever has the most emblems by the end of the school year will be chosen to take part in this mission. Lady Cooper, please stay after training. I need to speak to you. Other than that, you all are dismissed."

Luella brushed past Ella, whispering in her ear, "Guess she finally realized that you aren't worthy of being here."

Clenching her fist, Ella waited for all the girls to leave. Then she followed Madame Briar to her secret office.

The tasks always seem simple at first glance but are far more difficult than they seem. Even if you keep your eyes open, things are not what they appear.

Nora "Cinders"
Report 10, paragraph 2

Chapter Fourteen

Nervous at what Madame Briar might want, Ella sat in front of her, waiting for her to speak. Instead of forcing her to wait like she normally would, she began speaking as soon as Ella sat down.

"Lady Cooper, due to the nature of your circumstances, you will be having a harder task. The other ladies, if they get caught, will be forced to do a punishment, not unlike yourself with the horses. But you, on the other hand, are supposed to be sent away. If you get caught, it is the end. According to the school, you should have been punished for attacking a noble. If you are recognized, it would show that you were not sent away. Because of the mess involved, we would have to send you away for the protection of the Fan Society. Do you understand what I mean?"

Ella hung her head. "I'll make sure that I will stay within the walls and only make attempts during class."

"Heavens no, child. I'm not asking you to stay in the walls. I am trusting you to not get caught. Make good use of your Assistant, since she is able to be outside the walls. That is what they are supposed to help with if you took anything from my lessons."

The weight of what the madame said still sat uncomfortably about Ella. She still hadn't shown her skills. Even though she hated to admit it, Luella was far better than she was at the spy thing. Unoriginal, but well trained.

After reading about her mother, Ella wanted to do as well as her. During the summer when the girls were gone, she had spent her time pouring over the pages that Madame Briar had given her. But after reading reports and other papers written of her, she doubted she could live up to her mother. She had examined every little thing, and she was even more amazing than Ella's scant memories held.

Madame Briar must have seen her unease, as she spoke again, "You are very much like your mother."

"I look nothing like her." Ella pouted, remembering her mother's portrait in the Legacy room. Her mother's red hair and vibrant smile looked nothing like Ella's frizzy brown hair and gangly features. Just sitting for a portrait, her mother looked elegant and refined. Ella was still trying to figure out what fork to use.

"I wasn't talking about your features. I was talking about your drive and stubbornness to be the best and not let anyone tear you down."

Ella still didn't think so; none of her mother's writing ever showed any of the doubt that Ella had last year. Her mother's goals were to protect the royal line to keep this country safe, just like the Fan Society's mission statement. Ella, on the other hand, was only trying to get close to her mother.

The madame continued, "I have seen many girls go through my doors, and I have never been wrong about a single one. I may have been wrong about their goals, but I was never wrong about their talents. Now, you have a lot to think about. And also, since you will not be able to do classes with the other girls during the day, you will have classes with me. I will help you catch up on what you have been missing. But for today, you will be free to think about your task. You may go."

Ella left, still thinking about the words the headmistress spoke. She was trusted with the weight of a higher standard. She could do this, couldn't she? After all, hadn't she lasted a long time against Luella? She had never trained with either the sword or the fan. Ella had no doubt that Luella had been trained, considering her stance and easy confidence with the sword. And yet Ella had still kept up. Madame Briar thought she had talent, and now it was time to prove to the others that her faith was true. She could do this, as long as she had Clementine's help.

By the time she made it back to her room, she had a plan; it all depended on her speed and Clementine's resources.

The plan was simple. During the run, pilfer as many emblems as possible without anyone noticing. All it took was her being faster than anyone else and having quick fingers. During the last few runs, Ella was faster than everyone else, having more stamina from hard work. But it would only work in the beginning. Because with the rate they were going with their physical training, it wouldn't take long for the other girls to catch up to her. Soon, they would be good enough that they would be more aware of their surroundings when they were running. For now, they just tried to not pass out.

After collecting the emblems, all that would be left was retrieval. And Clementine would know the perfect person to help with that. After talking to Clementine to set their plan in motion, they were all set to go the next day.

Since nobility were not early risers, due to the late-night schedule they kept, the girls all had morning classes together. The Assistants were servants and had their own hard work to do during the day. Madame Briar said that they would be joining them in their classes together next year. But for this year, they would only be together after classes.

The class normally started with a run, but this time they had obstacles as well. They had to climb over boxes and barrels, while servants tried to knock them off with padded poles. During their stretch, Ella scanned the room and spotted a servant with her hair in a bun tied with a red ribbon. The sign that she was willing to help. A smile came on her face; Clementine worked fast. Now she needed to do her part. Casting her eyes over the Fan Society members, Ella picked out who would be the best targets.

Eleanor interrupted her thoughts as she leaned over to touch her toes. "Eyeing Luella still? I thought you did a great job yesterday no matter what she says."

"Thank you, Eleanor. That means a lot to me." And it did. She flashed Eleanor a warm smile.

"Luella has a chip on her shoulder, so don't take what she says to heart."

A burning question leaped out of her lips at that statement, "Do you know why Luella hates me? I didn't do anything to her."

It had never occurred to Ella to ask the other girls. She was so used to doing everything with only Clementine that it took a bit to realize that she was now a part of something. And there were others on the same side. Not only that, but she knew Luella better.

Tilting her head, Eleanor replied, "You are a Legacy. Only a child of a Legacy can come directly into the Fan Society like you. Luella, on the other hand, had different circumstances. Her parents were Ghosts that became friends of the Society. Due to that, the Fan Society made it so that her family received a title, and in turn, they had their daughter become a member of the society in repayment. There was a lot of effort and hard work she put in so she could be considered part of the Fan Society. She put in that effort due to the stories about your mother. She idolized her."

It must have pricked at Luella to know that some upstart was able to come in just because of her heritage. And with how poorly she had done during the first year, that only showed her that Ella was nothing like her talented mother. But none of that was anything that Ella had a choice in. And besides, Ella had been working hard to catch up to everyone. She hadn't even known that her mother was a Legacy until Madame Briar told her a couple of months ago.

"Thanks for letting me know, Eleanor. I knew it was personal, but I didn't know why."

The girl shrugged, stretching her arms. "You're welcome. Don't let her get you down. Oh, it looks like it's time to start." Then she took off at a run.

Distracted by Eleanor, Ella missed seeing where her targets had gone and had to take a few seconds to look for them. One of them being Luella, who was already at the head of the pack. Ella would have to hurry if her plan was going to work.

Kicking up her heels, she caught up to the one in the back of the pack. She was the quiet girl from the first class named Flora. She had on a few different emblems. Never the strongest runner, it was easy to catch up to her. As she ran past and jumped the first box, she pulled the decorative hairpin out of Flora's hair, hiding it in her palm and continuing onward. And when she got to the servant with the red ribbon, she dropped it in front of her. If the girl stuck to the plan, she would then kick any snagged emblems out of sight until it was time to leave, then retrieve them and pass them on to Clementine.

With her heavy skirts weighing on her, Ella hurried to catch up to the next girl when there was suddenly a commotion behind her. Everyone came to a halt.

One of the girls had passed out next to Flora and lay sprawled out, a pin clutched in her hand. The girls had started huddling around the fallen girl. Before anyone could panic, Madame Briar came forward, shooing the girls away. Bending down, she looked at the girl's fingers, then to Flora.

"How long do you think she will be out for?" Madame Briar asked.

"No more than a few minutes, I would say," Flora replied.

"Seems that someone was well prepared for defending their emblems." Madame Briar raised her brow at Flora.

Flora smiled in return. "It is only right to be well prepared considering what this class is for."

"Indeed." Madame Briar clapped her hands. Standing, she turned back to the girls who were milling about trying to get a good look. "Ladies, time to get back to class. Lady Williams will be fine."

And just like that, the girls returned to their exercise, albeit with more chattering between them. Eleanor came up beside Ella and said, "Flora did a great job."

"What are you talking about?"

"Flora is training to be a nurse. She knows a lot about different plants." At that mysterious comment, she headed off at a run.

Thinking on it, the girl that had fallen was one of Ella's targets. She wasn't a fast runner, and her bracelet was tantalizingly easy to slip off. As the servant's helped move her to a comfortable spot, Ella noticed that fallen girl didn't have her bracelet on her, which Ella had spotted earlier. Thinking back on the conversation Flora had with Madame Briar, it sounded like Flora did something to make the girl faint. Remembering the last emblem she had stolen had been from Flora, Ella looked at her gloves. As she did, she saw that white satin now had a greasy substance on the fingertip. Eleanor had said that Flora was good at plants. She must have put something on all of her emblems, and when they touched it, the substance caused them to faint. And it would be so easy to steal something from an unconscious person.

Ella glanced back at the quiet unassuming Flora. She had forgotten one simple thing: All the girls here were picked to be part

105

of the Fan Society. No one was as they seemed. If she wanted to be a member of the elite Guardians, she would have her work cut out for her. This task had just become a lot harder than she thought.

The creativity that the girls have shown this year is inspiring. This year's girls are proving to be rather talented. It will be interesting to see how this all plays out.

Madame Briar
Progress Report 2, Year 1826-1827

Chapter Fifteen

Because of the limits set on her, Ella used her knowledge of the secret passageways to get around. Some of the passageways had peepholes to gain information. It came in handy when she was keeping an eye on Luella.

Her observations paid off. As afternoon classes ended, Ella had managed to catch a conversation between Luella and Audrey. She was too far away to hear it, but the peephole hidden in the wall gave her a rather clear view of what was happening. Annoyance built within Ella as she watched Luella talk to Audrey, two people who had caused Ella nothing but trouble. Wishing she could hear them, Ella pressed herself against the stone wall as much as she could to get as clear a view as possible. The conversation ended without Ella hearing anything.

As Audrey and Luella parted ways, Luella gave her stepsister a box that had a bracelet in it, one Ella recognized as an emblem that Luella had. She knew that this would only be a massive detriment to Ella. That vindictive girl had it out for her. But at least Ella knew where one of the emblems was.

Ella continued to spend her time watching the hallways since she couldn't leave during the day or risk getting caught. During her time staking out the hidden passageways and peeking through peepholes, she also managed to find where three of the other six girls hid their emblems. Since they had classes together, they tended to use the same hallways.

One of them was a calm girl that didn't really stand out much named Dorothy Stratton, who hid hers cleverly in her vase used for flower arranging.

Olive Williams, the girl who passed out during class that morning, had snagged two different emblems from Ivy Parker, who had promptly stolen one back the next hour. There were only two girls she didn't see doing anything with the emblems.

Flora, who Ella now knew was a commoner from Clementine's information, was training to be a nurse, so she wouldn't be seen in the nobility hallways.

The other was Eleanor, who Ella had seen talking to some of the other girls but hadn't done anything with the emblems.

After those classes were done, the Fan Society girls had class together. This was another lesson on weapons. Madame Briar was going through all the different weapons and tools that they would be using.

"What do you think this is?" Madame Briar asked, holding up a golden locket.

Everyone knew by now that that the answer couldn't be as simple as a necklace and only glanced around at each other until Eleanor raised her hand. "Is it a necklace?"

"Very good, Eleanor. You are correct in that this is a necklace, but to all those who are eyeing each other, it is also much more than that." Madame Briar opened up the locket, revealing a white powdery substance. "What is currently in here is talcum powder."

"The same used for makeup?" Ivy questioned.

Eyeing her for the interruption without raising her hand, Ivy shifted under Madame Briar's gaze. After she was thoroughly uncomfortable, Madame Briar continued, "Though a lady should never interrupt that way, Lady Parker has correctly stated that it is used for makeup. But as I'm going to teach you, there are many different uses for it. I will demonstrate now."

Blowing gently on the locket, a puff of white smoke fell onto her table. Madame Briar closed the locket and blew it again. With a wave of her hand, she motioned for the girls to gather around. As Ella moved closer, she could see that the dust had collected on certain areas of the desk.

"As you can see," Madame Briar said, "you can tell where people have touched. Mind you, it only works on certain surfaces, but it can be useful. What else can you use it for? Lady William?"

"You can blow it into another's eyes," Olive suggested.

Madame Briar nodded. "That is an option of last resort. It is perfect for defense, though you would need to be close enough for them to see you. Lady Jones?"

Luella smiled. "You could use the powder to fake an illness. Or help make you look more like a lady." The unmentioned, unlike you, hung in the air between her and Ella, though Ella paid it no mind.

"Yes, applying the powder could make you paler. Faking an illness can be used in multiple situations such as escaping a meeting, or distractions if your acting skills are up for the challenge. And yes, considering it is makeup, it can be used in that fashion. Lady Cooper?"

Ella's brain was rattling around as it came up with multiple uses. She hadn't even paid any attention to Luella as ideas blossomed. When Madame Briar called on her, ideas started spilling out. "Well, technically, the weapon is the necklace itself, so you could whack someone with it. And you can even change out the powder for something different such as a powder to make someone sleep and pour it into a drink. Or you could—"

Madame Briar held up a hand to put a halt to her words. "Very astute observation, Lady Cooper. You have gotten ahead of me in the lesson. Anything can be used as a weapon. That is the art of ninjitsu, or the art of unconventional warfare. It was part of the teachings that Queen Jane had learned herself from a Japanese diplomat 500 years ago. Using that principle, what about these shoes? What can we use them for?"

"You may have gotten the right answer, but at least I didn't lose my emblem," Luella whispered in Ella's ear.

Startled, Ella looked down at where the broach had been, seeing that now it was a bare silk bow. Ella searched for where it could have gone and saw that her broach was now pined to Ivy's collar. It had been such an enthralling lesson that one of her emblems had been snatched by Ivy. Distracted for the rest of the lesson, Ella had to stay more alert to her surroundings and could only give some of her attention to Madame Briar, much to her own disappointment.

By the time she returned to her room, her brain felt like mush.

"That was a long day," Clementine sighed as she came in after Ella. She slumped in one of the chairs next to Ella and started redoing her hair that had fallen out of her normally pristine bun.

"Aren't you supposed to attend to me first?" Ella teased, glad that she wasn't the only one who felt tired.

"Aren't you supposed to be a slave in the Americas?" Clementine retorted, then came and started helping Ella with her complicated hairstyle that Clementine had put it in that morning.

Smiling at the friendly banter, glad that they were back to how they used to be, Ella asked, "So what did you find out?"

"For your information, this information was difficult to get."

Knowing that her friend was fishing for a compliment, Ella replied, "Oh you are wonderful, Clementine. You work so fast, thank you for everything that you do. With your winsome smile and great acting skills that are far better than anything I can do. How can I ever do anything without you?"

A smug smile came on her friend's face, "Of course, you can't. Flora is a little clumsy on her feet, but she is an expert in stitching. She is really good at fading into the background. Now, for your information, Flora is even better with herbs than I am. She is on course to be a Medic. It was a good thing that you had gloves on, isn't it?" Clementine nudged her in the shoulder.

"It's not as bad wearing gloves as I thought. And Madame Briar taught us uses on how to use them in a fight." Doing her best to not flush, she changed the topic, "Did you get the emblem?"

From her skirts, she pulled out the hairpin wrapped in a hand-kerchief and passed it to Ella. "Thanks for the heads up, by the way. It was hard work getting Eve to help in the first place. If she had passed out because she helped you for the class, she would have gotten so mad."

Ella nodded absently as she opened up the kerchief and looked for the emblem. Inside one of the gems in the flower design had an open fan.

She said, "From what I saw, Ivy and Olive will be more prone to picking pockets to get the emblems. Ivy already managed to snag one during class today. Dorothy is playing the defending game. I have no idea what Eleanor is doing, other than making friends so they wouldn't want to steal from her. And Luella wants a fight."

"Did that glare of hers give you a clue?" Clementine retorted, brushing out her hair and starting to braid it.

Ella snorted. "No, it was when she gave one of her emblems to my stepsister."

Clementine paused briefly. "Which one?"

"Audrey."

Clementine breathed a sigh of relief and continued her braiding. "Oh good."

"Do you think you can handle Jenny and find a time to clean their room?" Ella asked as Clementine finished tying her hair.

"No problem. So, what's your plan for the others?"

Leaning back in her chair, Ella thought about it. "Dorothy should be easy enough. As long as I can see her stash them, then I can give the info to you and have you snag it. The problem is Ivy and Olive. I don't know what I'm going to do with them unless . . . Clementine, do you think you can make the same thing that Flora put on her emblems?"

Clementine held out her hand for the hairpiece that she got from Flora. Smelling it and rubbing it with the cloth, she said, "It shouldn't be too hard to do. I can whip up a batch tonight and get it to you tomorrow."

"Thank you, Clementine. I don't know what I would do without you."

"Nothing, and don't you forget it." Clementine passed the hairpiece back to her, then gave her a grave look. "Now, what are we going to do about new Luella's declaration of war?"

New declaration? More like she doesn't want to admit defeat. What to do about Luella? At first, Ella thought that she was just mad at her for no reason, but after reading all her mother's exploits in the reports Ella had received last year, she could see why Luella acted that way. Single-handedly stopping a war with France by leaking information to the lover of one of the lords was a stroke of brilliance. And that was only one of her missions. Not that she agreed with Luella being such a punk about it.

Though, it would be better for Ella if Luella continued to think that she wasn't worthy to be part of the Fan Society because of her mother's name. Because then she would underestimate Ella and give her the openings she needed. And Luella, as talented as she may be, was not very creative, much to Ella's advantage. When the school year was over, Ella would prove that she belonged here by being the one who went on the mission.

"For now, we get the emblem from my stepsister, then we shall see how she reacts."

Clementine shrugged. "If that is what you want to do. I'm going leave so I can get to sleep at a decent time. All this spy stuff is really messing with my beauty sleep. Ta-ta."

Waving goodbye, Ella plopped on her bed and spent the night running through plans and counter plans until she finally drifted off to sleep.

Every year, the trials are different, a newly designed opportunity for the girls to grow. But the second year always has a war. It is there you find out how good you truly are.

Nora "Cinders"
Report 50 page 2, paragraph 3

Chapter Sixteen

And so, the war began in earnest. Before, it was only them testing the waters, but now that traps had been sprung, everyone had grown more creative. It was difficult to keep track of how many emblems each person had. Especially between Olive and Ivy.

Ivy was very fierce and even after passing out a few times from other ladies copying Flora's trick, she still attempted to pickpocket emblems whenever she got the chance.

Olive, on the other hand, was more warry after having fallen for Flora's trap once and went around wearing gloves, as well as a few other girls. It was difficult to know when she would strike; there were more than a few times after classes when a girl would gasp at a missing ring and wonder when it had been stolen.

Dorothy became a fortress. She was able to hide her emblems so well that even Ella had a hard time finding them. Especially since she could no longer spend as much time watching and had her own private lessons with Madame Briar.

No one wanted to mess with Flora, as all of her emblems had traps on them. The worst made them spend a few hours in the lavatory.

And Eleanor? No one seemed to know what Eleanor was doing; everyone assumed that she was going for alliances with everyone.

Luella, of course, made it a point to come after Ella's emblems. And Ella reacted in kind.

"Ella, the social field is a battleground. Very rarely does anyone speak the full truth outright. That would be impolite. Everything must be done from a delicate approach. Now, the question is, how do you find out the truth if everyone speaks in half-truths and lies?"

They had been sitting in Madame Briar's secret office, taking lessons, since she was unable to leave the hidden passageways as easily as the other girls.

Furrowing her brows, Ella thought about it. "Catch them contradicting themselves?"

Madame Briar smiled. "Yes, very good. Just make sure when you are thinking that you don't furrow your brows. It gives away your thoughts. Now that you know that you need to get them to contradict themselves, how do you do it?"

Ella held back a grimace. "I don't know."

"One of the easiest ways I've learned is to get them on a topic that they really want to know about. If they are over-eager, they are less likely to pay attention to their words. And it is very easy to trap them in that case. It is difficult to keep up the lies when your mouth is running. Find the weak point of their words and at the right moment, attack. Understand?"

"Yes, Madame Briar," Ella answered thoughtfully. This could be very useful.

"Now, we need to talk about the etiquette of conversations . . ."

Madame Briar continued until it was time for weapons class.

As the weeks went on, Ella found her footing in the physical classes. Since she had been a servant in her own home, she was used to doing hard physical labor and had far more stamina and strength than the other girls. Only Luella could keep up. During weapons class, they began having more active fights with those who were proving more talented in this area. Ella was one of them, much to Luella's chagrin.

At first, Ella was annoyed at the constant glare and snippish remarks that Luella gave her during class. But as they sparred, Ella thrived.

The class today was dagger against parasol, with Ella wielding the parasol. Luella was quick, flitting in with swift strikes and then backing out of range. Eager for the challenge, Ella knocked the dagger away. Then, stepping closer, she slid the parasol from behind Luella along her arm before twisting it towards herself. Stepping in, the stick now held Luella's arm lock in place behind her back. Luella then ducked under Ella to twist back. As she did so, the handle slipped from her silk gloved fingers, allowing Luella to get out of her hold and strike back.

"Still not good enough," Luella said smugly. She crossed her arms and admired her dagger, quite pleased with herself.

"Oh Luella, you may have won the battle, but I will win the war." Grinning back, Ella opened her other hand and showed her what she had been hiding there.

Dangling between her fingers was the bracelet that had been on Luella's wrist. Ella had managed to pull it off during their quick exchange.

Unable to stop her pale cheeks from turning pink, Luella pulled out her fan, covering her face. "Just one emblem doesn't win the war. Just because you have managed to snatch these two doesn't mean I haven't gotten others. I will be the one to go on the mission."

Two? The one that had been hidden in Audrey's room had turned out to be a fake. There was no emblem on it. For now, the only one that she had gotten from Luella was the one she currently had in her hand.

Hiding her confusion, Ella pressed for information, "Do you really think that the broach you took from me during the obstacle course was worth it?"

Her opponent stiffened at her words. "You mean that flimsy copy. I was just wanting to see how horrid it was. I had to throw it out because it was so bad that it would give the Fan Society a bad name."

Questions bombarded Ella as she held her smile. Why did she get a fake? The broach that she had on then was the real emblem. Did she still think Ella had it? And if what she got was a fake, then what happened to the real one? Who was the one who took it?

Stalling for time, Ella said, "And yet you took it. Such a shame. But it's time for a rematch. Are you sure you are going to win this time?"

Luella snapped her fan shut, tucking it into her skirts. She held out the dagger to exchange weapons with Ella. And then they began to spar again.

"But then who could have stolen the broach?" Clementine asked as she picked her nails clean.

"I don't know. That's the problem," Ella sighed as she paced back and forth.

The decoy situation was bothering her. The emblems were given to them directly from Madame Briar. But considering the girls didn't know what the mission for the year was until they were in school, it was odd that decoys were appearing. Either someone was a masterclass craftsman, or someone who knew what the mission was beforehand crafted them well in advance and was purposely causing trouble.

"It must have happened before the end of class," Ella muttered. "If she received a decoy directly from me, it must mean that I had a decoy on me at the time."

"But I'm pretty sure that I oiled that thing the night before, and it was the emblem," Clementine chimed in. Ella glanced at the vial now in her hands. She added, "This oil rubs off quickly. I have to oil the pieces every day for it to be viable the next day."

"Did you check it when you put it on me that day?"

"Sorry, I don't think I did." Head downcast, Clementine looked as if she wanted to kick herself.

Grabbing the bottle from Clementine, Ella waved off her concerns. "It's alright. I just needed to know." Ella paused, then thought out loud, "So, the only thing that can be positive is that it was between the time you put the oil on and the end of the obstacle course. It had to be during that time. Did it have the oil on when you put it on me?"

"That I'm sure of because I had to change gloves."

"Hmm. Then if the oil was on it, it had to be someone who had gloves on unless . . . did you make sure that no one came in your room during the night?"

"The line of salt was unbroken," Clementine assured her.

Due to the nature of the task, they had learned to take measures to see if anyone entered their rooms. One of them was to put a line of salt in front of their doors during the night so that when the door was opened, the line would be disturbed and couldn't be fixed unless they fixed it and left through another exit. Assuming that Ella's investigations for any secret passageways were accurate, there wasn't any other way to leave or get into her room other than the front door.

"Then it must have been during class. At that time there were still a few who didn't wear gloves, like Ivy, Flora, and Dorothy. And I know it wasn't Luella. So that leaves Olive."

"Don't forget Eleanor."

That was right. Ella had forgotten Eleanor. Why had she forgotten her? Even Flora, who didn't have much of a presence, she didn't forget. But Eleanor hadn't been doing anything out of the ordinary for her. She was just talking to people. Something she was constantly doing. And even though Ella knew that she was a likely candidate for changing it, she kept avoiding the thought.

"These decoys are bothering me. I have a feeling that they are some sort of test. We don't know who is doing it, so the first thing we need to do is get information. Can you speak to the other girl's Assistants and see if they know anything?"

Giving her perfect bow, Clementine replied, "Of course, my lady." Her proper manners shattered at the smile she gave Ella afterword. "Now, what are you going to do?"

"I am going to set a trap."

I have learned that there are many ways to go about missions, and they are as numerous as the stars in the sky. The best thing to do is know what your strengths and weaknesses are. And, better yet, know what your opponent's strengths and weaknesses are.

Nora "Cinders"
Report 101, page 1

Chapter Seventeen

I t was a week before Ella was finally ready to enact the plan, but it was well worth the wait. Decoys kept cropping up, and no one knew where they were coming from. During the week, Ivy had snatched five emblems, but according to her Assistant, they all ended up being decoys. Olive only made three attempts, but two of them were decoys. The others hadn't tried for any, or Clementine was unable to get information about it.

Today for their morning exercise, they practiced running up and downstairs, all dressed in their finest. Even though Ella had difficulty running up the stairs in her heeled shoes, which still made her uncomfortable, it didn't matter for this plan. Ella was wearing her emblem on a pink ribbon that was tied around a braded bun. The emblem was a pink rose that was attached to the ribbon.

It wasn't until after the running that someone took the bait. The girls stretched and chatted together to cool down before their next class. Ivy was the first one who came up to talk to her. The petite girl came up to her with a smile, her blonde hair almost yellow in the light of the room and green eyes glinting with a hint of mischievousness. "That was a crazy class. I don't think I've run up that many steps in my life."

Wary, Ella put on a smile as well. "Yes, I don't think I can ever get used to these shoes." She turned and twisted her ankles, trying to get the blood flowing back into them.

The girl's quaint smile turned into a full-on grin as she came forward conspiratorially. "That is why I wear these."

Ivy lifted the edge of her skirt and showed that the shoe's heel was much lower than was fashionably standard, making it more comfortable. "You never saw this."

Ella held back a laugh. "No. I didn't see a thing."

"I've got to get to class. We should talk more often. Even though with this test, it will be hard. But we are going to be on the same side eventually."

As they talked, Ella's eyes found all of the insignias that Ivy had. It was hard to tell if any of them were decoys; she would have to check later, but for now she had given Ivy ample time to exchange or steal her emblems.

"I would be happy to," Ella said as Ivy gave her a secretive wink as Ella headed off a little ways away to do her own stretches. As she did so, she check over herself to make sure that Ivy hadn't snagged any of her emblems or that any of them were changed out.

After finishing her stretches, Ella headed over to where a few servants were waiting with towels to dry off any sweat, as well as help the ladies redo their hair and makeup before they had to go to their classes. Ella sat before the girl with the red ribbon in her hair. She pulled the flower from her hair and adjusted her locks until they looked presentable. Then she replaced the flower with one that Ella had prepared beforehand.

Ella stood up to leave just as Eleanor came up to her. "Ella! Are your feet doing okay?"

"I'll survive. I just hope we don't have to do too many classes like this," Ella replied with a fake smile. She hadn't wanted to suspect the first person who was kind to her, but this was part of what she needed to do. For as long as this test was going on, she would have to suspect everyone.

"It seems Luella still has it out for you, even though you have been doing very well in these classes."

Ella turned to where Eleanor was looking. And not to her surprise, Luella was getting her hair adjusted and giving Ella her perpetual glare.

Sighing, Ella responded, "I've gotten used to it by now."

"Wouldn't it be better to show her how great you are?"

"How? Luella is very talented, and I already have a hard time beating her in class. What can I do to show her?" This was a problem that she had been mulling over, on top of practicing her skills and trying to do the task. And she hadn't found the best way to do it.

Leaning over, Eleanor said, "Well, if you do the best, then you will get the chance to go on a mission. That is something that Luella can't go against."

"Thank you, Eleanor," Ella said.

Eleanor bobbed her head and beamed, "No problem! Good luck." Then she bounded away.

Thoughts flooded Ella's brain as she walked to Madame Briar's secret office, where she was taking her lessons. But she did retain enough presence of mind to pull off the ribbon with the flower on it and replace it with one that Clementine had placed earlier that day.

"Tell me why connections are important in society."

Ella blushed. She was in her class with Madame Briar and her thoughts had drifted to thinking about what she was planning to do in weapons class. Grasping for an answer, Ella said, "Because with more people, you will be stronger?"

"Not necessarily," Madame Briar replied. During these lessons, Ella was taught various things about society and the history of nobility. This time was about the different houses. "Do you know why this is?"

Ella shook her head.

"It is all about the balance of power. Certain families are in alliances with some and against others. So, if you are friends with one family, you have to be aware of all of their connections as well. Then you also have to be aware of what ties they have. Every family has alliances between different families, as well as individuals. Depending on what is most important to them, they may break an alliance with another family to keep their connection to an individual. Think on why this may be so."

Ella nodded and headed to the training room, lost in thought. The last thing that Madame Briar had said nagged at her. Breaking ties with a family just to keep a connection to an individual. This brought to mind the decoys that were floating about. Considering they had the Fan Society symbol on them, that made it likely that it came from someone who was a part of or who knew of the Fan Society.

Madame Briar hadn't said anything about them, meaning Ella's guess that they were part of a test was likely valid. But considering Madame Briar still had to run the school, that meant that perhaps she might have someone placing the decoys on her behalf.

Meaning that someone had to be willing to go against all the other Fan Society students. Someone who thought that their connection to Madame Briar was worth more than the extra ire that may be gained due to the decoys. Most of the students viewed them as cheating since they had no time or money to make such great copies, allowing the student who was spreading the fakes have a greater advantage over everyone else.

When Ella arrived at the training room, some of the other girls were there. Thank goodness Luella was not there or else things would have been more difficult.

Ella headed towards where Olive was stretching.

"Hello, Olive," Ella greeted her.

The reaction she received was unexpected. Instead of any greeting, Olive gave her a raised brow, then went back to stretching. Ella tried not to panic. This would not work if she couldn't get close enough to her. But the girl wasn't going to speak to her, and if Ella pushed it, the girl would be even more suspicious of her.

Instead, Ella started stretching next to her. Olive didn't react. It was difficult for Ella to get a handle on Olive. She was not really a talker like Ivy and Eleanor. She wasn't showy like Luella. And she didn't have an invisible presence like Flora, nor a steady presence like Dorothy. Olive was always on the fringes of things. She didn't really speak much, and her dull brown hair and slate green eyes made her easily ignored.

And yet Ella had seen some of her pickpocketing skills and found she was capable of taking the initiative to steal from the other girls, but it was only when she knew that she could get the emblem and get away without anyone noticing.

So, Ella gave her the opportunity when Luella came in, ready to pick a fight, like usual.

She strode over to Ella in an instant. "If you think you won in the last weapons class, think again."

"Don't you every get bored with antagonizing me?" Ella snapped.

Luella flushed at the retort but kept her higher-than-thou look on her face. By now, Luella's repetition and lack of any originality in her bullying had worn on Ella. If anything, it was annoying, like a yappy dog constantly nipping at your heels. If only Ella could do one thing to prove that she did deserve to be here, Ella knew that Luella would stop.

Ella continued, "How can I win in a class? We are just learning. Now a battle I can win, considering how I beat you during our last class."

Luella flushed, while still keeping her glare on Ella, "You can still win in a battle, but you won't win the war."

"Thank you for saying I can win. It is very thoughtful of you. But Luella, you still can't win the war when you can't beat the opponent in battle."

Sniffing, Luella turned and walked off. Ella could tell that she was resisting the urge to stomp off because it would be improper for a lady. A smile crept up her face. After Ella's lessons with Madame Briar, it had been getting easier to talk back.

After finishing her stretch, Ella walked over to where the equipment was stashed near the back of the room and pulled out her flower ribbon and grabbed another that had been sitting there.

Tying it on, she made her way back to class as they all gathered around Madame Briar.

Madame Briar taught me a lot of things. And as the year went along. I found ways to implement them to varying degrees of success.

Arabella Cooper "Cinders"
Report 30 Paragraph 3

Chapter Eighteen

"What are you going to do now?" Clementine asked as she helped Ella practice her dodging before bed. "Now that you know who is doing the decoys."

"I'm not sure. I still feel like I'm missing something," Ella said, breathless.

Being extra careful during the day and only be near certain people during certain times, they tested to see who the person was who had been exchanging the decoys. They had found out that her emblem was changed to a decoy when her ribbon was pink. The only person she had gotten close to at that time was Olive. Olive was smart enough to pull it off, but something still felt wrong. Another person could be doing it, but Ella pushed that thought aside.

Ella marked each of her copies with a different mark. That way when she found the decoy, she would know which person could have done it. But something was still nagging at her. She would need help from someone who she knew would never do anything that was considered cheating and would never have it in herself to use the decoys. Someone who could help her lure out the real culprit.

"What are you going to do about it?" Clementine asked as she tried to poke Ella again with her stick.

Dodging, she muttered, "I think it's time to make an alliance with Luella."

Clementine smacked her in the shoulder with the stick.

"Hey." Ella rubbed her shoulder. "Be careful."

"Did you just say make an alliance with Luella?"

"Yes." Ella rolled her eyes.

"The girl that thinks you shouldn't be part of the Fan Society. That Luella?"

"Yes," Ella said she moved the stick that Clementine was pointing at her to the side. "That Luella."

"Why would you want to do that?"

Ella eventually wrangled her thoughts together into a cohesive sentence. "It was something that Madame Briar said about making alliances. Sometimes it's about giving them what they want. And with Luella, I know what she wants. She is someone who fully and truly believes she will prove she is better than me. If she cheats, she can't say she is better than me. Not only that, but I know she is not the one doing the decoys; it's not really her style. She had been very open about her hatred of the person using decoys. And if she finds out that I have nothing to do with the decoys, she might be willing to help us find the real person behind all this."

"If you say so." Clementine rolled her eyes, then leaned on the stick. "So, how are you going to get her to help you?"

And so, they began planning on how to bait Luella and the person with the decoys.

Getting a chance to meet up with Luella was difficult. Considering their relationship, it wasn't surprising. So, the only choice Ella had was to make her come to Ella.

After everyone had arrived at the training room, Ella made her way toward Luella. She ignored Ella and continued to talk to Eleanor. Knowing that Luella wouldn't be the first to initiate the conversation, Ella said, "It is time to finish this, Luella."

Spinning around, Luella raised a brow at her. "Finish what?"

"Do you still believe I have no talent after having stolen your bracelet in the middle of a fight?"

"That was a cheap move, and you know it," Luella sniffed and avoided looking at Ella. "At least I worked hard to get here, unlike you."

After everything Ella had gone through, Luella still dismissed all the work Ella had done since coming here. Pursing her lips, Ella refused to let her get a rise out of her. That was not what she was there for. "Then why don't we have a duel to fight for it? If you win, I will give all of my emblems over to you. That should help you with earning the right to go on the mission. And if I win, you will treat me as you do everyone else in class."

"Why would you propose such a lopsided proposal? I thought you were smarter than that?"

Sighing, Ella said, "Because you don't see me as an equal, so I thought that you wouldn't agree to a proposal that was equal. Besides, all of the animosity has been annoying me. And the deal is only bad for me if I lose. I don't intend to lose."

Narrowing her eyes, Luella hissed, "And how do I know that you will keep your promise?"

"What is there to lose? I will also be willing to tell you where my emblems are beforehand." Ella shrugged. "I thought that it would show your superiority over me should you win, but if you lose—"

"I won't lose."

Ella fought a smile. "Then there shouldn't be a problem."

Luella paused. "When and where?"

She was right where Ella wanted her.

That evening, at the appointed time, Ella met with Luella. If looks could kill, Ella would be dead. Wearing a red outfit and one of her ring emblems, Luella waited with her foot tapping impatiently in the darkened hallway.

When Ella stepped out of the shadows, Luella stopped tapping. "Glad you appeared. I was afraid that you would be too scared to come."

"Of course I came. But there is something I need to show you first."

Folding her arms across her chest, Luella sneered, "There is nothing you can say that will stop this duel. I thought this was what you wanted."

This was going to be the tricky part. Trying to get Luella to do what she wanted was like trying to shove a boulder up a hill. But Luella was good at what she did, and Ella needed her help.

"We can still have our deal, but instead of saying anything, how about I show you something?" Ella hoped she would take the bait.

Looking her over, Luella didn't say anything for a few moments as Ella hid her nervousness. When she finally opened her mouth, Ella almost sagged with relief.

"Alright, show me. But if I find that it was worthless, you will give me all of your emblems regardless of the duel or not because of wasting my time."

"Deal." Now Ella could only hope the second bait had lured the decoy maker. "Follow me."

Ella moved towards the wall across from them and pushed inwards, revealing a dark passageway. After a few seconds, Ella could hear a shift of fabric behind her, but Ella couldn't hear any steps. Relieved, Ella moved forward and followed the path to the left until they came to an alcove. Feeling Luella's presence beside her, Ella pushed up a plate that was on the wall, revealing two pinpricks of light.

Ella looked through the holes to see an empty room with a table in it. On the table held all of Ella's emblems. Then, as previously planned, Clementine started making noise back at the hall they had just left. She started banging a stick and a parasol together at odd intervals to hope that the person who was switching out the emblems would think that Luella and she were dueling. After a few seconds, a figure pulled herself from the shadows and headed for the table.

Clenching her jaw to stop her gasp from escaping, she moved aside to let Luella take a look at who was messing with Ella's emblems. When Luella pressed her eyes against the holes, only a little light escaped, and Ella could see a flush of red grow across her cheeks as she saw who was in the room. As she pulled away, she left the flap up so Ella could see her nod and motion for Ella to lead.

Leading Luella through the passageways, Ella was glad for the dark to deal with her thoughts. She hadn't wanted her guess to be true, but now that it was, what was she supposed to do? This was how the task is supposed to be done. It was only right to pay her back in kind.

They arrived at a well-lit area hidden deep within the recesses of the academy. Ella led Luella to her room to discuss what they had seen.

Moving to a chair, Luella sat back, ever the proper lady, and asked, "What did you show me, Ella?"

Ella leaned over and pulled a box from off a nearby table. "You know how lately there have been a lot of fake emblems that have been found during the task?"

"I thought it was you."

"I thought the same of you," Ella replied with a shrug. "But obviously that is not the case. I made sure that someone would be able to overhear our conversation of the duel and set a trap to see who would try to get the emblems."

As she was talking, Clementine came in bearing a box, and Ella continued pulling out the jewelry from the box that Clementine held and from the one on her lap. "I marked all of my fakes with a flaw. Do you notice a difference?"

Taking it from Ella, Luella studied the two pieces. Within moments she had noticed the mark that Ella had left on hers.

"I assume that this was left in its place?" Luella asked, holding up the fake that Clementine had brought.

"Yes."

Luella sat thoughtfully, while Ella hid her nerves. How would Luella take the information? Ella had only known the girl for a few months, but she had hoped that her instincts were right.

"Thank you for this information. Then shall we get on to our duel?" Luella stood and started to head for the door.

"That's it? That's what you are going to do about this information?" Indignation flooded her. After everything she had planned and everything she had put forward, that snooty girl was just going to get up and walk away? Had she still not proven herself to Luella?

Tilting her head, Luella looked at her. "Yes. You said that after you showed me the information that I would decide whether to take your emblems or not. I am happy you showed me the cheater who has been placing decoys around the place. The information was solid, but I never said I wouldn't duel with you."

Ella sat in stunned silence.

"What were you expecting from me? We are against each other for this mission," Luella reminded her, genuine curiosity lacing her voice.

Momentarily at a loss for words, Ella spilled her genuine thoughts, "I thought that we could form an alliance against the person who has been spreading the decoys."

Luella's face was stoic at the word, and when she spoke, her face was blank, never giving anything away. "And why would you want to form an alliance with me? I have always shown how much I dislike you."

Ella shrugged. "Why would I not want to ally myself with anything other than the best?"

Her blue eyes reflected nothing as she stood in contemplation. "Stand up. It is time to do the duel."

Ella could only do as asked and hoped that what she had said would be enough to change her mind.

The girls are performing wonderfully. They are performing as well as the batch that Cinders was a part of. I can expect great things from them. I wonder if they will be the ones to rid the Fan Society of its black mark.

Madame Briar
Progress Report 3, Year 1826-
1827

Chapter Nineteen

The girls decided to change the location of the duel to the training room since it would be safer to be there. Their Assistants came to witness the duel. Ella and Luella stood across from each other, each holding their favored weapon. Luella with her daggers and Ella with the fan.

Circling each other, they paced until Luella struck with her daggers. Flitting in, she stabbed her blunted blades forward in hopes of catching Ella off guard. But they were constantly paired together during weapons class, and Ella knew her patterns. With her fan closed, she knocked each of the other girl's attacks away like an umbrella ignoring the patter of rain from above. With more ferocity than normal, Luella stepped into her attacks, coming at Ella in every direction.

Ella was forced back from Luella's attacks but still managed to block them. When there was a hesitation in her attack, Ella leaped at the chance. Flicking her fan open, she thrusted its edge towards Luella's unprotected neck. Luella managed to bring her dagger up just in time to block the attack, causing Ella's fan to close.

Not giving her a chance to respond, Ella jabbed her closed fan into Luella's elbow. With her years of training, Luella managed to keep hold of her dagger, then attacked again.

The girls danced around the training room, with neither one gaining the upper hand. During their classes, Ella had steadily caught up to Luella's skills, and now they fought on even ground.

As their duel dragged on, their attacks slowed, and they were less quick to react. Ella knew that if she didn't attack now, she would lose. So, when Luella stepped in to attack her side, Ella slid to the side, grabbing her wrist. And with one smooth motion, she twisted her hand behind her back and flicked her fan open at Luella's neck.

Luella opened her hand in surrender, holding her daggers only by her thumbs.

Releasing her, she stepped away. And when they looked at each other afterward, Ella saw something that she never thought she would see on Luella's face. A smile. Instead of that perpetual glare, Luella gave her a genuine smile.

Clementine came over and took Ella's fan to put it away and Lilly, Luella's Assistant, came and took her daggers.

"You win." Luella pushed it out like it was a vulgar word, though she still smiled at Ella.

Ella smiled back. She understood Luella's reluctance to call her opponent a winner, but that was a good duel. It was a close match. "Now you can't say I don't belong here."

"What if we change what the winner gets?"

Already, Luella looked to be the picture of a noble lady. Only Ella, who knew that they had been dueling, could see the slight glisten of sweat on her brow and her chest rising faster than normal. Her face showed nothing of the exertions that they just went through, let alone revealing her intentions.

"What do you want it to be instead?" Ella asked, trying to get her breathing under control.

"An alliance."

Curiosity gave way to surprise at Luella's words. A grin grew on Ella's lips. "I will accept that. Though, that would mean that you would still have to beat me in the mission for me to accept you."

"I can deal with that," Luella said, a hint of a smile touching the corners of her mouth.

And for the first time, they looked at each other as if they were truly rivals.

After accepting the alliance, things changed. They discussed many topics, but the main thing was that they work together and how they could catch the counterfeiter to stop the spread of fake emblems.

Classes also felt different to Ella. They had both agreed to pretend to not be in an alliance, and so Ella was still constantly teased everyday by Luella, but during the sparing and duels, they both felt a growing acceptance of each other. It was no longer a fight to prove the other didn't belong. It was now a challenge between equals.

And after the last class of the day, they came together to plot. As they did so, Luella also took it upon herself to catch Ella up in other things that the girls already knew, such as the language of the fans. The version that most nobles used. She thought it was horrid that she had gotten so far in classes and still not learned it.

It was odd for Ella. They still didn't particularly like each other, but they had gained respect for their skills. But it still annoyed Ella every time Luella found something else that Ella didn't know. It made for an interesting collaboration.

"Why don't we just sneak into her room?" Luella questioned. "Do you know how to pick a lock?"

"Yes, I know how to pick a lock." Ella just barely managed to refrain from rolling her eyes. Just how much did she think that Ella didn't know? "But we don't know that the emblems are in there. Plus, she might have a system that lets her know when someone is in her room."

Now that they were in an alliance, she almost wished she wasn't. The debate on what to do had gone on for a week, and still, they didn't know what to do about the copier.

"What about if we set another trap?"

Sniffing, Luella retorted, "Do you think they would fall for the same trap? The same person who bamboozled all of us would fall for the same trap twice? They probably already know that all they got were fakes. And since it was with me, they could suspect me as well."

Throwing her hands up, Ella stood and paced. "Then what do you think we should do? We only have a few days left until the end of the school year."

"You didn't like my idea, remember?"

This was getting them nowhere. Ella paced as she thought. She wished Clementine was here, but both of their Assistants were keeping watch so no one could sneak up on their planning sessions. In frustration, she flopped on her bed.

"That is not ladylike."

Ella snorted. "So what? It's not like I'm in public."

Luella gave the "look" that spoke volumes about what she thought about Ella's logic. Ignoring her, Ella pinched her nose, hoping to bring out a plan as she wracked her brain. What was she doing wrong?

Ella turned to look at Luella, who appeared as if there were two of her because of her hand between her eyes.

A realization smacked Ella in the face. She had been going all wrong about this. Even though they had been talking about plans, they were not thinking about each other's strengths. It was as if they were two separate people. They needed to be able to work together seamlessly if they were going to catch the counterfeiter.

"I have an idea. And I think you are going to like it."

You can't change people overnight. You have to learn to work with them. And those faults can turn into gems when you make them shine.

Book with fan on cover
Chapter 4

Chapter Twenty

Ella's lesson with Madame Briar seemed to drag on. Normally, Ella actually enjoyed how Madame Briar taught, even though she hated the subject, but now that they had a plan, it was difficult to pay attention.

"Is the lesson on the different nobility houses boring you, Lady Cooper?"

"No, Madame Briar," Ella quickly replied.

"Then what has been keeping your attention away from my class, one which you desperately need to take to catch up to the other students?"

The question made her embarrassed. There was no reason for her to get this distracted. Nothing was going to happen in this class, and Madame Briar was right about her needing this. Considering how nobles viewed houses and lineage, knowing this was going to be vitally important when she was sent on her own mission for graduation.

Bowing her head, she said, "I'm sorry, I have no excuse."

"If you cannot keep your attention on things around you, it will be difficult to pull off other missions. You must always act like a lady at all times. It can be used as a disguise as well as a distraction from what you are doing. If your attitude is one of a lady, people will not expect you to be picking locks and will ignore your lockpicks as some sort of hairpin. Keep up the act at all times. You never know when someone will come around the corner."

She looked down her nose at Ella, making sure she understood. With a small nod from Ella, the madame continued with her lesson.

Ella paid extra attention after that and made sure to answer every question until it was time to head to the next class. As she was about to walk out, Madame Briar stopped her. "Don't forget what I said."

Her voice made it clear what she was referring to. As always, Madame Briar knew what Ella had planned with Luella. Ella nodded, then began making her way to the training room.

All the girls had arrived ahead of her this time. Letting her gaze wander over the room, Ella marked in her head where all the girls were. She took a deep breath to steady her nerves, trusting that Clementine would do her part.

The headmistress glided into the room and all the girls gathered round. Once they settled in, she started, "Today, we will begin working on putting together everything we have learned. You will be putting your combative as well as your spy skills to the test. Everyone will be handed your weapon of choice. Around your waist, we will tie a rope, then we will tuck strips of cloth around the rope. Your goal will be to steal as many strips of cloth from the other girls as you can while also defending your own. This will be a free for all. Ladies, prepare yourselves."

While tying on her rope, Ella steadied her nerves. All the girls held themselves at the ready spaced across the training room floor. At the sound of the snap of Madame Briar's fan, Ella stood in place, warily watching to see what the others would do.

Ivy, equipped with a drawstring purse, started first. Heading towards Olive, she swung the purse by its string. It wrapped around Olive's wrist, which had been darting forward to snatch a cloth.

Stepping back, Olive opened her grip and pulled the parasol out of the string with her other hand. Then, gripping the drawstring, she yanked Ivy close to her. When she was jerked closer to her, Olive used the handle of the parasol to twist around the cloth, tugging it from her waist.

A thud sounded nearby, causing Ella to turn just in time to see Flora wielding a wicked-looking medical saw, edges blunted, at Dorothy, who was holding her off with her open parasol. It was rather odd to see a girl who usually hid in the background fight someone with such ferocity, but that just went to show to not judge someone by how they looked.

As she was watching, it was only by luck that Ella felt the presence of someone nearby and whirled away on instinct. Eleanor had come up to her with her fan across her face like she was going to lean over and whisper some juicy gossip like she normally did. Laughing at getting caught, she missed Luella behind her, who had pulled out a cloth from her waist.

Ella backed away from the two of them when Luella used her hat pin to try to stab another cloth from her waist. Doing a complete turn, Ella flicked her fan in the middle of the turn, bumping Luella's arm out of the way and allowing her room to steal a cloth back from her. And so, the battle continued between them as the class went on.

It ended when everyone had managed to lose their strips of cloth.

After class, they stretched to cool down, and Luella came over to Ella. "My hairpin is now a copy! You are the only one who could have done it. There have been so many decoys that it's ruining the test. I'm supposed to be wearing an emblem on me at all times, but for some reason, things turn out to be a copy. And the only one who could have done it during that fight was you. I did manage to seal all of your strips from you."

Red flashed across Ella's face as she stood up to confront Luella. Even though this was part of the plan, Luella's attitude still irked her. "I have done nothing to you. Why do you always blame me?"

Folding her arms, Luella gave a smug grin. "I don't know. Maybe it's because I am always by you when things go wrong?"

Ella threw her hands up in frustration. "It could be someone else." Turning to Ivy, Ella asked, "Have you had your emblems changed to copies?"

Ivy gave a jerky nod and backed away, not wanting to get involved in the conversation. Though, the rest of the girls showed curiosity and irritation on their faces. They all wanted to know who was dealing with decoys. But one of them was faking it.

Turning to her new victim, Ella asked Olive, who nodded in the affirmative and went back to stretching, while still keeping an attentive eye on the proceedings.

"I couldn't have done it to everyone. If you think I did, then that would be admitting that I'm better than everyone and deserve to be a part of the Fan Society."

Snorting, Luella asked, "Then if you didn't do it, who did?"

Rolling her eyes, Ella retorted, "We are doing the task with all the other girls. It could be any of them. But I know who did it." With a pause, she looked around as each of the girls looked back at her, desire to know written on their faces.

"Well?" Ivy pressed.

Turning away from Luella, Ella headed back to her room. She paused to say one last thing, "I would not tell you who it is since I plan on stealing the emblems back today."

With that said, she turned back to her room and hoped the plan worked.

* * *

Luella and Ella waited for Clementine to arrive. Lilly, Luella's Assistant, was guarding their emblems. It didn't take long for Clementine to arrive, and they followed her out. Using their lessons of walking quietly, they didn't make a sound on the stone floor as they headed through the corridors.

Apprehension filled Ella as they steadily approached Madame Briar's secret office. Thankfully, they stopped at a small alcove before the office.

Pressing a brick with a small Fan Society symbol emblazoned on the wall, the small alcove opened to a larger space, though not by much. It had just enough room for the chest set at the back of the room and a few people to stand uncomfortably close. The room was dark. Its shadowy corners made the room feel even smaller.

"Open the chest and let's get out of here," Ella said, a chill creeping down her spine as she felt as if someone was watching her.

With a huff, Luella knelt in front of the chest. "Let me check for traps first."

"There are not going to be any."

Both girls turned to the third voice. From the dark recesses came a hooded figure. They didn't notice her hidden in the shadows.

"Eleanor, I'm not sure how you managed to do all of this, swapping out real emblems for forgeries, but you managed to trick every one of the girls. And considering how many emblems are here, it was more than anyone thought it was. I don't think that anyone could have guessed it was you doing this all along. After all, you are such a bright and caring person, you could never betray your friends, even if it was a mission."

After everything, Ella still had hoped that it wasn't her. Even after seeing Ruth, her Assistant, take the emblems during the duel, she had hoped it wasn't true.

Yet now she was standing in front of her. The friendly, bubbly girl who was getting along with everyone was standing in front of her with a bright smile on her face. Still looking as sincere as she always had.

Giving her a crooked grin, Eleanor shrugged, "It is not what you think it is. Those in there are all copies as well. It is not as it seems."

"How did you keep everyone—"

A question that had been burning within her flew from her lips, interrupting what Luella was going to say, "Were we really friends?"

Throwing her arms around her as she had done just that morning, she beamed at Ella, "Of course, nothing personal. This is just the name of the game that was set before us. No hard feelings?"

Ella couldn't quite push away the hurt she was feeling, but Eleanor was correct in how the task was set up. Eleanor hadn't done anything wrong.

Forcing a smile on her face, Ella replied, "Yes. No hard feelings."

"Not to get all mushy, but can we get back to the matter at hand? What were you doing here anyways if you are not the one who is spreading the copies? And how did you keep everyone from targeting you?" Luella demanded, now standing and brushing nonexistent dust from her skirts.

"Always in business mode," Eleanor sighed, then leaned forward and whispered, "There was an odd number of people."

Confusion washed over Ella until things clicked into place. Thinking out loud, words tumbled from her lips, "You kept us fighting each other. Me and Luella, and Ivy against Olive, and Flora and Dorothy. If they were focused on each other, you could slip through the cracks and pick up the pieces with none the wiser."

"But that still doesn't answer to how you are not the person leaving copies and why this is filled with copies of the emblems," Luella retorted.

Ella turned to her, a question in her eyes. The only person that she could think of would be Madame Briar, but she wouldn't go that far, would she?

With a glimmer in her eyes and a wink, Eleanor said, "You will find out on the final test at the school year. Since you found this, I can say this much: I am not the mastermind behind the switching of the emblems."

Circles within circles. At that, she left the girls in stunned silence. They had hoped that by causing fear that the copier's stash may be stolen, they could catch her in the act, but instead, they were left with a puzzle. One they couldn't do much about until the end of the week when the last day of class was.

Always be aware of your surroundings. Keep an open mind. Tasks are never as they seem. Make alliances but be aware of betrayals. Don't be afraid to strike when an opportunity arises; they might not come again. But only strike when you can get away with it. These are some things I've learned during my second year in the academy.

Nora "Cinders"
Report 20, page 2

Chapter Twenty-One

The last day of class started with Ella being a bundle of nerves. Today, only the Fan Society girls and a smattering of servants were left in the academy. The others had gone home for a break until the next school year. That left the school open for the girls to do the final test for the year.

They went to the training room as usual, only this time, things had been set up differently. Instead of the room split in half with the tea sitting room on one side and the mats on the other, everything had been pushed to the sides. In the center were twice as many tables as normal, and there were already people dressed as if they were at a garden party situated amongst the tables. The guests were dressed in light colors and had bonnets covered with flowers. A few were standing amongst the tables holding parasols. Also amongst the guests were servants. They went about the tables giving food to the guests. Ella didn't recognize any of them.

Her Fan Society classmates, already dressed for a garden party as they had been asked, stood on the outskirts waiting for Madame Briar to arrive. Refraining from fidgeting, Ella peeked at the near-by girls. All wearing their emblems, they stood with a noble's grace. Even though their faces were passive, a nervous excitement filled the air with energy. As they waited, Ella did her best to stand as a noble would while she glanced curiously at the girls nearby.

When Madame Briar arrived, every eye followed her walk down the stairs. They all waited with anticipation wishing that she would hurry down the stairs. Acting as if it was any other day, Madame Briar didn't rush and didn't slow down, though to Ella, each methodical step made her want to run over and drag her to her spot. But Madame Briar was a lady and they never showed that they were in a hurry. It was a breath of fresh air when she stood before them.

"Welcome to the final test of this year," Madame Briar said as if she was doing her normal morning greeting. "Sitting before you girls are alumni who will be helping with this test."

The girls turned and studied the people before them. Some Ella could recognize from her lessons on the different nobility houses. As she studied them, she realized that she didn't recognize any of the servants mingling with the ladies.

"This test will show what you have learned during this school year. As a member of the Fan Society, you will have to be aware of multiple events going on at once. You will also have to try to prevent things without having all the information you need, all while still keeping your cover as being only a lady," Madame Briar continued. She looked every girl in the eye, giving weight to her words. "For this test, you will be finding out who has been passing out forgeries. You know that this person is attending this party. You will act as though this is a real event. How you react as well as what information you find will determine how well you do. Do not forget you will also be playing as another partygoer for your other classmates."

That last sentence bugged Ella and brought questions to mind. Questions buzzed around her head and were about to be released when Luella raised her hand. Madame Briar nodded, allowing Luella to ask her question.

"Do we know who the mastermind is? Or anyone in connection to this person?"

A smile graced Madame Briar's lips. "Very good questions. You know that counterfeit jewelry has been passed around. Everyone attending is part of the jeweler's community or has ties to that community. But the forger does have a connection to the person who has been spreading decoys during the school year. Any other questions?"

The question that had been forming burst through, and Ella said, "Can we steal emblems during this party?"

Raising her brow at the outburst but allowing a grin to cross her face, Madame Briar answered, "A lady should never interrupt, but yes. You have until the test is over. And before you raise the question, the test is not over until the party is over. But I will be awarding more emblems to those who do the best in this test."

Ivy raised her hand. "Are there any specific rules we have to follow?"

"You are training to be spies, dear. Don't get caught and don't blow anyone's cover."

Ivy shuffled sheepishly at that answer, bowing her head to keep a flush from rising to her cheeks.

"What will our covers be?" Flora asked.

"You will not have another identity and will be playing as your own self other than Flora and Lady Cooper. Flora, you will play the part of the daughter of a jewelry merchant. You will be part of the nouveau riche." Flora nodded, and Madame Briar turned to Ella and gave her a gentle smile. "Lady Cooper, you will be playing as yourself if your parents had not passed."

Madame Briar's eyes looked over the girls for any other questions and seeing none, called, "Let's begin."

Emotions flooded Ella. It was not the kind that froze a person in their tracks; it was the nerves that made her hyper-aware of what was around her. A smile grew on her face as her long hours training to be a lady with Madame Briar clicked into place, and she started moving as a noble would.

Grabbing a parasol that was nearby, she strode into the center of the room.

Ella made a mental note of where everyone was seated and also where her other classmates were. She headed towards who was acting as hostess and made her way to greet her, making sure she was facing the most people.

When she greeted the hostess, Ella dredged up information that would tell her who she was. Noting a family ring, Ella made the connection, "Greetings, Lady Fairfax. It was an honor to be invited to this event."

"Lady Cooper, what a pleasure. Please have a seat," the genial girl said, motioning to the seats that were furthest from the head of the table.

Bowing her head in gratitude and reining in her annoyance at being looked down upon, Ella thanked the host and moved to her spot.

In a way, she was lucky. Being at the edge of the tables made it easier to see everything, though it did make it more difficult to get to places. Ella would just have to make do. At least it was a garden party where it wasn't unusual for guests to get up and move around. For now, it would be best to take stock of her surroundings.

Ella noted her other classmates and how many emblems they were wearing. Dorothy and Flora had the least. It was difficult to count the rest because it was hard to see where all of them were placed. Spying Eleanor nearby, Ella analyzed what she had.

She didn't seem to be wearing any emblems. She wore a garland of real flowers and had a simple gold chain, which Ella knew was not one of the emblems. For all appearances, it looked like she was telling the truth. Though something still nagged at her, like an itch she couldn't quite scratch.

But for now, it was time to put that on hold. It was time to find who had a connection to the forgeries. The other girls were scattered about the party, each keeping to their own sides, wary of getting close to the other girls for fear of losing their emblems.

As Ella sat, making small talk to the woman at her table, she started to understand how difficult this task would be. It was difficult to keep up with appearances while investigating everyone. Normally, she would send Clementine to go help, but assistants had their own finals to do. She needed some assistance. Ella's eyes rested on another girl at the party.

A smile formed on her face; it was time to rein in on their alliance.

There will always be times when your Assistant cannot help you. It is always a test when you are in these situations. If you ever get into these situations, look for potential allies that can help you achieve your mission. Just be aware of their motivations. It can be dangerous if . . .

Book with fan on cover
Chapter 12

Chapter Twenty-Two

B owing her head to Lay Fairfax who was the table's head and giving a proper excuse to leave, Ella meandered towards Luella. As she saw Ella heading towards her, Luella's expression turned blank. Pulling out a lacy white fan, she covered her face.

When she was close enough, Ella gave her a proper greeting, just like the one Luella herself had taught her, and said, "Greetings, Lady Jones. It is so wonderful to see you."

Closing her fan, Luella bowed her head to the appropriate height for someone of lower rank. "Greetings, Lady Cooper." As she spoke, she rubbed the edge of her fan, far more roughly than was necessary. Ella translated it from the fan language to be "What do you want?"

Using her own fan, she intertwined two of her fingers while motioning fluttering her fan between them. She had hoped that their alliance was still valid considering Luella now knew who was spreading the decoys. Speaking out loud, Ella said in character, as if they truly were at a garden party, "The gardens are beautiful this time of year."

Luella nodded, "Yes they are, but one can wonder why the roses are blooming so early this year."

Taping her fan as she said why was a signal that the why was the important part of the sentence. The rest was to make it seem like an ordinary conversation. Taking the why as Luella questioning her as to why they should work together, Ella replied, "It could be the weather. But it's hard to find the roses, even though they are in bloom because the garden is so large."

Picking up her emphasized words Luella tilted her head and looked around the training room, "Yes, quite large. It would be difficult to find the roses."

Ella had to restrain herself from smiling. It looked like Luella understood that this task was too difficult to do on their own.

"Of course," Luella continued, "we could look for it. It would be like a quest to find the flower. Then as a prize would take a rose as repayment."

Ella did her best to keep her face relaxed as she tried to figure out the meaning. Quest must mean the mission, and considering how she twisted her fingers in the fan language for alliance, she must have been thinking of agreeing if she received a prize.

"What rose could you be speaking of?" Ella asked, bushing her finger across the fan as she tried to figure out what she was asking for.

With eyes glittering with a hint of greed, she said, "The special rose that is an invitation to the ball."

The mission was given to the girl who scored the highest. That was what she was asking for. It was a high price to pay for help. Ella wanted to get the highest score, as well. To prove not only to the others that she belonged here but also so that she could somehow feel closer to her mother by becoming a spy as good as she was. The image of her mother beaming at her floated through her head, but she quickly shoved it back down. This was not the time for that; this was negotiation.

Sighing, Ella gave her reply, "That would make a wonderful prize, but we would have to ask the host if we could do that."

Ella looked back to Madame Briar who had been observing from the stairs, then back to Luella. Luella nodded back in understanding. In the end, Ella was not the one who chose who had the highest score, it was Madame Briar.

"Then let's make it a race. Once we find the rose, we will tell the other, and then who can get to the center of the garden maze wins. Would that suffice?" Luella asked.

It seemed that Luella wanted an honest competition. Once the other had figured out who the target was, they would tell the other. The race must be in reference to the emblems that they were still supposed to steal. It was just like Luella to suggest a compromise like that.

Bowing her head, Ella smiled. "That would be wonderful. Thank you for this exciting conversation."

Giving a nod of acknowledgment, Luella flicked her fan, motioning to one side of the room. Turning in the direction she motioned to, she started to converse with another of the guests. Ella headed in the opposite direction from where Luella gestured. Now that she had less ground to cover, it was time to find the target.

There are as many things that can be considered poisons as there are sands on the beach. But not all are used. There are many reasons for that. The main reasons are availability, what evidence such a substance leaves behind, and what the purpose of poisoning the target is. For instance, if a commoner was going to poison someone, it will not be a rare plant used. And if you are attempting for the target to look as if they died of natural circumstances, you don't want random rashes and other such oddities to appear. Many poisons react to silver and cause it to tarnish. That is the reason why many nobility use . . .

Book with fan on cover
Chapter 13

Chapter Twenty-Three

T he party had been going on for a while, and the only thing that had happened was Ivy trying to swipe an emblem as she tried to pass Ella. Thankfully, Ella saw it coming. After speaking to some of the other "guests", she still found nothing of note. Another quick glance at Luella showed that she was having the same troubles.

Holding back a sigh, she excused herself and headed to a more isolated place. With a deep breath, she tried to ease the tension in her chest that had been growing as time ticked away. This wasn't working. There had to be another way.

Across the room, Eleanor caught her eye. The one person she knew did have something to do with the decoys. She hadn't done anything out of the ordinary since the start of the test, but Ella might still get something from her. Ella followed her hunch and edged closer to Eleanor.

As she watched, something felt . . . off. Eleanor was chatting away with everyone as her perky self, but there was a sense of tiredness around her rather than her boundless energy. Her voice felt hollower and her brilliance dimmer. Things became stranger when Ella noticed her switch her spoon for another and used it to stir her tea. After looking at her spoon, she laughed and leaned forward, which caused the teacup to fall to the floor, shattering.

The head of the table motioned for a servant to come. Eleanor held her fan in front of her face, fluttering it as if embarrassed.

Something was wrong. The Eleanor that Ella knew would not be that clumsy. The head motioned the ladies to continue their conversations as the babble began once again. Ella moved forward, doing her best not to get caught in any conversations, as she headed toward Eleanor's table.

"Greetings again, Lady Fairfax, I believe I forgot to greet Lady Jones," Ella said with a bow of her head.

Lady Fairfax offered her a genial smile. "Of course you must introduce yourself to Lady Jones. She is the life of the party." She gestured for Ella to sit at an empty set near Eleanor. "Though, please do be careful. We had an accident with a teacup recently."

"Yes, Madame." Ella took her set and turned to Eleanor. "Lady Jones, I am so sorry that I forgot to greet you. You just always seemed to be talking to someone else whenever I wanted to."

With a smile and a wave of her hand, Eleanor said, "All is forgiven. There are always so many people you have to remember to greet. This is Lady Clifford and Lady Gray," she said, pointing to the other two guests at the table. "Did you think about what we spoke of last time?"

The glimmer in her eyes told Ella exactly what conversation she was speaking of. That the mastermind would be revealed at the test. Glancing at the other two ladies at the table, she turned to Eleanor and said, "Yes, such a curious riddle you left me with." As Ella spoke, she noticed the spoon that Eleanor had switched out. It was pure silver, and the head of it was tarnished.

In one of her lessons on dishware, Ella remembered that silver reacted to certain poisons. The spoon was tarnished just as it was shown to her. Why would someone poison Eleanor during the test? Was this just part of the plan? Or was it just a part she was playing? Why was Madame Briar allowing this?

"Do you need help?" Ella asked. "With the riddle you left me, I mean."

"Did you solve it yet?" As Eleanor spoke, her face brightened like normal, and the odd sense of distance evaporated. The other girls looked at them with curiosity, peeking behind open fans as they leaned eagerly towards them.

"No." There was no one other than Madame Briar who had the authority to tell Eleanor to do anything. And Ella hadn't recognized anyone else in the party as someone who could order her to spread the decoys. Ella glanced again at the spoon that Eleanor had tucked behind her cup and was about to ask about it when another chirped up.

"What are you trying to solve?" inquired Lady Grey. Though her face was covered by a fan, Ella could see interest as she watched them. Ella didn't know who she was, but that was not surprising. But based on her clothes and jewelry, Ella assumed that she held a decent rank.

Putting on a polite smile, Ella replied, "Lady Taylor gave me a riddle to solve, and I'm still trying to solve it."

"Oh, a mystery? I love a good mystery! What is it about?" said the boisterous Lady Clifford next to her. She had leaned closer to them, her fan no longer hiding her face.

Ella shrugged. Considering they were alumni, they may be able to help. "It's about a constable who found a counterfeiter, but he had only found a low-ranking member of the counterfeiting ring, and he is trying to find the mastermind. The only information that he received was that the mastermind would be at a certain party, but the constable had no idea who it could be."

"What sort of party is it?" asked Lady Grey. She was more sedate than the over-eager Lady Clifford next to her, with fewer decorations on than one would expect from one as young as her.

But considering who they were, Ella knew better than to base anything on appearances.

"One like this," Ella replied, motioning to the party around them.

"You mean one for business?" chimed in Lady Clifford, twisting her fingers in her side curls, her eyes gleaming with curiosity.

Ella frowned. "Business?"

"Yes. If you notice everyone here is in the jewelry business. Lady Fairfax likes jewelry and likes to do her best to endear herself to all of those who are in the jewelry business so she can get the best items," Eleanor clarified. "No one says anything since she does a lot of promoting and donations for them. Lady Clifford owns a gem mine, and Lady Grey's family holds the market on fine necklaces."

"Ahh." Ella tucked that piece of information into the back of her mind. This was what Madame Briar had mentioned at the beginning. And if Madame Briar had mentioned it, then it must be important. As she worked to connect her thoughts, Ella continued to converse using her made-up story to ask questions, "Yes, the constable was at that kind of party. Considering that he was investigating a counterfeiter and from what he knew from the grunt that he had found, knew that he would be at a jewelry business party. How would you go about finding the mastermind?"

"Oh, oh, I know." Lady Clifford almost bounced out of her chair with excitement. "It could be the hostess."

"Why would the hostess do that? It would only cause problems for her," the other guest answered. "I would look at who the grunt may be connected to. Or connected to a place they have been near recently. That would show who they had contact with."

What Lady Gray said struck a chord with Ella. Eleanor spent most of her time inside the school and didn't have contact with anyone outside the school. So, the mastermind that Eleanor had spoken about would be someone from the school. But it had to be someone who had the authority to tell her to do it and could interfere with the test. A person who Ella's mind had pushed away initially just as it had when she had thought of Eleanor as the one spreading the fakes. Ella turned towards Madame Briar, who was observing everyone.

"But if the mastermind was truly evil, I don't see why he would keep his grunt who spoke alive," Lady Gray said as an offhand remark.

Ella blinked at those words. Madame Briar did say to treat this like it was a real-life situation. Lady Grey was right; a mastermind would want to get rid of the person who could interfere with their plans. And considering the tarnished spoon, they had already tried.

If Eleanor was playing the part of the person who had been found out, she would be in danger. Scanning the room, Ella caught sight of a server who was moving rather quickly.

And his eyes were on Eleanor.

The art of attacking someone without looking like it is an art that one must possess to be a Guardian. A lady is always to be seen with poise and grace and must never show too much emotion. Yet there are times when you must still maintain that aura when fending off an attacker. The best defense is to act like a lady at all times. Would they expect a lady to trip a person or that it was an accident?

Book with fan on cover
Chapter 15

Chapter Twenty-Four

Ella thanked all of those who were seated at the table and excused herself. Picking out Luella on the opposite side of the room, Ella cursed at herself for being so far away from Luella that she couldn't help.

But now wasn't the time. Reminding her to maintain her lady-like aura, she grabbed a glass of fruit juice from a nearby server and headed towards the suspicious serving boy. As she brushed past him, she bumped into him, pouring the drink on him. His tray of cucumber sandwiches fell to the floor, as well as the long needle that he had hidden under the tray. With a kick of her foot, she sent the needle under the neighboring table.

"Oh my," Ella exclaimed as she pulled her fan out and fluttered it in embarrassment in front of her. At the commotion, the other ladies in the room turned to look at what had happened.

Lady Fairfax spoke up, "My, it seems as if we are having a lot of accidents today."

With her genial smile, the other guest laughed off the accident and went back to their own conversations as Lady Fairfax ordered another server to clean up the mess.

Coming up beside her, Luella asked, "Is everything all right over here?"

"Oh yes. I was just distracted from finding the rose that I didn't pay attention to where I was going. And Lady Taylor had just been so kind as to give me advice and I was so excited that I didn't pay attention." Tapping her finger on her fan with the tip of her nail, Ella pointed it at the table where Eleanor was seated at, indicating that assassins were targeting Eleanor.

"It seems you are still needing lessons. A lady must control her emotions. It would look poorly upon you if you went about being vulgar like that. I would be willing to help you with some lessons." Luella twisted her finger showing that she would help defend Eleanor.

Ella smiled and opened her mouth to speak but hesitated. Spotting a few servants making their way to Eleanor, she instead said, "If you would be so kind, I would happily accept your offer."

Closing her fan and tapping it in the sign for danger, Ella pointed it at the two servers on the right.

Luella's polite smile turned to one with restrained eagerness as she eyed the men who Ella had pointed at. "Then let us return to protect the rose."

With a polite goodbye, they headed toward their targets. All the practice on stealing emblems was going to come in handy as Ella spied a knife on the target. It looked like they were no longer keeping quiet.

Ella made sure to pass the servers and with quick hands pulled a dagger and a vial from each of his pockets. With a wary eye for anyone who could spot her, she stood in front of a table, hiding what was in her hands. Ella pulled a vial of oil from her skirts, the same oil that Clementine dipped her emblems in every day, and dripped it onto the handle of the knife.

Careful not to touch the handle, Ella meandered through the tables again. She waited until the server passed by her and deftly slipped the knife back into its hiding place.

Now he just had to touch it. And when he did, she would be far away from him, so no one would suspect her.

Checking to see if any of the other girls noticed, Ella scanned the room. Dorothy and Olive were glancing at the commotion but hadn't connected them back to Ella. Ivy was using the disturbance to try and steal some emblems, and Flora was keeping to her corner.

Glad that no one had caught on, Ella turned to see how Luella was doing. But she didn't need to worry. Luella had already stopped one of the server's progress by sending him off to get some things for her and had damaged the other's uniform. It would not do to have a damaged uniform, and Lady Fairfax had already sent him away to get a new one.

Luella glanced back at Ella and looked at the server that Ella had allowed to get close to Eleanor.

Flicking her fan open in front of her face, Ella hoped to stop Eleanor from messing with her plans. A small furrow grew between Luella's brows as she glared at Ella and headed to intercept him, ignoring Ella's signs.

With a sigh, Ella headed to stop her. Ella had thought that she had enough respect for her skills, but it seems it still wasn't enough. Seeing Luella pull a hat pin and taking aim at the man, Ella stepped into her line of sight. If she hit the servant, then he wouldn't touch the knife, and it would be more likely for their cover to be blown.

Anger flared in Luella's eyes, though she kept her face the typical serene mask of a lady. And Luella was about to move to find a better line of sight but was stopped as the servant made a grab for the poisoned knife and collapsed.

The knife skittered across the floor to stop before Eleanor. Seeing it and the man, Eleanor let out a squeak and fainted on the spot. Lady Fairfax came forward to calm them, but it was too late. The party couldn't be saved, and the killer would have been captured by the house guard. At that moment, had it been real, Eleanor would have been able to leave the party unharmed.

Madame Briar came forward, clapping her hands twice. All the guests got up and left the room. Two dressed as servants picked up the one that had attempted to "kill" Eleanor, leaving behind all of Ella's classmates. A few were confused at the "fight" that had just happened, shifting glances between each other.

They gathered around Madame Briar as she smiled at them. "That was a great test. You all did a wonderful job. Now it is time for me to award points. I will call you up one at a time and tell you how you did this year and what you need to work on. After that, I will award the extra emblems based on how you did."

That nagging thought that had been in the back of Ella's mind since the conversation at Eleanor's table bothered her. And the idea that had formed grew more concrete as now she had time to think about it.

"Lady Parker, you did very well with the pickpocketing, but all you do is attack. You have no defense. You still were not aware of who spread the decoys by the end of the party. Though, when a servant was revealed to have a knife, you reacted very quickly.

Keeping only half a mind on what Madame Briar was saying, Ella came up with a plan.

"Lady Williams, you did a good job observing, but you need to practice being a lady more. Sometimes, there will never be a perfect moment to act. You have to act before it becomes too late."

As the plan came to Ella, nervousness came upon her. If she was wrong, she might not ever become a full Fan Society member. But if she was right . . .

"Lady Jones, you used your alliances to good effect and helped put a stop to the attack. Just be aware of the capabilities of your allies. You almost put yourself in danger of being caught when your ally had things well in hand."

Then it came to Ella's turn. Her silk gloves were growing damp from her clammy hands that were clenching her fan. But she couldn't lose heart now; she had to stick to her instincts.

When Madame Briar stepped up to her, Ella flicked her fan open, holding it to Madame Briar's neck. Ella held her arm steady even though she wanted to drop the fan. Luella was about to come forward to yell at Ella, but Madame Briar held out her hand.

"Why are you doing this, Lady Cooper?"

Madame Briar's calm voice almost made her lose her nerves, but she could not turn back now. "You were the mastermind behind it all. You were the one behind the copies, as well as the attempted assassination against Eleanor."

Still not giving anything away in her expression, Madame Briar asked, "And why do you think that is?"

The thoughts that had been forming in her head bubbled out, "The only counterfeits that we could use came from you. None of us could have had the time to make such well-made fakes in the time we had. It had to come from someone who knew well beforehand what the test was going to be."

Raising her brow, Madame Briar questioned Ella. "Is that all?"

Now that she was thinking of Madame Briar as the culprit, more things started to connect. "We caught Eleanor with a box of fakes, but she said she wasn't the mastermind. Considering that the test should be fair to all the girls, she couldn't have known ahead of time and made the fakes. That meant that someone had to give it to her. Considering the box of fakes were found by your office, and that we caught her by your office, the only place we didn't check for eavesdroppers, you were the only one who could have known that Eleanor was caught. And as per the test rules, to act as though it were real, as the mastermind, you would have been the one to have her killed."

"That is a great story," Madame Briar said. "Are you sure that is the story you want to tell? Because if you answered wrong, then I'm afraid you would no longer be able to be a Guardian."

Madame Briar eyed the girls that had half gone into a defensive stance, and half looked at the conversation with confusion.

Everything had fit. Ella knew that she was right. "No. I'm sticking to my answer."

Giving her a smile, Madame Briar brushed the fan away from her. "Lady Cooper, you are correct. I was the mastermind behind all of this, but do remember you need more than gut instinct to answer your problems. With this, you are the one who is able to go on the mission next month."

Joy filled Ella. The trust that Madame Briar had placed on her, and the burden of her mother's excellence, as well as the nagging fear that she wasn't good enough that had plagued her, lifted. She was good enough to be a part of this grand thing that her mother had been a part of.

"Well done, Lady Jones." Madame Briar said, offering her light applause.

Ella looked around at the other girls. Eleanor gave her a beaming smile, Ivy was clapping enthusiastically, and Flora, Dorothy, and Olive were giving her a polite clap.

Then her eyes fell on Luella. Ella could see the war going in on her head. The anger that Ella had supposedly pulled one over her, the respect that had grown for Ella, the jealously that Ella would be going on the mission, and disappointment that she knew she lost fairly.

An uncomfortable feeling tugged at her heartstrings as Ella looked at Luella. She had made a promise, and Luella had helped. Even though they would never be friends, she still tried to get along with her. Ella had gained respect for Luella, and she couldn't leave her like this.

Turing to Madame Briar, she asked, "In the mission, is it alright if she has two daughters?"

Madame Briar looked from her to Luella, a contemplative smile on her face. She nodded. "I do believe that would be fine. Having two of my finest students have this experience would be good for you."

The war of expressions on Luella's face changed from bewilderment to one of excitement. A genuine smile graced her face, one that was bigger than was appropriate for society, and Ella knew she made the right choice.

Dressed in clothes of a seamstress's daughters, Luella and Ella followed their "mother", each carrying a basket that had a wrapped package hidden beneath balls of yarn. They entered a clothing store where the shopkeeper led them to the back.

Twisting her hands around the handle, Ella looked to see if Luella was as nervous as she was. The only thing that gave away Luella's anxiousness was her clenched jaw and pale face.

Shaking her head, Ella focused on what was going on. They weren't told much about the mission, only that they were acting as Cloak's support. They didn't know her real name, only her code name, but were told to refer to her as Mary. A Ghost of hers was a bit skittish and didn't trust Cloak to not be a scammer and had asked that her daughter pass off the package to him. Seeing the shifty-eyed waif in the back corner, Ella could see why.

"I'm here, Shifty," Cloak said to the opposite end of the room where the boy stood.

"Why are there two of them? I only asked for one," he demanded, looking ready to bolt out the door at any moment.

"I can't just leave one of my daughters at home now, could I? And having the package split between the two would give you a better chance of having one should we get caught."

He wrung his hands as he thought about her words, eyes shifting constantly between the door and the two girls. "H-have your ddaughter-rs set it righttt there in the middle. Right there," Shifty replied, pointing a generous ways away from himself.

Cloak nodded to Ella and Luella, waving them forward. Ella walked slowly, making sure that Shifty wouldn't bolt out of the room. Her fingers twitched with excitement, or maybe nerves. Ella couldn't tell which as they made their way across the floor.

As soon as the made it to the center, Shifty said, "Stopp. That is fffarrr enough."

The waif darted across the room and scooped up the baskets, then skidded back to his corner. He reached into the pile of yarn and felt around.

"Is the deal done?" Cloak said as the girls made their way back to their side.

Shifty nodded, then disappeared through the back door.

Cloak led them through the other door and back through the way they came. They changed back into their normal clothes and were shooed into a plain black carriage that would return them to the academy.

Ella sat back on the bench and stared outside in silence. The buzz she felt during the mission was dying down. The mission was easy, as was expected. It was nothing more than a drop with an informant that was well-known and trusted in an area that wasn't too dangerous. But this made her feel as if she was getting a glimpse into what her mother had once done.

They continued to sit in silence until Luella spoke up, "I won't thank you, since we were in an alliance."

Holding back a snort, Ella replied, "You are welcome."

Shifting back on her seat, Luella folded her arms. "Just because you did the best this time, don't think I won't come after you should you fail to meet Fan Society standards."

"I wouldn't dream of it." Ella rolled her eyes and looked out the window at the passing city. Luella's attitude didn't bother her. Much. And she had many things to think about.

Now that she had a solid footing in her academy classes, she now had to think about what path she was now walking on and whether it would lead her to her true desires.

This connection she had been feeling with her mother, where would it lead her? And what would she become?

Year Three

After reflecting upon this year, I had never realized how much I was lacking in connections. Connections to myself, connections to others, and connections to where I belong.

Arabella Cooper "Cinders"
Report 32

Chapter Twenty-Five

"That is not how you do it," Luella chided again as she watched Ella try to stitch a flower.

Ella had just placed the tip of the needle into the silk square, and already Luella was throwing a fit. After last school year, when Ella had generously suggested to have Luella go on a mission with her, she did not expect her to take it upon herself to teach Ella to be more ladylike. Ella really wished she hadn't. Luella would tell her something was wrong and yet never tell her how it was supposed to work. All she ended up doing was annoying Ella.

Refraining from tossing the whole thing at her, Ella took a deep breath and asked, "Why are you here so early? I didn't think that classes for you started until tomorrow."

Unlike Ella, Luella did not have to live within the wall of the academy. Due to circumstances that happened the first year, Ella had to hide within the walls to keep her stepsisters from finding out that she hadn't been punished like she should have been. If she was caught by her sisters, the Fan Society couldn't keep her safe. Which meant that she couldn't escape Luella. Instead, Ella was now stuck as she sat in on Ella's and Clementine's sewing practice.

"I decided to take it upon myself to make sure you didn't screw up pretending to be a noble because you can't do needlework.

And since for now I am an only child, I don't have to help a sibling get ready for the season."

Ella couldn't miss the anger when Luella said "for now" but didn't bring it up. She only got hints of Luella's family situation but she has learned to stay away from it if only her being annoyed at her family situation didn't mean her coming to force some extra unwanted attention on Ella. Attention that was extra harsh, because of her irritation.

Instead, Ella turned to Clementine, who was sitting in their sewing circle, and said, "It doesn't look bad. Clementine, what do you think?"

Looking up from her elaborate stitches, she asked with a raised brow, "What did you say?"

In her small, well-lit room, it had been easy to see her flower that had been stitched with complicated knots, all done to perfection. Ella glanced down at her simple flower, then back at the garden that was on Clementine's square. Clementine had known full well how terrible Ella's sewing was, and had tried to politely not be forced to say so.

A blush flaring on her cheeks, Ella muttered, "It's still good."

Tuning back to her stitching, Ella started adding another flower. She didn't want to get into another argument with Luella. They did not have a good relationship. For most of the last school year, Luella had been trying to prove that Ella didn't belong in the Fan Society. She had thought that Ella had gotten in due solely to the fact that she was a Legacy, the daughter of another Fan Society member, her mother Lady Nora.

Thinking about that, a question popped out of Ella's mouth, "Why did you fixate on my mother?"

Anger filled the room as Luella gave Ella that perpetual glare that had been on her face for most of last year. "What are you trying to say?"

Even though they had acknowledged each other's skills, that still didn't mean they were friends. It would be more prudent to say they were friendly rivals. Holding her hands up innocently, Ella said, "What I'm trying to ask is that of the many Legacies that are out there, why did you focus so much on my mother specifically?"

The anger faded at Ella's words, and Luella went back to focusing on her own stitching. "My parents were Ghosts for the Fan Society. They ended up stopping an assassination attempt and also saved one of the members of the Fan Society by bringing them to Eleanor's parents."

"I've heard this before," Ella reminded her.

Luella glared at Ella for interrupting her, and Ella instantly shut her mouth. After a few seconds of silence, she continued, "What you didn't know was that the person my parents saved was an operative codenamed Cinders."

Cinders. Her mother's codename. Ella never knew of Luella's connection to her mother. No wonder she hated Ella at the beginning. "I didn't know that they did that."

Luella raised her brow, very reminiscent of what Madame Briar would do. "The things you don't know could fill a study. How do you think people become Friends of Society? Do you think they just fall out of thin air? Most of them are originally Ghosts who have proven themselves worthy of the Fan Society or are children of previous members of the Fan Society."

"But then how did you become . . .?" Ella let the question die. Just because Luella was snooty didn't mean she could be that rude. It was obviously a touchy subject for her.

Luella gave Ella a look of exasperation, knowing what Ella was going to ask. "For your information, the Fan Society had me adopted by another Fan Society member, which gave me the title needed to become a full-fledged member of the society."

"Oh." Ella didn't say anything more.

An awkward silence filled the room, and only the Assistants, Clementine, and Lilly were calmly sewing away already, used to how Ella and Luella reacted to each other.

With a sniff, Luella stood. "The mood has been ruined. I am going to go elsewhere."

Relief filled Ella as she gave a polite farewell to Luella. When the door closed behind her, she fell back on her bed. "I thought she would never leave."

"I'm surprised you guys managed to last that long together," Clementine commented as she continued to work on her stitches. "And by the way, you stitched that wrong."

Looking down at her square, Ella realized that Clementine was right. She sighed again and got to work fixing the stitch and hoping that when classes started tomorrow, things would be better.

Due to nerves, Ella arrived very early to class. None of the students had arrived, but a few of the servants had started stacking boxes for the obstacle course they typically did in the morning. Ella had started memorizing all the servants during the second year. They also helped her with some classes that she took while the others went home for break.

"You are here early," Eleanor remarked.

Ella turned around at the sound of her bubbly voice. After last year, Ella still couldn't feel quite as close to her as she did during the first year. Even though in her head she understood why Eleanor acted the way she did, it still felt like a betrayal to Ella. "Hello, Eleanor."

Eleanor must have caught the tone in Ella's voice but chose not to comment on it. Instead, she smiled brightly and asked, "How was your summer? Did Madame Briar give you a break?"

Remembering all the lessons about being a member of nobility that Madame Briar taught her when everyone was gone made Ella wince.

"That bad?"

"I still have to catch up. Most ladies have been taught this stuff since they were children. I'm nine years too late," Ella replied with a shrug.

After being here for a while, it had become apparent that Ella was sorely lacking in many areas of being a noble, and it was hard trying to catch up. Even at the pace that Madame Briar was going, it still was taking her longer than she thought it should. And many of the rules of being a noble were nonsensical and just made things harder. Especially the dizzying array of clothing that could only be worn a certain time of the day or at certain events.

"I'm sure you will do fine. Anyways, it looks like everyone is here."

While they had been talking, the other girls had arrived. Calm, steady Dorothy, perky Ivy, observant Olive, and obstinate Luella were all here and ready for class. Flora would no longer be joining in all of their classes due to her becoming a Medic and needing different expertise.

Four more girls were with them. Ella recognized Lilly, Luella's Assistant, and an older woman who was standing next to Eleanor. She was familiar, and Ella recognized her from the tea party the first year. She did not recognize the other two girls. They must be the other Assistants. Clementine came rushing in behind them just as Madame Briar entered to start their classes.

"This year, you will be learning about gaining connections. Ghosts are an integral part of the Fan Society. We are unable to be everywhere at once, so having loyal, well-trained Ghosts is essential to gaining information. This year's task will have you working in tandem with your Assistant to gain a Ghost. Many ladies here come from powerful families and though they are young, they will be powerhouses in society in a few years. Working in tandem with your Assistants, you will gain one of their personal maids to be a Ghost for you. By the end of the year, you will have them give important information to you for your finals. Lady Cooper, due to your circumstances, I will change some of what you need to do. After class, come speak to me."

Madame Briar continued with an in-depth lesson on the groups that supported the Fan Society members. The two important ones that Ella would be working with the most would be the Friends of the Society and Ghosts.

Friends of the Society was a group that supported what the Fan Society was about and were trustworthy enough to know about the Fan Society. Ghosts were people that members turned into informants; they could be anyone, such as men, women, or children. They could be in any position such as footman, housemaid, or stable boy. Any of these were in positions to get information needed.

Ella felt her heart fall as the class went on. After class, they went on their usual run. But her fears bombarded her with each step. She now had to gain the trust of a stranger by the end of the year. Considering her circumstances, she didn't know how that was possible, but Madame Briar did tell her to come to her secret office at the end of class.

Now it was to find out what she needed to do.

This year will be the hardest one yet for a few of the girls. But should they overcome this, they will be better for it.

Madame Briar
Progress Report 8, Year 1827-1828

Chapter Twenty-Six

Nerves tingled through Ella as she waited for Madame Briar to let her into her hidden office. Finally, Madame Briar called Ella over.

"Come in, dear. We have much to speak about."

It always made Ella anxious when she was called over to Madame Briar. Even when she didn't know that she was an elite spy. Her commanding but quiet presence made everyone turn to her even when she didn't speak. But now, after having been trained by her, Ella was even more awestruck.

She sat before her, this amazing woman, who also had a connection to her mother.

"Lady Cooper, you know that this task will be difficult for you because of your unfortunate circumstances. You stepsisters are going to make things difficult for you."

Ella nodded. She was right. Ella had gotten used to the bliss of not having her stepsisters torment her every day. But for now, according to the world, it was like she didn't exist. If she left and got caught or noticed by her sisters, her work with the Fan Society would be over.

Madame Briar continued, "Due to your success last year, your task this year will be harder."

Pride filled Ella. But considering her difficult her task was last year, she wondered how much more difficult the madame was going to make it.

"What do I have to do? Will I be dressing as a servant so I can get closer?" Ella asked.

Shaking her head, Madame Briar answered, "No, the servants all work together, and they may be able to recognize you. But the ones you worked with will be in classes of their own at this time, and personal maids wouldn't recognize you. No, this year, you will be acting as a new student and go to classes with them."

"But what about my stepsisters? Won't they recognize me?"

"Yes, they will, if you get caught. They will be in different class- es. We will also have a wig on you just in case, so hopefully seeing you in passing, they wouldn't look too hard. But the biggest thing you can do to not be recognized is to play your part to perfection. They wouldn't expect the stepsister they have always seen as a servant to act as a noble, understand?"

Ella nodded her head, remembering her classes. People saw what they expected. With no physical evidence, as long as you played your part to perfection, it would cause doubt.

Continuing, Madame Briar said, "The same thing I told you last year is applicable this year. If you get caught, we cannot protect you."

The challenge excited Ella. But she still wasn't sure how this would all work. "Do I have a cover?"

Madame Briar nodded. "You are lucky you have common enough features. We can change a few of your looks and have your name be similar to what you have. We will keep your story similar to your own, so it will be easier for you to remember. And that way when you leave the academy and become a member of society, they will think they just misremembered you. Especially if you are considered unimportant."

Thinking on it, Ella was starting to understand. Servants were naturally more observant; they had to be to do their job, but they had a blind side. They only tended to pay attention to those they deemed of worth or were a higher class than who they served. If Ella came in as a lower-class nobility, then they wouldn't really pay any attention to her, nor would they try to remember her. There was only one question left.

"What is my cover?"

Madame Briar gave her a knowing smile and handed over a set of papers. "Are you ready?"

Ella looked over the pages with Clementine. She was lucky that this time Clementine would be able to help her, and the cover was not that much different from the one she had in the first school year at that disastrous tea party test.

She would be an adoptive daughter of a baron who had hopes that getting Ella into this prestigious academy would help him rise in rank. Which it would have, had she actually been his daughter. Her cover also showed that she would be new to nobility and was still fumbling with the ropes. She would be an awestruck country girl who now was a noble and was like a princess taken to a castle.

"I'm supposed to shorten my name to Minnie. Should I create a persona to go with that name?" Clementine asked as she looked over the papers with Ella. Once again seated in Ella's room, Clementine was helping Ella memorize the part she must play.

"As if your real name works with your personality." Meek and mild were not things that Ella would call Clementine.

"Did you see what your name is going to be?"

Ella sighed, "Yes, Pricilla Cook. I'm going to have to get used to that. That, and she is planning on having me wear a blonde wig."

"You don't like long names. Considering most people don't even realize your name is Arabella and not Ella because you would rather go by Ella," Clementine said as she moved and sat next to her on the bed. "But it shouldn't be too bad. A bit tedious to have to put a wig on you every day, but at least you only have to do this for a year."

"Maybe." The talk with Madame Briar brought the realization she could become anyone since people would not be expecting her. Her family wasn't looking for her. She didn't have anyone else who would worry about her. She could leave and look for her mother and no one would stop her.

"What are you thinking about so hard? Worried about the classes you have to take?" Clementine interrupted Ella's thoughts.

Giving her friend a smile, Ella shook the odd thought from her head. "No, just lost in thought. Though, I thought she said my name would be close to my own. This sounds very different. And what classes am I taking?"

Clementine looked at the list again, biting her lip thoughtfully. "You will be doing classes on sewing and letter writing."

"They have whole classes dedicated to letter writing?" Ella exclaimed.

Clementine snorted in a very un-lady-like manner. "You should realize by now that nobility has their own set of rules."

"That is true, and Madame Briar always has yet to steer me wrong." Fiddling with the papers, Ella glanced at the pages, not really reading anything. The thought that she had pushed down kept coming back. Ella wondered if this was where she was supposed to be.

She didn't even notice Clementine reaching over to take the papers from her until they were already gone. Clementine stood and had started organizing the pages.

"Hey, I was reading that!"

Clementine, setting down the papers on the vanity, looked down at Ella. "No, you were not. Now, when you are ready to talk about whatever you are chewing on, let me know."

"You're not going to ask me about it?" After the messy situation when Ella had been trying to protect Clementine and they stopped talking to each other, she had made sure to tell Clementine all of her thoughts after that incident.

Clementine shook her head. "You are still working through it. I trust that you will talk to me when you are ready."

"Thank you, Clementine. What would I do without you?"

Giving her a proud smile, Clementine replied, "You wouldn't be able to do anything, because I'm awesome. Now, make sure you get some sleep and rest your head. Don't stay up too long thinking. Goodnight, Ella."

With that, she left. In the darkness of her room, Ella ruminated on her thoughts.

There are many things you can do to gain the loyalty of a Ghost. The first is to find common ground. It can be difficult when you are acting as a noble, but there are always things that you can complain about. If the relationship is one of different classes, this is especially easy.

Book with fan on cover
Chapter 15

Chapter Twenty-Seven

The day started earlier than usual for Ella. She had to go to the Fan Society's mandatory physical training in the morning. Panting from the morning run, she met Clementine at her room, who rushed her inside. Looking frazzled, Clementine came in to attend to Ella but had to quickly leave to do her other duties since she was still attending the academy as a servant, as well as having her own classes to attend, on top of her classes with Ella.

They didn't even have time to chat with each other but instead, Clementine hurried in and helped her into her dress, since she couldn't go in her training clothes that now smelled of sweat. Having already pulled out Ella's day dress and peeled off her damp clothes, Ella quickly wiped herself down with a waiting rag and basin. She couldn't do a proper cleaning, so Clementine made sure to spritz her with ample perfume to hide the smell. Pushing her down into a chair, Clementine wrangled Ella's frizzy hair and tried to tuck it into a blonde wig.

"Ugh, your hair won't cooperate," Clementine hissed as she grunted with the effort of trying to wrangle Ella's hair.

Ella winced and blinked as her eyes watered from the tugging on her hair. After the wig was properly settled, Clementine quickly set to making sure the wig was still styled. After a swift onceover, she said, "Good luck." Then off she went.

Sighing, Ella watched the disappearing back of her friend as she hurried down the hallway. Today, Ella could have used their usual banter, because then maybe her nerves wouldn't be wound so tight.

This would be her first time having to play a role for a long time, as well as playing a part with her stepsister nearby. They could catch her at any time should she take the wrong hallway or they change their routine. Not to mention she had to play the part of a noble, surrounded by people who had been training their entire lives. Meaning that she would be looked down on by everyone around her. And to add one last thing, she also had to find a way to make one of their personal maids become one of her Ghosts.

Ella ambled through the passageways to one that would lead to a usually empty corridor near the nobles' halls. Pushing a Fan Society symbol on the wall made the bricks swing open to the empty corridor.

With a few deep breaths, Ella took her steps out of the walls into the academy proper for the first time in two years.

And the wall closed behind her.

It was like a leaver flipped in her mind. And she was Pricilla Cook. A young girl who needed to do well in this school to make her family proud. With all the grace Ella could muster, she strode down the halls to her class. Clementine joined her as she moved through the hallways after finishing up her work. When they arrived, Clementine opened the door, head bowed as Ella entered.

The room was large for the smattering of girls who were seated in a loose circle made of couches and chairs. A few were already stitching kerchiefs as she walked in. They looked up, but noticing the way she was dressed, in a nice but out-of-season dress, they quickly turned back to their stitches.

Letting her little noble training take over, she found a spot away from what was considered the "head" of the room. Though in circumstances like these, rules were laxer. Clementine passed Ella her handkerchief already placed in an embroidery hoop.

Ella sat and began stitching, while from the corners of her eyes she took stock of the girls. Based on how early they arrived and how they were dressed, they were likely children of barons. None of them were what she was looking for. She needed a maid of a higher-ranked member of society.

The door soon opened, and a few other girls arrived. These girls were obviously of higher rank. Dressed in day dresses of a floral print and heads held high as if expecting everyone to fall over themselves to obey, they floated in and sat down.

These were the girls that they needed information on. Instead of looking at the girls, Ella glanced at their personal maids. They were well-trained. No emotions peeked through as they moved to stand at the edge of the room with the others. It was going to be difficult to get them to be flipped to her side. Ella would have to keep an eye out for cracks that she could use to turn them.

Within moments of their arrival, the teacher came in and instantly jumped into how to do fifteen of the most basic stitches. She didn't stay long since everyone picked it up easily and she let the girls practice. It took no more than a few minutes.

After the teacher was finished, the girl at the "head" of the room nodded and started talking to the round-faced girl next to her. That was the signal for the girls to speak.

"Lady Cecil, it is so good to see you again."

"It is good to see you as well, Lady Byron."

Lady Byron was the leader of the conversation, and from her lessons, Ella could guess that the girl was Mary Byron, the only daughter of Marque Byron. Lady Cecil was Beatrice Cecil, the daughter of Viscount Cecil, who was in a trade alliance with the Byrons. As the greetings went on, there was a girl she hadn't noticed before. She was one of the first greeted, so she had to be of higher rank, but Ella recognized her as one of the girls who had been in the classroom before her.

After her introduction, she paid close attention to the afore-mentioned girl. The lady's name was Lady Hill. The dark-haired girl sat almost outside of the circle, in a padded chair. She didn't speak up much and only answered when someone asked a question. Ella looked to her servant, who hovered about behind her, trying to keep a worried look off her face. Ella recognized the Hill name as being influential but didn't recognize this girl from the descriptions of the Hill family. She would have to look it up when she returned to her room.

Ella caught Clementine's gaze, then looked to the worried servant before continuing to try and keep pace with the conversations that were going on over her head.

Class ended when Lady Byron stood and gave her goodbyes. One by one, the rest of the girls headed out the door to their next class. Ella slowed her steps so that she would exit around the same time as Lady Hill did. She decided to adopt the manner that Eleanor would take, feeling it would help her to get the girl to open up.

"Hello, Lady Hill. I'm so excited to come to this school. But I'm so nervous to talk to the other girls."

The shy girl stumbled in surprise at Ella's conversation. Looking up, she stuttered out, "Hello."

Ella smiled back, hoping it was a calming smile and the girl wouldn't be too jumpy. "I didn't mean to scare you. I've never been in a place like this before, and it's been a little scary. I was trying to gather to courage to speak to you but didn't quite know the social protocol to do so."

The country girl persona seemed to work, as the Hill girl smiled in her direction.

"There is a lot to know about social protocol," she said, her voice quiet, and she peeped in Ella's direction. "I still get stuck on it."

"How about we help each other on it?"

The girl nodded, a flush of red on her pale cheeks.

"Call me Pricilla."

"Helena."

They soon reached a corridor that Ella needed to turn down or she might end up running into her sisters. "I've got to go this way. I guess I will see you next class."Helena nodded and headed in the opposite direction. Going down the hallway Ella had indicated, she waited until the other girls were far enough away and slowed her steps enough for Clementine catch up and whisper over her shoulder.

"We are good to go."

This day started going well, and now that she had chosen her Ghost, the hard part was getting the maid on her side. And getting close to her lady would give them more time together.

Marriage is a pivotal point in a noble woman's life. Marriage is a business contract. They are used to move forward in business ventures, gain prestige, and hold alliances together. The better you do in gaining a proper husband, the better off you will be.

Nobility and Marriage Arrangements
Chapter 1

Chapter Twenty-Eight

The next class Ella had was letter writing. It was much the same as the last class but involved desks instead of couches. At the end of class, they were supposed to write a letter to all the other students to invite each other to a tea party. Ella had forgotten that everything had to be written with nuances depending on who you were writing to.

It would be easier as a commoner. The thought crossed in front of Ella's mind as she had to rewrite her last sentence three times. She brushed a blonde curl that had fallen in front of her face again. At least she wouldn't have to wear a wig if she was a commoner; no one would recognize her anyway. Her hand froze at the thought, but then she shoved it away. Yes, being a commoner would include less random rules, but after being treated like a slave in her own home, Ella knew that they had their own problems.

She continued her class, but the thought that it might be easier to find her mother if she just went to the streets herself kept coming back like a bad cold.

After writing, the teacher came over an looked over all the letters. She hovered behind each lady as she read the letter, with only a nod of acknowledgment if they achieved their assigned goal. As she moved over to Helena's, she spoke the words, "You did very well."

Bowing her head as her cheeks flushed, Helena couldn't see the angry glares directed at her from Lady Byron.

It was the very same look that Ella's stepmother used to give to other ladies who she believed had stolen her attention. A look of inferiority. But why would she feel inferior, considering she was still in charge of the classroom?

Standing by her shoulder, the teacher picked up Ella's letter. "Lady Cook, this wording is too inflammatory. It needs to be more subtle. Considering your peerage, the person you are writing to has a higher rank, so the words need to be even more polite."

Ella bowed her head and nodded.

The teacher nodded to Lady Byron to have the class exit, and everyone was dismissed.

Ella glanced one last time at Lady Byron, who had thrown another glare at Helena's direction as she left. It still bothered her as she left the class and slipped inside the hidden corridors to her Fan Society lessons. Even a lesson on various ways to communicate to Ghosts couldn't pull her out of her thoughts.

Only when Clementine was helping her get ready was she finally able to think straight.

"Clementine, what did you learn from the servant?" Ella asked, trying to keep focused on the task at hand.

Braiding Ella's hair, Clementine answered, "Ada is very worried about her charge. Lady Hill is the second daughter of Marquess Hill and is considered worthless to the family."

"Ahh." That made more sense. Helena was from an influential family, but her position was not rated high enough to be considered worth much. It wouldn't be good to have her servant as a Ghost since she was not in a high position. Unless . . . "Are there any plans on her getting married?"

Clementine tilted her head, thinking. "I don't know. Since we have been hiding in the academy for a while, it has been difficult to know the outside situation. I suppose it would depend on the politics. But considering her family position, they would want to have her marry into a family that would further their power."

"Then can you find out?"

Snorting, Clementine declared, "Of course I can. Who do you think you are talking to? Ada will be much easier to turn to a Ghost than any of the others."

Ella insisted, "But she still has to be in a prominent position. A second daughter is not a prominent enough position."

"For now. I'm sure that considering she was chosen to be in the school, she will be." Clementine tilted her head. Eyeing Ella, she said, "I can see the wheels working in your head."

Now that her hair was braided, Ella plopped down on her bed and looked up at her white ceiling. "All the girls here are considered by Madame Briar to be worth her time. I would be remiss if I didn't consider all of them worthy of my time, as well."

"Going to class one day and already talking like a noble." Ella was going to deny it when Clementine stopped her, "It is good that you speak like them. Then it will be easier to do your duties as a Fan Society member."

Fan Society member. The first year was just surviving, the second year was just trying to prove to herself that she could do it. But the question was, did she even want to be a member? The one thing that still kept her here was her mother. Staying here gave her a chance to find her. With their resources, they could help. But was there a better way?

"Yes, it would be easier to be a Fan Society member."

With a jaw-cracking yawn, Clementine said, "I had best get off to bed. Considering how tired we are now, think about how it's going to feel tomorrow. It's going to be an exhausting day."

"Go get your beauty sleep. See you tomorrow." Ella kept a smile on her face as Clementine left the room. Her expression fell when the door shut, leaving her to her troubled thoughts.

This time, when Ella went to sewing class, she made sure to sit near Helena. It was difficult to get her talking, but Ella did her best to act as Eleanor would and made some progress.

"Who is it you admire?" Ella asked, trying to get the girl to open up more. Most of the girl's answers were one-worded or included a mere shake of her head.

But for once, she actually exclaimed, "Sir Robert Peel."

"Who is that?" Still not having time to catch up on the outside world, Ella had no idea who this person was. She hadn't expected Helena to answer so excitedly, though.

"He is putting forth a vote for the Metropolitan Police Force to help protect the city. Considering how there is no official police force, and how the policing is mostly done by volunteers or by the church, it makes it difficult to feel safe on the streets. This will change things so that it won't get bad enough for military forces need to come in," Helena babbled. She must have seen the surprised expression on Ella's face since she looked down at her sewing. "I'm sorry, I know it is impolite to get involved in politics."

Blinking at the sudden shift in conversation but not wanting to let go of this chance, Ella hurried to calm her, "No, I was just surprised. I didn't know that such a thing existed. I have been out of the city for many years."

Helena gave her a small smile, her cheeks flushing pink as she continued to work on her stitches.

A dark memory surfaced that Ella hadn't thought about in years. It was the day that a night watchman came to her door and her sobbing father. The day they found out her mother had gone missing. What would have happened had they actually had someone investigate the matter at that time? What if they were able to follow the clues of what happened that night and found her mother? Would she had been properly taught by her mother to be a member of the Fan Society? The lack of learning, the torment of her stepsisters, would have never happened.

Holding her tongue about the questions she truly wanted to ask, instead, Ella said, "It is amazing that you know so much! I can see that he is such a wonderful person. The only person I know as a hero is the Duke of Wellington. He was an amazing war veteran and a great strategist. He still has his looks, too. I wouldn't mind being married off to an older man if he looked like him. After all, it is my duty to be married to further my family's name."

The happiness that had been in Helena's blue eyes changed to one Ella couldn't recognize. It was like a cross between happiness and worry.

"Worried about your marriage?" Ella asked. This was her chance to get the information, but she didn't want to push the girl too far.

"I . . . Look, class is over. Farewell, Lady Cook—I mean Pricilla," Helena muttered as she hurried out the door.

Brow furrowing, Ella watched as she scurried away. Disappointed at the turn of events, she headed out the door. Thoughts tumbled around as she wondered why Helena pulled away.

Did it have to do with her marriage? Did she not want to get married?

Ella paused and looked at a Fan Society symbol that was hidden within the fancy brickwork as another question came unbidden to her mind. Did Ella want to continue being a member of the Fan Society? Other than her mother, what other reason did she have for being here? Why was she trying so hard for something she wasn't even sure she believed in?

Shoving that thought back was difficult as her mind tumbled around. Putting her head down, she shook her head and made her way to class.

Ella headed to the hidden hallways. She kept busy by making sure each line was constructed carefully while her mind wandered down the dark corridors of what if. She didn't even notice that Clementine had been following behind her as she entered the hidden passageways.

When it came time for her Fan Society class, Ella's doubts that had been pushed away now haunted her every step.

Pulling her out of her thoughts and causing her to jump, Clementine asked, "What is wrong?"

Ella had thought she had been doing a good job keeping her fears from her face, but Clementine knew her too well. Grateful for the dark, Ella asked, "What would you do if I decided to leave the Fan Society?"

"I would leave with you. What would you do without me?"

The reply was instantaneous.

"Are you sure?" Ella pressed. Clementine had done so much for her. She didn't need to follow her when it would certainly be more difficult for Clementine. "You have been doing so well here. They treat you well and you are talented for this type of stuff, too."

Clementine snorted. "I could say the same for you, as well. But before we leave the academy, may I ask why you want to?"

The what ifs that had played in her mind now poured from her lips, "I think that I would do better finding my mother on my own outside the academy than I could in here." The conversation with Helena about the police force still bounced around in her thoughts. Ella glanced at Clementine, worried what she might say.

Clementine was silent as she took this in. The dark pressed in on Ella as she waited in silence for Clementine's answer. After hearing her reason, would she leave her?

"I think there are still things to learn here before we leave," Clementine broke the silence, and Ella's heart fell. But Clementine continued, "I suggest you wait until the end of this school year. Then, if you still wish to leave, I will leave with you."

It was a very rational decision, and anyways, she would still need to talk to Madame Briar if she chose to leave. Ella nodded. "I agree with that. Thank you."

"And this is why you speak to me. Because I'm amazing. Now, let's get to class. If this truly is going to be your last year here, then you should learn everything you can."

Clementine was right as always. With a smile on her face, Ella followed Clementine down the dark corridor to the bright classroom next to the training room.

A code, when properly constructed, will be detectible only by the intended recipient.

Book with fan on cover
Chapter 15

Chapter Twenty-Nine

The classroom that they had been learning in was not the training room that they had been using for the past two years. This room had just enough space for all the girls to have breathing room with their desks. Now that they were working on codes and messages, they needed a place to write. The person teaching this class was Ruth, the older woman who was at the tea party and Eleanor's Assistant.

Unlike when she was at the tea party, now she had a warm smile. Her hair was auburn with white at her temples. She wore the black uniform of a personal servant as she stood before them.

"Can anyone tell me which of these three sentences are written in code?" Ruth asked, pointing to the words written on the chalkboard behind her.

Looking over the words, Ella tried to see if anything would be out of place. But they all seemed like a sentence you would write in a letter. After a few minutes of looking it over, all the girls slumped in their seats, defeated. Even Luella had a hard time with it. Her eyes squinted at the board as if in the hopes that if she looked at it hard enough, the answer would come to her.

Ruth gave them an encouraging smile. "The answer is all of them are written in code. They are passphrases that must be used in answer to each other in the third sentence. A common phrase, but it has to be answered on a certain line with an exact phrase. There are many different codes, and they all have their weaknesses. What would be the weakness of this one?"

Ivy raised her hand. "Oh, I know. If you have a lot of letters, you can find it since they would use it often."

"Very good, Ivy," Ruth beamed. "This is fine for certain correspondence, but you have to be aware of who can get your letters. Now, the next code I'm going to teach you is . . ."

The lesson continued, leaving Ella enthralled. It was much easier to pay attention after talking to Clementine. Yet she still had to come to a decision of what she wanted to do. Should she leave the society? But something else was nagging at her, something that she had forgotten.

It was answered when a servant came to the class and gave her a message that Madame Briar wanted to see Ella after class.

And there it was. The cause of that feeling.

After all the time spent within the walls of the academy, Ella had spent the most with Madame Briar. Ella looked up to Madame Briar and admired her, as well as felt a connection to her mother through her. Guilt was setting in her like a rock sitting in the back of her throat and the fear that had been settling in her awoke aggressively, reminding her that she was in a secret society. Could she leave even if she wanted to?

When class ended, the doubt that she thought she had waylaid started to creep back, step by step as she made her way to Madame Briar's secret office. The guilt that sat on her made her so sick that she was sure she would pass out before she was able to knock on the door.

Inside, Madame Briar sat at her desk as usual. The Fan Society emblem on the wall mocked her as Ella sat down.

Placing the full weight of her gaze on Ella, Madame Briar said, "It has come to my attention that you are having a trying time, Lady Cooper."

That was an understatement. Of course, she knew, but how did she know? She always had information that she couldn't possibly have. If Madame Briar had told her she had telepathy, Ella would have believed her.

Ella swallowed. Trying to keep her face relaxed, she pushed back her guilt.

"When we spoke at the end of last year, I asked you what kept you in the Fan Society," Madame Briar continued. "And you replied that the only reason you are staying is because of the connection to your mother. Is that correct?"

Ella couldn't open her mouth but forced herself to nod in reply.

"You also had a conversation that you had plans on leaving the organization. Is that correct?"

Fear pierced Ella's heart. That only happened an hour ago. How could she know?

Was this the end? What was going to happen to her? What would Madame Briar think of her?

"Oh, don't be so afraid, dear, you are allowed to have feelings." Madame Briar's words warmed the thick fear that had frozen Ella in place, until the headmistress continued, "But we cannot have you changing your mind all the time. Should you wish to not be a Guardian for the Fan Society, you do not have to be. Considering that you were chosen for this, we can rely on you to keep your mouth shut, and instead, your position would be changed to Friend of the Society. We aren't barbarians. But I agree with Miss Clementine and think you should take time to think about your choice." Madame Briar looked past Ella, her expression wistful. "I once came to a decision with too much haste, with disastrous consequences. I do not wish for you to make the same mistake."

Ella wondered if that decision had something to do with her mother. Desire to know pressed against her, and she opened her mouth to speak.

But she was stopped as Madame Briar went on, "You have until the end of this school year to make your choice. I would make a suggestion, however: Make an attempt to get closer to those around you before you make your choice. Choose wisely."

That was a clear dismissal, but Ella had one question. One that she hadn't dared ask before.

"Are you searching for my mother?"

Madame Briar, who had started working on her papers, looked up. Setting the papers aside, she sighed, "Yes, we have looked for your mother. But by the time we got the information that she was missing, any clue that we could have found was gone. You can't search for something if you have nothing to go off of. We do keep our ears out for any information, but we have little hope of finding her. I'm sorry."

Ella refused to allow her shoulders to slump. She had expected this answer, but she had still feared receiving it.

"I understand. Thank you, Madame Briar." Ella gave her best curtsy and then headed back to her room to organize her jumble of thoughts and feelings. Grateful that the next class was physical fitness, Ella let her mind circle as she made her way around an obstacle course.

One never knows when information will come. Always be aware of others' behavior, as when they are acting differently is when information is most often found.

Book with fan on cover
Chapter 11

Chapter Thirty

The weeks that followed Ella's conversations went as thus:

Wake up early to do morning exercises, then off to class to try to get closer to Helena, and afterward, there was practice with letter writing, and finally lessons with the Fan Society about other forms of communication.

And yet Ella still didn't know what she was going to choose. She was no closer to finding her answer as she was getting Helena's maid to become her Ghost.

"What am I going to do? Nothing is working!" Ella complained as she lay on her bed.

In a nearby chair, Clementine looked up from her sewing that she was working on for Ella's dresses. She had been sewing in some hidden pockets in the skirts. "Well, you could actually follow Madame Briar's advice."

Propping herself up on her elbows, Ella gave Clementine an incredulous look. "What are you talking about?"

Clementine shrugged as she continued stitching. "I believe that she said to get close to others around you."

"I have been trying to get closer to Helena," Ella sighed, scratching at her hair. Even with the wig off, she still felt itchy.

Raising her brow, Clementine sniffed, "I do believe that Helena isn't everyone. What about Eleanor?"

"What about her?" Ella questioned, trying her best to refrain from glaring at her friend and barely succeeding.

"Oh, I don't know. Maybe since she has been trying to get you to forgive her for most of this year, and you have been avoiding her, you could try mending that relationship. It's at least a start. Who knows? Maybe she will help you," Clementine said as she finished knotting her stitch and began to clean up.

The guilty feeling along with anger that burned anew within Ella whenever she thought of Eleanor. Before class, Eleanor had come up to her to have a friendly conversation, but Ella always rebuffed her attempts. She knew that Eleanor hadn't done anything wrong. Yet Ella couldn't help but feel betrayed. It had always been difficult for her to trust people, and she had placed her trust in Eleanor. Yet she was the one who had been getting close to people to replace their emblems with counterfeits. It still left a bad taste in Ella's mouth.

"How does talking to her help with the predicament of getting a Ghost?" Ella said, avoiding the real point of contention.

Clementine rolled her eyes and walked over to Ella's vanity table, looking into the mirror. "If that is how you feel then I guess I should prepare myself to leave the academy," Clementine muttered as she looked at herself from different angles and fixed her blonde hair so it looked just right. After she was done, she walked past the stunned Ella and started to head out the door.

"Wait. That is all you are going to say to me?" Ella demanded, coming out of her stunned silence.

Sighing, Clementine turned to her. "We have known each other for many years. I have watched you grow up. I know that you know what you need to do, but you are avoiding it. I sure hope that you can figure it out before the end of the school year."

At that, she exited the room, leaving Ella in silence. Anger at her friend flared first but then puttered out with guilt.

Clementine was right. She needed to forgive Eleanor.

Ella made her way to morning class the next day with determination. Eleanor was already there chatting away with Ivy. Feeling her determination waning, Ella clenched her fists, held her head erect, and strode to Eleanor.

"Eleanor, I would like to speak to you," Ella said, ignoring the surprised look on Ivy's face. Eleanor merely nodded, telling Ivy she would talk to her later before following Ella a little ways away.

"What do you wish to speak to me about?" Eleanor asked in her signature bubbly voice, a bright smile across her face.

A flash of irritation ran through Ella. This was the same smile she had when she first introduced herself. The same smile she gave as she lied to Ella. But that was what they were supposed to do.

Instead of saying what she planned, questions poured from Ella. "How could you do it? How could you lie with a smile on your face?"

Eleanor's expression turned serious, and the answer she gave was unexpected, "I believe in what the Fan Society stands for. If smiling to someone will protect the royal line, then I will smile until my face becomes so sore that it will be stuck in place.

"We are all supposed to gain information by standing by important figures and helping to change things by changing the minds of those around us. That sometimes involves us playing a part we don't wish to play. But those in the Fan Society know that we are playing a part. We all have to trust one another to do what is best for the Fan Society. This is what we stand for. To play a part we may not like for the good of everyone. Ella, you are very talented when you have the desire to be. What are you standing for?"

With that, Eleanor's face returned to its bubbly smile as she bounded off to greet the others who had arrived. Eleanor had hit her where it hurt. Did Ella even know what she was standing for? If she truly believed in the Fan Society, then she wouldn't have been so annoyed with Eleanor. Did she even truly trust any of these girls?

As she did her morning run, Ella realized that she didn't really talk to any of them. The one she was closest to was Luella, and they hated each other. Ella's troubled thoughts echoed in her head with each step of her run. It haunted her as she got ready to go to her sewing class. So much so that Helena had to say her name three times to get her attention.

"I'm sorry, Helena. I was lost in thought," Ella said, trying to ease the worried look on Helena's face.

It didn't work.

Ella sighed, "Any news on if we will be having a police force soon?"

That did the trick. Helena's face brightened, and she nodded. "Even though people don't like the idea, it is still pushing through."

Seeing the delight on her face, Ella couldn't help but ask, "Why do you like it so much? The thought of a police force?"

Helena set down her sewing to look at Ella, then seeing how it was a serious question, went back to her needles and answered, "Having the power to help and using that to do so. Also having the courage to do so. I have seen so many people have power and only abuse it, but Sir Peel and the others are the true heroes. They have to courage to change the situation around them. I wish I could be like them."

Understanding filled Ella. Helena was the unwanted, useless daughter, and Ella doubted that anyone cared about her, let alone tried to change her situation. Because of that, she was very timid. Seeing the courage of others and how they wanted to help people must have made a lasting impression on her.

In an attempt to get closer to her, Ella said, "Sorry, I don't know much about the police force, but I do know about the night watchman. They do their best to change the people's situations; it is very admirable."

Ella did her best not to wince at her words. The night they came to her door to say her mother's carriage was found empty still haunted her to this day. If only the Fan Society informants had been there. Or better yet if she were there, then she could have given information to them. Acting as nobility didn't come naturally to her.

Would it truly be better for her to become a Guardian? She was nothing like her mother.

And if she was part of the Fan Society, she would have to put her focus on other things instead of helping her mother. Was putting other missions ahead of her mother the best course of action?

"It's true that they do help, but there is no organization in the night watch," Helena replied.

"What?"

Babbling, Helena continued, "Well, I mean they have some organization, but they were all volunteers. Some information may be the same. And since they are volunteers, some have more knowledge and others may not know what they are looking for. But if they had a central force that trains everyone on how to look for information and pass information between themselves, they would learn more. Not only that, but they can consolidate information and have one person look at all the information. It makes it much easier to catch criminals. And that is what the police force is trying to do."

Helena's babbling puttered out as she looked at the door. "Oh my, it's time to go. And I forgot that I need to talk to Lady Hastings. I'm sorry, Pricilla. Farewell."

She dashed away as fast as was proper, and Ella slowly followed her out the door.

As an observer, you must be able to work with those you hate should it help with the mission you are on. You will have to act like you are friends with people you despise because you need them on your side.

Book with fan on cover
Chapter 21

Chapter Thirty-One

The question that Ella had been avoiding all school year tightened its grasp as it forced her to face the truth. Ella was grateful that Helena had hurried off. It was easier to keep her façade up without having to answer Helena. But it started to crack when she heard a familiar voice in the hallway.

Effie, her stepsister, was talking to Helena nearby. Someone who knew Ella very well and expected her to be a servant far, far away.

The fear that froze her for a moment burned away with the desire to find out what her stepsister was doing with Helena. Using the hand signals that they were taught in class recently, Ella motioned for Clementine to listen in on her stepsister's conversation. Taking a deep breath, she resisted the urge to look at Effie again and headed to writing class at a slow pace.

At first, Ella received a few odd looks when she walked in without her personal maid, but after Clementine came in carrying a pen and some ink, the other students turned back to each other to talk.

Clementine passed Ella the writing implements and a letter. Using the letter opener that was already at the desk, Ella sliced the letter open and read the words that Clementine had freshly written. Ella had no idea how she wrote it and came back that quickly, but if she ever asked Clementine, she would only give a smug smile and act mysterious.

Reading the coded message, Ella could tell that there wasn't much to go off of from the conversation. Ella wrote a reply in her letter that they were supposed to write for class. The challenge made the tedious class go by quicker. This was the first time she felt this joy in a while.

When class ended and Ella and Clementine were in the hidden passageways, Ella asked, "Do you think you will be able to find out more information on the conversation with Effie?"

Following Ella in the dark, Clementine replied, "By the time I arrived, the conversation was almost over. They were talking about a man and Ada, Helena's servant, seemed worried by the conversation. I'm not sure how much information she can give me. I might need some help on this one."

Ella gasped, "You need help? The amazing Clementine needs help?"

"I have no problem asking for help." She snorted. "I can take my own advice. But you won't like who I need help from."

"Don't tell me it's Luella." Though talented, the thought of having to work together with Luella again made Ella groan. It was hard getting anything done with that personality of hers. Ella started prepping herself for the long conversation about how Luella's ideas were so much better than Ella's that she nearly missed Clementine's answer.

"No. We need Eleanor."

That stopped Ella in her tracks, confusion rising.

"Why do we need her?" Ella asked, her stomach turning in knots. Even after their last conversation, she still didn't want to talk to her.

"You really don't know? I thought you came up with the plans? If you don't know, then I guess I can do my best."

Clementine walked off ahead of her, leaving Ella in the shadows to catch up.

During class, Ella kept glancing at Eleanor. Ever since she walked up to Eleanor, Ella felt even more guilty whenever she saw her. With a glance at Clementine, she saw that she was steadfastly ignoring her. Rolling her eyes, she turned back to the teacher as she discussed methods of information transfer.

Anger filled Ella as she ran through her mind what her friends had told her.

Friends. Ella's anger died as she realized she thought of Eleanor as a friend. The whole reason why she was so angry at both of them. They had spoken the truth, and Ella didn't want to hear it. But she needed to.

Ruth echoed what she was feeling throughout the lesson, "Do not get angry at the messenger for the information they bring. They knew that it was bad, which is the reason they brought it to you. If you get angry, then you will only get information that you want to hear and not information that you need to hear. This is why sometimes it is better to do what is called dead drops . . ."

Ruth was right. Clementine was right. They all were right.

They were just trying to help her, and Ella had lashed out at them.

Making up her mind, she thought about what she should do, and the dark that had hovered over her this school year lightened with each decision she made. All that was left was to apologize to Clementine and the others.

The remaining time in class made Ella want to wiggle in her seat. Only her training kept her from moving too much. When it was time to leave, she hurried over to Clementine and pulled her to their room.

"I'm sorry, Clementine. You were right," Ella said, the words tumbling out of her mouth as soon as the door shut.

"About?" Clementine raised her eyebrow.

"That I need to start working with Eleanor and not dwell on things in the past."

"Oh really? And why is that?" Clementine stood there, arms folded across her chest.

"Because all of this is not actually helping do the task that I was assigned and is just me being a total idiot because I can't forgive my friends. And that I've been taking my emotions out on you because I still haven't come to a decision," Ella sighed. She had been such a jerk to everyone for doing their task. Something she should have been doing herself. Instead, she had been dancing around feelings that she hadn't wanted to feel, which had caused her to fail at everything.

"What else?"

Ella could see that her friend was holding back a smile. "That Clementine is always right, and I need to stop being an idiot and do what needs to be done."

Clementine smiled and put her hand on her hips, replying, "I know I am right. It's a good thing you are back to being the planner. It was exhausting. Glad you are out of your idiocy and ready to actually do the task."

The tension and guilt that she had been carrying released at the easy banter with Clementine. "Yes, and I will make sure you have time for your beauty sleep, as well."

"Good." Clementine sat on Ella's bed and started fixing her hair. "Now, have you figured out what we need to do to gain Helena's maid as a Ghost? Because these half-hearted plans are never going to work."

A smile grew on Ella's lips. "Yes, and now that we know Effie is involved with Helena, we have to do our best. It makes it even trickier; you know how she is."

"True, but you are even better. And you do better when your back is up against the wall."

Ella shrugged in acknowledgment. It was true. "Are you ready to hear the plan?"

Clementine raised her brow as she finished twisting her hair. "Does it involve Eleanor?"

She nodded. "You were right. We do need her. And it is time to work together."

Together, the girls must be able to stand. I fear that darkness is coming, and one mistake can lead to disaster. Should they fail, it will be the end.

Madame Briar
Progress Report 12, Year 1827-1828

Chapter Thirty-Two

The planning session with Clementine was what she needed. With a clear goal in mind and a better understanding, Ella could see how she could easily gain a Ghost before the end of the school year. But now it was time to truly talk to Eleanor. The poor attempt she made last time just showed Ella that she hadn't been ready to truly forgive her.

Talking to a few of the girls stretching, Eleanor looked up at Ella, who had shuffled up to her. With a quick glance, she turned back to the other girls and said she would be back in a moment. Eleanor stood up and followed Ella a little ways away.

"What do you need?" Eleanor chirped with her usual ever-present smile.

Taking a deep breath, Ella spilled out what she needed to say, "I'm sorry that I've been so rude to you. Please forgive me?"

Eleanor's smile froze. But then it spread so wide that Ella was certain it would break out of her cheeks. "Yes, I would be happy to forgive you if only you forgive me. I didn't want to lie to you, but it was for the Fan Society."

"I understand." And Ella did, in a way. Yes, she still didn't have as much devotion as Eleanor did, but she understood loyalty to family. To Eleanor, the Fan Society was her family. "I believe in what the Fan Society is doing."

Ella still didn't have the devoutness of Eleanor, but she knew that the Fan Society stood for something right. And if she truly wanted to find her mother, the only way she could accomplish that would be with their help. But for now, she needed Eleanor's help.

"Eleanor? Would you be willing to help me with something?" Ella asked.

"Sure. What do you have in mind?"

"I have a rumor that I need you to spread." Curiosity gleamed in Eleanor's eyes as Ella continued. "I need a rumor that will back Helena in a corner. Can you create a rumor that she is marrying someone that has a bad reputation within society?"

"I can do that." An understanding lit Eleanor's eyes she nodded in acknowledgment of what Ella needed.

"Thank you, Eleanor." And she truly meant it. All of the bad feelings she had towards Eleanor this year had faded their way out of existence.

With a bow of her head, Eleanor replied, "It will be a pleasure working with you." She bounded away with a bounce in her step.

Ella smiled. It was going to be a good day. One piece of the puzzle had been put into place. Now she only needed a few more.

It would take a week before the gossip could hit in full force. Or at least, that was the thought. But Ella should have known better when she asked for Eleanor's help. By the end of the day, the first piece was all set up, All Ella had to do was move.

Ella decided to wait a little longer and let Eleanor's work do its business. She could already see it starting to work when she entered sewing class, if the whispered glances towards Helena were any indication. The nervous girl kept her head down the entire class and as soon as she was able, she scurried out.

This continued for the next few days. As Ella sewed and Clementine talked to Ada, Helena kept her head down and didn't talk to anyone other than Effie. Ella needed to gain Ada as a Ghost, but she needed to know what Effie was trying to do. If not, anything she may plan could fall to ruin and get her kicked out of the school. But if either Clementine or Ella spoke to Effie or were near her, the chances of Ella getting caught grew exponentially. She would need to ask for more help.

Later that day, after a sparring match with Olive during their Fan Society classes, Ella gathered her courage and spoke to her. "Olive, may I have a word with you?"

She nodded politely, not giving away any emotion.

Ella gulped down her panic that this was a bad idea and that she would be betrayed. Stamping down that emotion, she blurted out what she wanted, "I was wondering if you would be willing to spy on someone for me?"

Tilting her head to the side, Olive asked, "What do you need?"

Relief flooded her. "Between first and second class, my stepsister Effie is speaking to my mark's charge. I need to know what they are talking about."

"I will let you know tomorrow."

Ella blinked in surprise. Olive had replied so quickly. "Are you sure you are willing to do this for me?"

"Of course. We are all working for the same cause. I am happy to help another member," Olive said with her brow starting to furrow.

Gratitude blossomed within Ella at Olive's words. Was this what she had been missing this whole time? And she was just being too stubborn to actually open herself to others? Smiling at her, Ella said gratefully, "Thank you."

A feeling that she couldn't quite place warmed her as Ella headed back to her room.

The next day, Olive gave her what Effie was talking about. They had both arrived at the Fan Society class early for stretches. "Your stepsister is wanting to gain connections to nobility through Helena."

That was unsurprising. Even though Helena was considered useless to her own family, that didn't mean she was useless to someone like Audrey, who had a very low ranking within nobility. No matter who the gossip is saying that Helena is marrying they are still of higher rank than they are.

"What is she offering her in exchange for the connection?" Ella asked.

"She was portraying herself as a friend who would stand by her during this crisis and that when this whole thing blows over, she should remember who her friends were," Olive said, stretching.

Helena was so starved for attention that she would jump at an offer like that. But Ella needed Helena to not be pulled down by these rumors. It would be better if she could push Helena into a higher standing. Ella needed to get Ada to her side for any of this to work. But first, she needed to see how the rumors had affected Helena.

"Helena, are you alright?" Ella asked, having managed to catch up to her after class the next day. This was a tricky part of her plan. She had to talk to Helena without meeting Effie. If Effie decided to go and find Helena and saw Ella, that would spell disaster. Ella would have to be able to win Helena over with as few words as possible without pushing her away.

"Yes, of course, I am. Why wouldn't I be?" It looked as if Helena was going to cry. A prick of guilt about Ella's part in this didn't stop her from doing what she needed to do.

"I'm so sorry. Rumors can be devastating. But may I ask what is the truth? Is your family really forcing you to marry that man?"

Helena took the bait when she answered Ella, "Do you really want to know? Are you going to accept my words as the truth? Because no one else does."

Grabbing her hands, Ella looked her in the eyes. "Yes, I would."

Opening her mouth to speak, Helena hesitated and looked behind Ella, then clammed up, "I'm sorry. Talk to my maid. She will tell you what you want to know."

She scurried off. This was what she was looking for. Smiling at what she accomplished, Ella started to head to class, but in front of her was Effie. Thankfully, she wasn't looking at her, but it was a near thing. She had to get out of this situation—and quickly. With Effie standing at the intersection to her next class, it was going to be risky.

Taking a deep breath, she put on her noble smile. The one that was not too wide or too small, but one that saw everything as pleasant. With small steps, she strode to her class, making sure to turn her face away from Effie while still keeping her in her peripherals. It was difficult to keep from running to the next class when her body was warning her that she was in danger. If Ella was recognized, she would be sent away, and then she would never find her mother. She would have to hope that her wig would be enough to fool Effie.

With steady breathing and her smiling mask on her face, she walked past Effie as she turned down the corridor. Even with her back to her, Ella still couldn't relax. Though the school was massive, they only took in a certain number of students, and the hallways didn't have many people that she could hide by.

After a few steps away from her, Ella could feel her stepsister's penetrating gaze from the prickling on the back of her neck. Still keeping her walk, Ella did her best to not react. Ella wished that she could get Clementine to intercede, but Effie would remember her, and that would make things worse. Swallowing her fears, she continued on her way even as Effie took a few steps toward her. Sweat beaded under the wig, making it itch. But Ella didn't dare to scratch it for fear of calling attention to herself.

Thankfully, luck was on her side, as another girl came up to talk to her and distract her until Ella was far enough away. But luck might have had nothing to do with it. The voice she heard was very familiar.

It was Eleanor's voice.

Even though she had been so rude to her this year, Eleanor had come to help her. It warmed her heart and thawed out the fear she had when she was close to being caught.

Ella finished making her way to writing class without issue. During class, they were supposed to write a thank you letter for a gift. Ella made hers for Eleanor, ensuring that anything about the Fan Society was in code.

She presented it to Eleanor before their class on codes began.

"I just helped out a fellow Fan Society member," Eleanor said with the same beaming smile on her face.

Because she was a member of the Fan Society, Ella wasn't alone. She didn't have to be, and the situation she was in wasn't as dangerous as it could have been. What would have happened if she was outside the academy and was in such a situation? Would she have been able to find her mother?

A smile lit up Ella's face when she replied, "A lady always makes sure to thank her allies. Isn't that what they teach us in class?"

"The best way you can thank me is to not let my work go to waste. Complete your task so I can see you next year."

"She took the bait. Let's see if we can hook a Ghost." All that Ella needed to do was get a meeting with Ada, and Clementine wouldn't let her down. Ella could only hope that she learned what she needed to turn Ada into a Ghost. But with Eleanor and Clementine, she knew that she could do it.

When Clementine caught up to her, she had the time for the meeting. It would be happening that night.

One trick to gaining a Ghost is to use the fishing strategy. The first is to leave bait. If they have a problem, make it your business to have a solution. If there is no problem, create one. You want your target to come to you. It will keep them from getting as spooked and more likely to be open to your suggestions. Second, get them hooked. Give them a solution to their problem, but make it so it would be detrimental to you. It will give them a sense of gratitude and will make them more loyal or favorable towards you. Third, you pull them up towards you. If you want them to be favorable towards you, one must keep their promises. If you don't fix the problem, they will run away and have a horrible impression of you. Making it even more difficult to gain a Ghost.

Book with fan on cover
Chapter 20

Chapter Thirty-Three

It didn't take long for Ada to meet up with Clementine after the incident. "She was jittery and completely worried about Helena."

"Did she say what time she wanted to meet with me?" Ella asked as they completed their evening run.

"Could you slow down a little? I'm not as fast as you," Clementine huffed as she struggled to keep up with her.Ella slowed her steps until Clementine could comfortably run beside her.

"Thank you. Now, Ada asked to meet in an empty room in a couple of hours."

"She must mean to keep Helena out of trouble." Ella remembered all the concerned looks that Ada had whenever she looked at Helena.

"Since she is putting you in danger, that means you can ask for more." They slowed to a stop as they finished their run, with Clementine gulping down air as she calmed her breathing, "Well, are you going to tell me . . . huff . . . why we are still having Helena's aid as a Ghost? . . . huff . . . Isn't she not important?"

A smile spread over Ella's face. "She is not important yet. But considering her obsession and her connections, I think I know what Madame Briar had in mind for her. For now, I need to concentrate on making a bargain with Ada."

Nodding in acknowledgment, they finished their class and readied Ella for her midnight meeting.

After lights out, Ella waited in one of the noble rooms that currently had no one staying in them. Clementine had already entered the room and lit a single candle in the parlor area. Two chairs had their dust cloths removed, and Ella was already seated when Ada entered.

With bumbling fingers, Ada snuck in with all the grace of a factory worker at a tea party. When she turned around, she let out a squeak of a surprise to see Ella sitting there.

Ella had to hold back a laugh. Considering she was the one who told Ella to meet her there, Ada was not a great spy. But then again, she didn't need to be. Ada only needed to be able to give her information.

But first, Ella needed to calm her down. "Ada, I'm sorry to startle you. Are you alright?"

Clenching her hand to her chest, she let out a sigh of relief, "Yes, my lady. I was just startled. There is no need to be concerned about me."

"Of course there is. You are my friend's personal maid. How are you to take as good of care of her if something happens to you?"

Ada flushed at the compliment. "Thank you for such kind words, Lady Cook."

Now it was time to get on topic. "What is wrong with Helena? I have heard rumors, and I don't know what to think."

"My lady did nothing wrong. They say that she is getting married to that ruffian Viscount Edmund, but she is not."

Ella knew that Eleanor was going to cause a rumor about a bad marriage choice, but she wasn't familiar with Viscount Edmund. She knew that he had some sort of shady dealings, but Ella was focusing on other things she needed to learn.

"Viscount Edmund is a part of underground dealings. This is horrible. What are you going to do?" Ella asked, concern filling her voice.

Wringing her hands together, Ada paced back and forth. "I don't know. This is going to ruin my lady. She doesn't deserve this! You believe me, don't you? That such a horrible man is not going to marry Lady Helena?"

At the last words, she came in front of Ella kneeling on the floor, pleading with her. Ella had needed her desperate, but she couldn't keep this woman in a panic for much longer. It wasn't right.

With a gentle smile, she lifted the woman's hand to lift her off the floor. "I believe you. But first, I need to know who her family is having her marry. If I don't know that, then how can fix the issue?"

Ada shifted from foot to foot, "I'm not really supposed to say such things. The marriage hasn't happened yet. If bad rumors were to spread, my lady would be in trouble, and her real marriage deal would fail. I couldn't do that to her."

Quickly thinking through what would be the best way to get her on her side, Ella asked, "Is she not in trouble right now? Why worry about things that might happen rather than what is happening right now? Helena is my friend. I don't want to see her hurt."

All of what Ella said was true. Even though she had set this up, as long as Ada became her Ghost, Ella would make sure that Helena would be okay. Helena was a good person, and it wouldn't take much to make sure that this mess was taken care of. But that would only happen if she stayed in the academy, and right now she needed to accomplish her task. And that was to get Ada to tell her information and become a Ghost for her.

Ada wrung her hands as she continued to fidget in front of Ella.

The twist of Ada's mouth said that she was going to back off. Ella couldn't let her spook. With a gentle voice, Ella said, "I need to help my friend. You are the only one who can give me the information I need to do that."

The wringing of the hands stopped, and Ada looked Ella in the eyes. "Do you promise that you won't do anything with this information that can hurt her?"

"Why would I hurt Helena? She is my friend. She needs our help."

And she was. But Ada was almost as naive as Helena. Ella knew that even friends in society could attack each other due to a change in power. She learned that from her lessons with Madame Briar. At least Ella didn't intend to hurt Helena. This would help her in the end. It would keep her from Effie, who only wanted to use her.

Ada nodded at Ella's words. "When the creation of the Metropolitan Police goes through, my lady is to be married to who is going to be put in charge. Her father is a supporter of Sir Peel, and he is having his daughter marry into the police department to show his support of the initiative."

That was great information. This was the sort of information that Madame Briar was looking for. Information on marriage connections could change the social and political field. And the information she received was not only about whom she was marrying, but it was also the reason why. The most surprising thing was how she knew all of this. But Ella wasn't going to ask those sorts of questions just yet.

"She must be ecstatic for this marriage. Helena loves Sir Robert Peel and would love to help him."

"Only if we can stop this rumor going around," Ada said as she clasped her hands together. The hope in her eyes as she looked at Ella only gave her a twinge of guilt, but she knew that this information would help other people. And with Ada being Ella's

Ghost, it would mean that the Fan Society would ensure that Helena would be put in an advantageous position.

"Then we must do what we can to help her. The first thing we can do is get the attention off of Helena."

"How do we do that?" Ada's earnest eyes pleaded with hers.

"Simple," Ella replied, "by creating an even bigger rumor. But the only way we can do it is if the rumor is real."

Ada's hand started fidgeting again. "What sort of rumor?"

Letting some of her feelings out, Ella shifted in her seat. "Well, one about myself. But I fear it may get me kicked out of the school . . . and my family."

Falling to her knees, Ada exclaimed, "If anything happens to you, my lady will help you! She may not be the most powerful now, but when her debut comes and her marriage goes through, she can protect you. Please help her, Lady Cook. I beg of you."

Ella shifted some more. The harder this looked for Ella to do, the more loyal Ada would be to her. "Alright. Since Helena is my friend, I will assist her in this. And you promise to keep in contact with me?"

Ada's head desperately bobbed up and down.

Still hesitating, Ella let the heavy feeling of anticipation stay like waiting for the landing just after fall. As the anticipation grew in Ada's eyes, Ella let the question be answered. "Yes, I will do it. But you must do exactly as I say or else this won't go the way I planned. Then both Helena and I will be in hot water."

"Yes. I will do as you ask."

Ada's eager answer lightened her mind. She had taken the bait, and now she was hooked. All that was left was to pull her up. And for that to happen, Ella needed to make sure that the last part of her plan went off without a hitch. Helena was counting on her.

Thinking ahead and knowing how a person's connection will affect the social climate is a must and is important for the completion of this test.

Madame Briar
Progress Report 10, Year 1827-1828

Chapter Thirty-Four

The plan that Ella had thought out was very similar to the one in her first year. That time, she was sentenced to become a slave, but this time it is only to get her kicked out of the academy. Ella had spoken with Madame Briar after class and told her what her plan was and obtained her approval. She did give her a warning that if the matter received too much attention, her stepsisters might find out that she was Pricilla Cook.

After morning exercise, Ella headed to her sewing class. When she walked in, she could see Helena brisling with nerves. It looked like she would jump out of her chair should anyone speak to her or even brush past her. Thankfully, Ada told Helena about the plan or else she wouldn't have been this jumpy, but with her nerves so tightly wound, Helena could mess things up.

"Helena, how are you doing today?" Ella spoke to her as she would talk to a wayward animal, hoping not to spook her.

Helena let out a squeak, "Pricilla, I didn't see you there. I mean, I saw you there, but I didn't mean to speak like this to you. The chair had you—I saw you in the chair. I'm going to be quiet now."

Ella would have burst into laughter had this not been an important day. If she didn't calm Helena down, the plan would get out of control, and it would be likely that her stepsisters would see her face. And Ella really didn't want to be sent away after all the work she had put into this.

Changing the topic to something Helena was comfortable with, Ella asked, "Do you have any news on the Metropolitan Police? Have they continued to pass the vote to continue with the police force?"

Some of the nerves lessened when Helena spoke. "Yes, it is still in motion. But the final vote won't be until later this year."

Continuing this line of conversation, Ella managed to calm her down by the end of class. But as the girls got up to leave, she froze, like a child being caught snitching dessert.

Turning towards Ella, Helena whispered, "I don't think I can do this. This is going to hurt your reputation."

Ella looked around them with a wary eye to make sure no one heard her. Then, leaning in, she whispered back, "Then you must be in a high position to help me out, and to do that, you must say those words to me."

"But I—"

"If you truly want to be like your hero, you have to be in a position to help others. You cannot do that with a horrible rumor floating around. Now, are you going to be brave and kind like Sir Robert Peel, or are you going to hide now that you can do something?"

It was like a leaver was pulled in her mind. Helena was the unwanted daughter and wanted to change her situation but didn't know how to do it. That was why she wanted to marry a police officer. She saw someone trying to change other people's lives and it thrilled her. Ella could see it whenever Helena spoke of the Police Act. She just needed a push to show that she was capable of changing her situation, and she had more power than she thought.

"Thank you, Pricilla, I will be in your debt."

A smile grew on Ella's face as she motioned her forward. "Now, as planned. I'm counting on you."

Helena nodded and held her head higher than Ella had ever seen it as she strode out the door. Now came Ella's turn to cause enough of a ruckus to get her kicked out but not enough to pull Effie's attention towards her. No pressure.

Raising her head and marching forward, Ella echoed Helena's posture as she headed out of the classroom. As she did, Helena was waiting for her just as planned.

"Can we talk, Lady Cook?" Helena asked.

"We just spoke. What more do you need from me?" Ella asked, lacing her voice with irritation.

"I need to speak to you about the rumor going on about me," Helena retorted, her voice pitched just a little too loudly to make it seem natural.

Ella tried to refrain from wincing, but at least Helena was doing her best. It wasn't like she was trained for this. Pitching her voice higher than Helena, she continued the conversation. "What do you want me to say? It was an accident. I thought that you were marrying Viscount Edmund. And besides, I didn't think that everyone would take it so seriously."

"But it was a lie."

By now, they had gathered a few of the ladies' attention and more were stopping to give them disgusted stares. Ladies did not show anger. A lady of society kept her emotions balanced at all times and never panicked.

"Since you didn't say anything about it, I assumed it was true."

Come on, just a little more, Ella thought to herself as she eyed the girls around them. Just a few more and it would get a teacher's attention.

"It was gossip," Helena sneered.

The girls around them gasped at that statement. Ladies were supposed to give the appearance of purity and innocence. Even though rumors spread in society, being accused of gossip could spell the end of you. If an accusation was thrown out, then you no longer gave the appearance of kindness. One would then be a slanderous woman. Which was exactly what she was looking for.

"You are going to put that on me, here, where everyone is at?" Ella replied, her voice rising just so that it pitched farther.

"That is because you spread gossip out on the open that it must be dealt without in the open." Helena was getting into the acting. She really could talk up a storm if she wasn't so shy. Ella was proud of her. Once this was over, hopefully she would keep some of the confidence that she was showing now.

"What are you going to do? Go back home to your father?" Letting jealousy lace her words, she spouted them out even louder. Ella was going to push the conversation further before she saw Effie coming to the see commotion and froze.

Helena is close to being in my hands. I'm sure I only need to talk to her one more time, and she will do what I want. She was so easy to manipulate. It almost makes me wish for a challenge like Ella was.

Euphemia's journal
April 1828

Chapter Thirty-Five

All the blood drained from Ella's face as Effie came closer. Ella continued the charade with only half a mind on it. She didn't know what Helena said, but Ella had to keep up the conversation. "For a so-called lady, I can't believe that you would mention another person's family."

Continuing on-script, Helena replied, her words hesitant as she spoke, "And yet you mentioned my fiancé as part of a conversation with others. A person you didn't know anything about. And told a falsehood about who that person was."

Flicking her eyes in Effie's direction, nerves filled Ella. Unlike the last time she came near Effie, Ella could not run or move away. She had to finish this so that Helena could get rid of the rumor. If she stopped here, it won't fully be complete, and that could cause problems to slip in. Glancing around, she could see one of the teachers coming, but she wouldn't get here before Effie arrived.

"And how do you know that it is a falsehood? Everyone believes that it is true."

Ella turned her head ever so slightly, using her peripherals to see if Eleanor was nearby as Helena said her line, "Considering I am the other party in your statement, I should know who my family plans on marrying me to. And would anyone really believe that the Hill family would dare associate with a scoundrel such as

Viscount Edmund?" The hesitance was fading as her voice grew firm.

"And why not?" Ella spat out the words she had planned as nervousness was turning into a panic. But her training kept her still.

If she did get caught, maybe she could bluff her way out. She was wearing clothes she never had worn in front of her sister, and she had a wig on. For now, she would stick to the plan. But she couldn't allow herself to panic. Forcefully, Ella shoved her anxiety back enough that her thoughts could run as she attempted to muster up a plan.

Ella could hear Helena speak her lines again, so slowly that it made Ella want to scream at her to hurry up.

And yet confidence that she had never shown before started to gleam through as she said the words, "Why not? Lord Edmund is a mere viscount. There is no way that one such as he could even touch a daughter of a marquess, even a second daughter. Especially one with differing political views."

Ella eyed the crowd, and she could see understanding starting to blossom in their eyes as they nodded in agreement when Helena spoke. But it was going achingly slow as both a teacher and her stepsister got closer; her thoughts still couldn't figure a way out of this debacle. Ella could see her sister's face clearly and a look of confusion that had appeared. Yet the only thing that Ella could do was continue to spout her lines at Helena. "Ummm, but what about an unwanted daughter? They might sell her off for that!"

The hope that Eleanor would come faded, as Ella steeled herself to bluff her stepsister. If she could.

Ella could see a curiosity glint in her eye as Effie furrowed her brow at Ella. Did she recognize Ella's voice? She just barely managed to hold back a wince as Effie stepped forward, only to be stopped by . . . Luella?

That was . . . unexpected. But Ella should have known better. Luella would do what was needed to help the Fan Society, of which Ella was a part of. Relief spread through Ella, relaxing the tension that had been building. She almost jumped in surprise as Helena was still continuing their little scene. "How can you call yourself a lady with those words? Oh, Madame Hilton, I am so sorry for the disturbance we have caused."

Seeing that Effie was trying to step away from Luella, she had to hurry and move this along. With one final glance at the crowd as they admired Helena, Ella said her final words, closing the scene, "This is such a farce. I'm going to show Madame Briar what really happened."

With a huff, Ella made her way to Madame Briar's Office, with Madame Hilton and Helena following at a more sedate pace.

When they arrived, Helena explained the problem as Ella had planned in advance. Giving a bow of her head to Madame Briar, Helena said, "I do apologize for creating such an incident. I did not intend to cause a scene, but I could not hear such slander in front of me. It would only ruin the reputation of this school that you have worked so hard to build up."

Weighing her down with her gaze, Madame Briar took in Helena's bow of apology and Ella's frowning form that had her arms folded and was tapping her foot.

"I see," Madame Briar said, and turned to Ella, "And what do you have to say for yourself?"

Ella didn't want be this disrespectful to Madame Briar, but knowing that Madame Briar would understand didn't make it any easier. "I did nothing wrong. I just said what was on my mind."

It was spat out, and it was hard to keep the sneer on her face as Madame Briar gave her a frown.

"I can see what is going on," Madame Briar said after several moments of silence, standing and moving around her desk to stand in front of them. "My dear Lady Hill, it seems there is still much to learn, but you have done admirably in such circumstances. Now, Lady Cook, I will not stand for such disrespect in my school. You are to pack your bags and leave immediately."

"But I—" Ella stopped when Madame Briar made a circle with her pinky, an indication that she wanted to meet with Ella in her secret office. She huffed, "Fine. I never wanted to be in the school anyways."

Ella stomped away, and as she left, Helena gave her a look of gratitude, then worry before Ella left the room.

Taking a deep breath to calm her emotions, she listened to see if anyone was in the hallway, then twisting a sconce on the wall, Ella entered the secret passageway and made her way to the secret office.

By the time she made it back around through the passages, the door was open to allow Ella in.

"Lady Cooper, congratulations are in order. There is still time left before you needed to complete this year's task." Seeing the look on her face, the madame ended with, "Well done for your performance. You did exactly as you should."

A blush crept across Ella's face at her mentor's praise, erasing the guilt she had from disrespecting her earlier. "Thank you, Madame Briar, but I had help."

Madame Briar continued with her report, "Lady Hill and Ada will be forever in your debt, and they won't soon forget that. It will be useful for you should you stay in the Fan Society or should you decide to leave. Though, I can see that you have already made a decision."

And she had. After Luella helped her, it was even more firmly cemented in her mind. "I have decided to stay."

"I see." Madame Briar kept her face passive as she continued, "Why have you decided to stay?"

Ella sat still, mulling over her thoughts until they were organized. "For my first year at this school, I was ill-prepared. I had to struggle to even keep up with lessons. And yet I stayed for my mother. For my second year, I knew how things worked and had to prove to myself that I was my mother's daughter and could be an amazing agent.

"This year, I didn't need to prove anything to myself. But it gave me time to think on whether I wanted to be here. I thought that If I left, I had enough skill that I could go look for my mother on my own. It would be better to do my own thing rather than follow the Fan Society rules and be stuck doing missions I was supposed to rather than the ones I wanted to. But then I realized something."

"What did you realize?"

Ella smiled. "I learned that I could be a part of something bigger than myself. During the task this year, I ran into some problems. There wouldn't have been away for me to safely get out of the situation other than to give myself away. But the other Fan Society members came and helped me. It was then that I realized that I needed help, and it is here that I can find the most help to find my mother."

The headmistress broke her passive expression and gave her a warm smile. "My dear, you living a happy life is all your mother ever wanted for you. After the incident with her friend . . . No, I shouldn't say anymore."

It was an odd thing to say, but the look on Madame Briar's face meant that even if Ella inquired further, the madame wouldn't answer.

Instead, Ella said, "Thank you for everything."

Straightening, Madame Brier's face turned serious. Looking Ella in the eyes, she asked, "I am going to ask you one final time. Should you say no, I will stop your training to be a Guardian and send you on your way with a new identity. Do you want to be a part of the Fan Society?"

Remembering how Eleanor and Luella stood up for her, Ella could only say, "Yes, Madame Briar, I want to be a part of the Fan Society."

Echoing one of the first things she had ever told her, Madame Briar said, "Lady Cooper, welcome to the Fan Society."

Year Four

Things are never as they seem. I learned that the hard way during my last year of training. But the information gained would change my life.

Arabella Cooper "Cinders"
Report 3

Chapter Thirty-Six

E lla sat in the carriage nervously itching at the red-haired wig as she looked through the window. The green hills were overshadowed by the grey fog that blanketed everything. Water condensed on the window, dripping down as Ella wrapped herself further into her blankets.

Northern England was far colder than she had expected. The carriage ride had been longer than expected, as well. It had taken a week to make it to the seaside town. Though, due to the cold and rain that had been perpetual for the trip, it had been difficult to enjoy the ride. The carriage took a turn down a gravel drive. Taking deep breaths to calm her nerves and her stomach from the swaying of the carriage, Ella turned her thoughts to what Madame Briar had told her about this year's mission.

Ella had known that the final year would be different, but she didn't realize how different. This year, Ella was being set to the far reaches of England. While there, she would be playing the role of Baroness Smith's second cousin once removed who was sent to the baroness's house to learn more about being a lady during the season. Or at least, that was the story. What she had actually been sent to do was to spy on the baroness.

"What do you need me to do?"

Ella turned towards Clementine, who was seated across from her. Since she was being sent far away from the academy, she had been sent with two others who would help support her. One was Clementine.

"I need you to get on the good side of the other maids in the manor. They won't look kindly to an outsider like you, but I trust you can get on their good side," Ella replied.

"Of course. Who do you think you are talking to?" Clementine said with a smug grin on her face.

Ella smiled warmly at her friend. She was only a few years older than her and had pretty blonde hair and rounded features that gave her an innocent look. One that Ella knew could turn nasty should someone push her too far. Ella was glad that they were together; they had gone through so much these past few years. From the disappearance of her mother, helping her through the death of her father, and the horrible years with her stepfamily, not to mention the trying times of her academy years, Clementine had stuck by her every step of the way.

The last few years had been life-changing for Ella. The biggest change came from how she thought of herself and the Fan Society. For most of her life, Ella had been forced into circumstances that were beyond her power to change. But now she was going to follow in her mother's footsteps, and maybe then she could be closer to her. And should any information on her mother show up, Ella would be the first to know about it.

Clementine leaned forward so her quiet voice could be heard by Ella over the creaking of the carriage. "What do you think we will find?"

Ella shrugged. She didn't know what to think of the task set before her. Madame Briar, the headmistress of the academy and head of the Fan Society, had sent her out here to watch the eccentric lady of the North Sea Manor. Baroness Smith wasn't seen at a lot of social events, and with her living away from the main hub of England, not much could be heard of her. Ella's task was, under the guise of being her second cousin once removed, to see what was going on in the manor for the last few years.

Since the North Sea Manor was away from prying eyes, it was a good place for her to do her "internship", as Madame Briar called it. This was a way to test her abilities in a real setting away from the safety of the school. And Ella would make sure that she did her best.

"We will find out soon enough," Ella said, looking at the cobblestone road that wound up to the manor on the cliffside. They had arrived.

The North Sea Manor looked like something out of a horror story. As it was near the end of October, the weather was chilly, and fog hovered over the ground covering most of the manor's brick walls. Its dark red roof was barely visible over the top of the clouds as it sat on the edge of the cliffs overlooking the North Sea, the manor's namesake. A light drizzle of rain completed the ambiance of a haunted house.

"That is where we are going to be staying for most of the year? Let's just hope the butler doesn't murder us in our sleep." Clementine shivered as she stared at their new home, albeit as temporary as it was.

"That is what we are here to figure out," Ella said, swallowing her mission jitters. This was not the time to be afraid. They hadn't even entered the house yet.

But as they came closer to the manor, ruins stuck up out of the fog like fingers from out of a grave. Her mother wouldn't have been scared of a house like this. From what she read in her mother's reports, nothing ever scared her.

The clop of the horse hooves came to a stop on the gravel drive. Ella nearly jumped out of her skin when the footman opened her door. Taking a deep breath and putting on a lady's smile, she allowed him to help her down out of the carriage. The footman was shorter than a footman normally was, and his hair was blond and curly, though it was less curly than her own. She could already feel the wig straining as her strands frizzed in the humid air.

After straightening her skirts, she was startled as a withered old man stood in front of her. It was the butler who bowed and said, "Welcome to the manor, miss."

With his gaunt features and skeletal figure, he fit in with dark and gloomy atmosphere of the manor. But she could feel his body heat as he stood beside her holding an umbrella, which meant he was living. At that thought, she relaxed some.

Taking a more objective eye to her surroundings, Ella could see buildings that had been hidden more clearly. She already knew that there were some historic ruins from the original inhabitants of this town. It only was creepy due to the swath of thick fog that blanketed the land, drawn in by the sea.

Ella followed along behind the butler with Clementine and the footman trailing behind her carrying all of her things. When she entered the manor, Baroness Smith was there to greet her.

"Welcome, Lady Beatrice Eden," Baroness Smith said, calling her by her fake identity and motioning for the servants behind Ella to take her thing to her room. Then she waved for Ella to follow her. "I do not know why your mother sent you to this place considering that I haven't spoken to her in years. But she was always prone to flights of fancy. A very odd child. I'm sure this is just another one of her strange ideas. I don't know what rules you followed before, but in my house, you will follow my rules."

Ella trotted behind her in an attempt to keep up. The woman was tall and skinny. Her face was severe, with its pointed chin and narrow eyes. Her grey hair was pulled up into a bun on top of her head, the strands thick but dry in the humid air. The odd thing was that she had very few wrinkles as one would expect with such grey hair. Her stride was long due to her height, and it made Ella struggle to keep up while maintaining a lady's dignity.

Baroness Smith continued with her rules as they walked through the hallways lined with art, "First, you must never interfere with my private affairs. It's my business and something you have no part in. Second, you will keep with the schedule that I set for you. Heaven knows what your mother was thinking of, sending you here, but I will make sure you are ready for your debut next year. I will teach you to be a proper lady, nothing like your mother. Third, I read from your letters that you enjoy horse riding, but you must never go down the cliff path behind the manor, as it is dangerous there. Your personal horse has already been sent to the stables. Ah, here is where you are staying," she said, stopping in front of a room in the west wing of the house. "You must be tired from your long journey. I trust that you will be on time for dinner."

And with that, she left Ella in her room that was with a flurry of activity from the servants putting her things away. Ella wandered into her large but sparsely decorated room. Considering all the ornate white molding and paintings that had dotted the walls, the lack of any wall décor made the walls very empty. The baroness had been very ill-prepared for Ella to arrive. The ornate carpeting that had followed Ella into the room clashed with the blank white walls, though it looked more grey at the moment due to the weather.

Ella sat down on one of the few pieces of furniture in the room and looked through the windows into the swirling grey fog. Ideas bounced around in her head as she thought about how best to proceed with the mission.

She was so lost in thought that she didn't notice when the servants finished and left the room. It was only when Clementine collapsed on the chair next to her that Ella realized everyone was gone. She huffed, "I'm glad bringing in all of the stuff is done. Next time you can play the part of servant and I can be the lady. Your things are heavy."

"You should still keep up appearances. You never know who might be listening or who is going to come in," Ella commented as she eyed Clementine, who was pulling off her shoes and massaging her feet.

"Relax, I told them that you will be taking a rest and that they are not allowed to come in until it's time for dinner. And I made sure I couldn't hear them anymore when I came over here." Clementine was now resting her feet on the low table and fixing her hair. "What are we going to do?"

"For now, we get ready for dinner and get a feel for the manor," Ella said, moving to her trunk. "And tomorrow, we go for a ride."

Grooms are a perfect messenger. They can be from outside the residence and don't always stay at the residence. They also can help a lady as an escort when there are fewer people around so they won't be overheard. This makes it so they can receive the message then leave and send the message someplace else without looking suspicious.

Book with fan on cover
Chapter 21

Chapter Thirty-Seven

The dinner was less ornate than Ella would have expected from such grandeur that filled the out-in-the-middle-of-nowhere manor. She seated herself on the left hand of the table. The baroness entered with a nod of acknowledgment and then sat across from Ella, the head of the table glaringly absent of the baron.

"Bring in the food," Baroness Smith ordered, nodding at the servants. They disappeared through a set of doors, and moments later, a man came out with a cart full of food. His youthful face twisted into worry as he wiped the sweat from his forehead with his elbow. The china clattered as he set the first plate in front of the baroness. Wincing at the sound and his madame's eyebrow raise, he hurried to place Ella's plate in front of her. After he set it down, he scurried away.

Odd. He seemed too new to be serving a guest. Making note of it, Ella turned back to her food, finding that it tasted plain. No small talk of commentary was made, only the clatter of silverware on plates. Baroness Smith didn't seem at all perturbed by the lack of her husband's presence, meaning that this was a common occurrence.

Once the meal was finished, she called for dessert. When the same servant came in bearing dessert, Ella worried that he would faint. His face was pale as he placed the dessert before Baroness Smith, but he managed to set it gently down. His relief was evident as he made his way towards Ella. But as he was setting down Ella's plate, he tipped it too far that the blueberry that topped the cake rolled off the table to the floor.

It was as if he had seen a ghost. His face paled as he turned to look at the baroness. Dropping to the floor like a ragdoll, he knelt before her. "I'm so sorry, Baroness. I didn't mean to—it was an accident. Please don't fire me. I need this job. Please."

This odd scene before Ella became stranger by what the baroness said, "Breathe, child. I don't dismiss people over things like this." The baroness looked to the empty chair, then back to the shivering servant. "My husband, on the other hand, might. If you can keep this quiet, you might be able to stay."

The servant bobbed his head and hurried out of the room.

Confusion filled Ella. What had she just witnessed? She would need to get Clementine to look into it. Hiding her emotions behind a smile, Ella tried to lighten the conversation. "Didn't know that my blueberry could cause so much trouble."

"Don't you worry about that. Many of our servants are new. They get a bit jumpy when they make a mistake." And that was all she would say on the matter.

Dinner ended in silence, and Ella was sent to her room. As she headed back to her room, she felt as if someone was watching her. Turning around quickly, she caught the glimpse of a dirty shoe heading around the corner. Ella was about to follow when another servant came asking her if she needed help to her room. Losing her chance to follow, she allowed the maid to lead her to her room. A thought nagged at her mind. The baron never did show up for dinner.

The next day, the sun drove away the drizzle, and Ella could finally see the rolling green hills that surrounded the countryside. The beauty almost made up for having to ride a horse.

Ella waited in the front circle for the groom to bring her horse, her second helper. Part of her cover was that she had a deep love for horses and would only allow her personal groomer to take care of her horse. The best person to play the part was William. No longer the scrawny stableboy she knew at the academy, William had grown in the few years since she had seen him when she first learned how to ride from him. He came under the guise of being a personal groom for her horse.

"Here you are, my lady," he said, offering her the reins. Ella half expected that he would go on about how this horse was finicky and loved it when you brushed his mane just so. Instead, he merely stood, waiting to help her onto her horse.

Ella had hoped he would babble about horses if anything to keep her mind off the fact that she was having to ride one again. Even though she now was competent at riding, she had never grown to like it. Ella had a distinct dislike for horseback riding because you were leaving your life in the hands of an animal that could easily trample you to death. And you could never tell what those black-eyed animals were thinking. They shifted randomly and spooked at the slightest of things. Ella eyed the horse with suspicion.

"My lady?"

Williams's question pulled her away from her thoughts. She was supposed to play the part of being an avid horse rider, and hesitating would look suspicious. Flashing William a smile, Ella maneuvered herself into the double horn saddle and strapped herself in.

"Since I don't know the area, I will just have you lead me down any good paths," Ella said, nodding to William.

With a bow in reply, he guided the horse off a side path that led to the ruins that she couldn't really see when she first arrived. Now in the sunshine, they were less scary and instead were merely rundown. The ruins were mostly old stone walls and loose stones scattered about. But looking at where windows once were, it must have been a beautiful sight when it had been originally built.

Once they were far enough away that Ella was sure that no one could overhear, she asked, "Since you were sent here earlier, have you noticed any people coming and going at odd hours? Or employees that keep showing up where they shouldn't be?"

Tilting his head, William paused before answering, "No one uses the horses to leave at night. And I'm not really allowed in the main house."

Ella's heart fell. She had always thought that he was a boy that only had horses on the brain, but when she heard that he was going to be sent to help her, she had hoped that maybe she was wrong about him. Refraining from sighing, she was about to thank him and give him a message to send to the Fan Society when he continued.

"But there are constantly having new people deal with the horses, and there is one guy named Arthur. He's an odd one."

That was useful information. Ella was surprised that he could notice anything other than horses. "Why do you say he is odd?"

"I was trying to work on Stella, your mare, and he kept interrupting my work and asking questions and talking to me all the time."

Ahh. That was why he was able to tell that a person was acting odd. It interrupted his time with his horses. But it was interesting that someone would try to question William when he so obviously cared more about horses than people. Arthur sounded like someone she should take a look into. "What do you know about this Arthur?"

Wrinkling his nose at the thought of having to think about that person, William started crooning at the horse. "He keeps asking about you and asks about how cute you are. And he is always asking if you like romance stories. He talks about romance all the time. Though, I don't see how anyone can be as beautiful as Stella. You are gorgeous, aren't you?"

That last sentence was directed at the horse. Ella sighed; he was a total horse lover, but he did give her good information. And why would a guy be asking about how pretty she was? They could never be in a relationship, and he had never met her. Ella looked down at William, who was still crooning over the horse. His muddy boots reminded her of the boot she caught a glimpse of. It could be Arthur. But why would be he be so interested in her?

"William. William? William!" He still didn't turn to her but instead continued to rub the horse's forelock. Ella sighed; she should have known it was going to be like this. "William. if you don't answer me, I will have to ask someone else to help you take care of my horse."

He was aghast as he turned to face her.

"Thank you, William. Now, I need you to send a message to the academy. Can you do that for me?"

William had already turned back to the horse, but this time he at least nodded that he heard her.

"William, I need you to let Madame Briar know that I made it to the manor safely. There are odd things going on. The baron is missing, and all the servants look to be relatively new to the manor. Are you listening?"

William nodded his head, saying, "You arrived, things are weird. The baron hasn't been seen, and all the servants are new. Isn't that right, beautiful girl?"

The question was stated at the horse. Sighing, she finished her message, "I will be looking into why the servants are new. And looking into a servant named Arthur."

Hopefully, William would remember to give Madame Briar her update on the mission.

As they made their way back to the house, Ella plotted what she needed to do to gather information. When she arrived back at the manor, those thoughts came to a screeching halt as Baroness Smith was waiting for her to appear. Ella looked to Clementine, who had been waiting for her to return, but she just gave a small shake of her head. Clementine didn't know what was going on either.

Nerves raked their way through Ella as she wondered why she was waiting for her. Her mind ran through the few times she met the baroness to see if she gave anything away as two servants helped her from her horse so she wouldn't flash her ankles at everyone.

Once she was down, William headed off with her horse as she stood before Baroness Smith. Her thin lips were even thinner as she loomed over Ella with her tall frame.

"I believe I told you I would do my best to make sure you are ready for society. I will not have you galivanting across the property every morning; a lady should have more than her hobbies. You will be allowed to do it twice a week until the weather gets bad. After that, it will be taken up by other activities such as having tea with me and a few other ladies, as well as getting you ready for the season. There is a lot of work you need to do to get ready. And it looks as though your mother foisted it all on me. You will be in my sitting room every day at 10 a.m. and earlier on the days you aren't riding."

"Yes, madame," Ella said. She hadn't expected such a thing from a woman who was considered eccentric, but then again, if she was eccentric, what should she expect.? Though this will make it easier for her to do her duty and keep an eye on her, but less able to get a Ghost in the household.

"I expect you to come to my sitting room after you get rid of that horse smell."

Ella gave her a polite nod. "Yes, madame."

For now, it would be better to stay on her good side. Ella could still get a Ghost in the house via Clementine. Ella could feel her presence following behind her as she headed to her room. When they entered, Clementine made sure to check to see if anyone was listening. Ella told her what William said about Arthur.

"That sounds strange. How are you going to get information on him?" Clementine asked as she helped Ella out of her riding habit.

"He is acting like he is interested in me. Why don't I play the part of a naive girl who loves the idea of a forbidden romance?"

Clementine nodded, weighing her words thoughtfully. "That could work. You can find out if he is trying to play the part of a guy interested in you or if he really is interested in you. Either way, it will give you an excuse to be near him. I'm assuming you want to discover more about the situation with the servants?"

"Of course." Ella smiled. Now changed and refreshed, it was time for Ella to find out what Baroness Smith wanted of her.

A lady must dance with perfection. This shows their grace and poise, as well as their competency in femininity. Many of those looking for matches for their children look at potential matches when they are dancing.

Book about manners
Written in 18th-century
author unknown

Chapter Thirty-Eight

Yet again, Baroness Smith defied expectations. The lessons that she set up for Ella were completely practical for getting ready for society. Some were even classes that she hadn't gone through with Madame Briar and were good for her to learn. Such as dance classes, which she should have started learning from an early age if only her mother hadn't gone missing and her father hadn't died.

"And one, two, three, four—stop, stop, stop. What do you think you are doing?"

The baroness stopped her clapping in time. She had taken it upon herself to personally teach her how to dance instead of sending for an instructor. Baroness Smith had also stopped her every few steps to say Ella was doing something wrong.

Ella thought she was doing well. Normally, things of a physical nature came easy to her, but the baroness keep tilting off-kilter.

"Reset and do it again," Baroness Smith ordered, pointing Ella back into position.

Gritting her teeth to keep from sighing, Ella moved back to position and waited for the count. The time grew longer as she held out her arms for her invisible partner. Ella peeked at the lady from the corner of her eyes to see what the hold-up was.

The woman was frowning at Ella as if puzzled about something. Finally, the woman held up a hand. "Stop, this isn't going to work."

Ella let her arms fall gratefully. "What is not going to work, madame?"

"Never let your arms fall like that. It's unladylike," Baroness Smith said with a sniff, "This whole thing is never going to work. You know nothing about dancing. These dances are complex and take years to learn. You are simply too old to learn them. Unless you learn that horrid dance called the Waltz. Hmm, I must think about this. Make sure you come down for dinner on time."

"Yes, madame," Ella said at the lady's dismissal and breathed a sigh of relief when she left the room.

Wishing she could stretch out her shoulders, she headed to her room to get changed for her horse riding. Due to the nature of the classes, Baroness Smith had allowed her to change when she went horse riding. This was due to the weather being rather chilly in the mornings as autumn turned to winter.

With Ella entering her room and Clementine shutting the door behind her, Clementine hurried over to help her get changed.

"Did you tell William what was needed?" Ella asked.

"Yes, but who knows if he actually paid attention to me rather than the horse?" Clementine rolled her eyes.

After her conversation with Clementine those weeks ago, Clementine had endeared herself to the other servants to gain information. But it had been difficult. Most of the servants were new and even in the few weeks they had been there, three of them had been changed out. And no one knew why. The only one who may know what was going on was Arthur. Arthur was one of the few that had not been switched out, making him even more suspicious. But a maid was not to be seen hanging around the stables, so they needed William's help.

Clementine wasn't happy about it.

Smiling at her friend, Ella said, "He knows what his duties are. Did you make sure he was looking at you and not the horse?"

Sniffing, Clementine pulled the strings on Ella's dress with more force than necessary. "I can't believe that he pays more attention to a horse rather than me. I mean, really, how can you avoid looking at me?"

Ella suppressed a laugh. Clementine was truly upset about her failures, and if Ella pushed her any further, she wouldn't be able to breathe. "That is why you are my personal assistant and not him. I couldn't do this without you."

"That's right," Clementine said as she finished helping Ella into her riding dress. She looked Ella up and down, tutted, then pulled out a thick woolen coat. "You have to hope that you can use Arthur because we are running out of time. You are going to be sent back to the academy without learning anything."

Looking out the window, Ella could almost feel the cold wind nipping at her face. Winter was going to hit full force, and it will be too cold for her to go riding on her own.

"Did you send the message to William?"

"About Arthur?" Clementine rolled her eyes and said, "Yes, but you know how that guy is about other people touching his horses."

Shrugging, Ella said, "It's my last hope to meet with him in a way that at least seems like it happened naturally. I just hope winter comes later than usual, then I would have more chances to talk William into it."

"I don't know why he is here if he's not going to help you," Clementine huffed.

"Technically, he is only here to send messages to the academy, which he is doing a great job of." It bothered her as well, but what could she do about it now? Ella could only hope that William did as asked.

Motioning Clementine to open the door, Ella made her way out front to where William was waiting with the horse. He helped her up with more difficulty due to the thick clothes she was wearing, but she managed to settle into the saddle and he led her away down a different path this time.

They headed to a safe spot where no one could overhear them, and Ella pulled out a letter from the folds of her coat. She kept it clenched in her hand so the wind wouldn't rip it away. "Make sure this gets the Madame Briar. It's my weekly report."

He nodded and shoved the letter into his coat pocket. Sighing, but glad that she wrote it in code, she continued, "Did you do as Clementine asked?"

"The annoying girl? I'm sure that she asked me something about the annoying guy, something about wanting him to come help with the horse."

Glad that Clementine was not with her, she would have been devastated to hear herself referred to as the "annoying girl", Ella hoped that she could still salvage this situation, "Yes, we need you to have him help me down from the horse when we get back so I can talk to him."

He didn't answer.

"You did ask to do that?" Ella did her best to keep her calm. But it was getting difficult as he kept his silence. "Did you do what Clementine asked?"

He held the horse closer to him and petted the forelock on the horse. Ella could barely hear his muttered answer of no over the wind.

Ella sighed.

"I thought she was wanting me to ask him to help me with grooming the horse. And I don't need help; no one should touch Stella but me," William countered. If only he wasn't so touchy about his horses, he would have been the perfect help. Why was he the one sent with her to send messages to the Fan Society?

But now wasn't the time to think about that. She had to think about a way to fix her problem. But she had to head back in because her nose was feeling the chill, and it wouldn't be proper to be out this long. She had hoped to use the need for two people to dismount to get the chance to speak to Arthur. Ella could only hope that he was chosen to help her down.

He wasn't.

Ella spent the rest of the day pondering her dilemma. Even discussing it with Clementine didn't help.

"I'm so sorry. I should have made sure that the horse fanatic was paying attention. Maybe we still have time to talk William into helping. And I checked into the servants. That boy who made mistakes during dinner has been fired, and he is not the only one. Several others have been fired as well since you've come." Clementine didn't play with her hair like she normally did. Instead, her head hung down.

Ella remembered the young boy who had dropped a blueberry from off her plate. She had wondered why he hadn't been serving the last few meals. It hadn't been that long since she had arrived, but already more servants had left. She needed to talk to someone who has been here for longer, and Arthur was the only one.

Turning to Clementine, Ella waved away her worries. "It happens. You already know the mistakes I've made. I should have started talking to William sooner. Once the snow hits and I'm unable to ride, it would seem odd if my maid still went to the stables and spoke to the groomer." Ella looked outside as white flakes fell. "Besides, it's already too late."

Winter had come early this year. Now how was she going to find a way to speak to Arthur before he disappeared as well?

The art of seduction has changed little over the years.
Though how one goes about it changes some due to
how society changes, the premise is still the same.
Keep him interested in you. Sometimes that means
acting weak, sometimes that entails acting the opposite of what society dictates. Just make sure that in the
end, you do not lose yourself to the power of emotion.

Book of charm
Chapter 2

Chapter Thirty-Nine

In the end, it turned out that Ella didn't need to worry. When she went to classes with Baroness Smith the next day, a young man stood next to the baroness.

Without dillydallying, the baroness motioned to the young man. "This here is Arthur. He will be joining us today. Considering how wretchedly horrible you were yesterday, I figured it would be easier to dance if you had a partner. You can't be called a lady of society without some dance skills, since most social activities are dances. Maybe with this, it might make you a passable dancer. Though he is just a groomsman, he will help you with dancing. And this young man knows the steps. Or at least, better than you. Come now, it's time to start."

It was odd that she brought in someone as lowly as a groom to help, but considering that it helped with her plans, she didn't question it . . . yet. Since he was supposedly in love with her, according to William, Ella wondered how he was going to act.

The young man in front of Ella was in his early twenties, only a few years older than her. He smiled with an easy charisma, very reminiscent of Clementine. His short dark brown hair curled at the ends, and his pale blue eye looked into her with questions.

Arthur came over and bowed over her hand, kissing it. Then he asked with a cheeky smile, "My lady, may I have this dance?"

It was then that Ella remembered herself. She was not some maid he could flirt with, though she did need to pretend to be one. And it would allow her to get closer to him. Maybe find out why he wanted to get closer to her.

Letting her embarrassment show through, she accepted his hand. "Yes, you may."

The baroness clapped. "Very good. Now, into positions. And one, two, three, four . . ."

And so, the lesson continued. Arthur did know the steps, and it was much easier for Ella to follow along with him leading. It was still difficult since there were usually more couples, but the baroness stopped her fewer times. However, to keep up her charade of falling in love with him, Ella stepped on his toes.

He kept his charming demeanor that would have made her fall for him had she not been on a mission. Though a few of her blushes had been fully genuine, not that she would admit it.

"Very well done. This will work." The annoyance that had been on her face since the last dance lesson had eased to just mild irritation. "Since the weather has worsened, I expect you to have dance classes every morning to see if we can get you caught up. Now, out with you. I need to have my morning tea."

With Baroness Smith's dismissal, they left. As they exited, Arthur kept pace with Ella instead of falling behind.

"I believe that you are supposed to be going back to the stables," Ella remarked, allowing her cheeks to flush red, in doing so making them flush darker than intended.

"Ah, but a good gentleman would never allow a lady to walk back by herself, Lady Eden," Arthur said, answering her with ease.

Ella blinked in surprise; she had almost forgotten that Beatrice Eden was her cover name. Flushing at her mistake, she blushed furiously.

Arthur took it as a sign to pursue further. "Since you are no longer able to ride, I can always show you around the stables. Baron Smith has some rather fine horses considering we are so far from the center of society."

Remembering her cover of being an avid horse rider, she nodded. "I would be happy to. But it's not really proper for me to be seen in the stables."

"That should be fine. There are a few underground passageways in these hills from the ruins. This manor is built on a ruin connected to some of the passageways."

His answer lit her mind with questions. "Do the other servants know about these passages?"

Arthur raised his brow and chuckled. "You are more curious than other girls, aren't you? I don't think anyone else knows about the passageways. You will not be seen doing inappropriate behavior."

Ella couldn't believe she dropped her cover again; he was easy to talk to. But he had sidestepped around the question. He was hiding something. Who knew about the passageways? He said no one knew, but was he just trying to throw her off the scent? Did the baroness know?

Regaining control over her emotions, she asked another question, "Why do you think my mother sent me here? You have heard of the lady's eccentrics."

Giving an easy laugh, he replied, "I see what you mean. Not to speak ill of the madame, but she certainly has odd nighttime activities. It would be odd to have your mother send you here to learn how to be a proper lady considering how the madame has her own eccentricities."

"Quite so. And I'll refrain from telling the lady about you believing she is eccentric. I don't want to see my dance partner kicked out like all of the other servants," Ella said, half to tease him, half to see if she could draw out any information. She had been hoping to lead the conversation to the baron, but Arthur's facial expression stopped her.

Arthur blinked at her words; anger filled his features for just a moment before showing her his charming smile. But Ella could see the pain in those eyes.

"We wouldn't want that," he replied simply, a smile tightening his lips. Arthur paused briefly. "Just be careful in those passage-ways."

"Why? Do people go missing in them?" Ella joked, trying to lighten the mood again. He would likely close up if he got too serious.

He didn't answer her question.

Unable to get any more information from him, Ella did manage to get him to tell her about how to get to the passageways and set up a time for them to meet. They parted ways at her study, where she was supposed to be learning more about economics and merchants. Not that Ella knew why she had to be studying this, but she did it anyway.

Entering a few minutes later, Clementine hurried over to her. "Why didn't you come back to your rooms to freshen up?"

Brushing away Clementine's fussy hands, Ella replied, "I was walking with Arthur, and this place took longer to get to than my rooms."

Clementine sighed, "Fine, but don't keep doing this. Parading about while you are sweaty is not something you should be doing. If you are going to be acting as a noble, you need to look like one."

"Yes, I know. I'll make sure I take extra care tomorrow and leave my lessons early so you can take care of things. Will this satisfy you?"

A smug grin sat on Clementine's face. "Yes, that will do."

"Good, because I need your help with things."

"What did you find out? I'm surprised horse boy managed to do his job." Clementine rolled her eyes and started fixing Ella's hair.

Ella allowed it. "No, he didn't. It was the baroness who had him as my dancing partner."

"I ought to slip something into his breakfast," Clementine muttered.

"Don't worry about it. For now, I have something I need you to do."

Clementine's expression turned brighter. "What do you need?"

Grateful she was able to pull her friend out of her mood, Ella continued, "I heard there are secret passages under the manor. The entrance is in one of the side corridors on the bottom floor. Can you keep an eye out on who uses those passageways?"

Clementine nodded. Ella turned back to her books on shipping times and how tides affect business. She trusted that her friend would do as asked.

Though I sent Ella to the North Sea Manor as her final, I hope she can truly find out what is going on. I'm sure that she is capable. She is as talented as her mother was, but she still has problems with doing things that she thinks doesn't make sense.

Madame Briar
Progress Report 10, Year 1828-
1829

Chapter Forty

E lla hoped that dinner would end faster. She still thought it strange that the baron did not join them; based on Clementine's investigations, he spent most of his time in his office. Instead, she was stuck eating at a slow noble's pace with multiple rounds of dishes with little to no speaking.

Ella was ready to claim sickness when the baroness spoke.

"Make sure that you go straight to your room after dinner. The baron will be having a late shipment in, and I don't want you getting mixed up with those ruffians."

"Yes, madame." Though Ella bowed her head in acknowledgment, her thoughts were racing. She was supposed to meet Arthur today, but it would be better to see who was coming to meet the baron at such an odd hour. And maybe answer some of the questions surrounding him. "May I be excused? I'm still rather tired from dancing today."

"You may go," the baroness said with a dismissive wave of her hand.

Ella nodded and then headed towards her room. It was time to find out what was going on in this manor.

Clementine was already waiting for her by the time she arrived to her room and helped her dress into more appropriate clothes. This time, she dressed in a gown for exercise and a thick dark cloak that a naive lady might wear, and Clementine added a lamp that she could cover quickly should anyone come along the passageway.

"Did you see anyone using the passageway?"

Shaking her head, Clementine replied, "Not when I was looking, but I was called away for a little bit, so someone could have gone during that time."

Ella nodded, taking in the information and storing it. "Let's go."

At those words, Clementine opened the door, checked the hallways, and allowed Ella through. They would have to do this fast since they were out where people could see them easily. But Ella needn't have worried. Most of the staff were still clearing away dinner.

They hurried as much as they dared until they reached the end of the hallway at the back of the manor. Remembering what Arthur had said, Ella slid her hand along the wall until she felt a loose panel. The panel opened without a sound, and a small room was revealed.

The room was the width of the hallway, and the walls were the same red brick as the outer walls of the manor. Near the back corner was a dark hole with a tip of a ladder peeking out from its depths. Hurrying in, Clementine shut the panel as Ella lit the lamp.

Ella went down first.

It was a short climb. Just enough to get underneath the building. Lifting her lamp, Ella looked around. She ended up in a small room that had been cut out from the cliffside or what could have been an old cave. Whoever had built it had died long ago, considering its condition.

There were two passages that led from the small room. The was a wide passage that smelled of the salty sea. The other passage wound around another direction that was much narrower. That was the path that led to the stables. But from the wide one, Ella could hear people's voices echoing down the rough stone passageway.

When Clementine stepped down, Ella hesitated, then descended towards the sea. Arthur would have to wait.

The stone floor had been worn smooth from the many years of feet walking its sloped path. Though the path was smooth, it wound back and forth, making Ella glad for the light. Soon, the stone walls turned green from the moss and lichen growing on it, and faint light shone up ahead. Closing the metal door on the lamp and hiding the light, Ella inched forward as the sounds grew louder.

Peeking out into the moonlight, Ella saw a hidden cove. And anchored offshore was a ship. The cliffs hid it perfectly from the sight of the village. Burly, tanned men were loading boxes onto the ship. Though the weather had gotten cold, the men didn't wear shoes and instead only light clothing as they easily lifted the boxes and brought them on the ship.

Standing near the entrance to the cave was the mysterious baron who Ella recognized from his portrait. Ella almost assumed that he had been made up so the baroness could maintain control over the house. But that was obviously not the case. With his round cheeks and fancy clothes, he was healthy.

He obviously was the one in charge as he spoke to the ship's captain, recognized by his fancier clothes. If you could call a jacket and boots fancier. What was he hiding?

Their conversation carried to her hiding spot, and Ella could pick up a few words over the sound of the waves.

". . . delivery will be . . . spring," the ship's captain said. "Supplies should last until . . . we will need . . . chains . . . water . . . rust."

The baron blustered, "You will get . . . later . . . The cost is too . . . high. Wait until I get more servants . . . I can't make . . . People will start noticing . . ."

A loud crash stopped their conversation, and the captain started yelling at one of his men who had dropped a box. Biscuits had fallen out of the broken box onto the sandy beach. It was time to go. Arthur would be waiting for her. With his connection to the passageways, maybe he could shed some light on the baron and what was going on.

With a nod to Clementine, they headed back up the incline to the other passage. Ella opened the shuttered lamp to light the way again.

Thoughts whirled around. Why was the baron dealing with a bunch of sailors? They looked like they were having a deal made. And one was for supplies. The other would be delivered during the spring. When they made it up to the top, a noise made Ella quickly shutter her light again. They had just started making their way down the path that led to the sables when the rhythmic creak of wood echoed behind them. They were lucky that they heard it since not soon after a figure made its way down the ladder from the manor above.

Ella and Clementine pushed themselves against the wall. A woman headed down the path to the hidden cove, not bothering to spare either of them a look. Instincts urged Ella to watch her as she edged around the corner.

She felt a sense of familiarity as the woman made her way further from them. It was difficult to see anything as the shadowed form disappeared down the path that led to the base of the cliff.

Feeling a tug on her sleeve, Clementine pulled her away from the path. Ella couldn't help but slow her steps and glance back. After moving a small distance away, she stopped Clementine. She had to wait for that woman to come back, but it was getting late, and who knew how long Arthur would wait? Her feet itched with indecision, but her curiosity got the better of her.

Thankfully, it didn't take long for the woman to return. Ella's eyes widened as a familiar face was lit by the lantern.

Baroness Smith.

It seemed she did know about the passageways. Ella waited until the baroness finished heading up the latter, then released a sigh.

"So, this is where you are."

Clementine and Ella spun with surprise toward a familiar voice that came from behind them.

He is into a more dangerous business than we initially thought. I worry about my charge. Things have become more dire than we had assumed. Your duty is to protect her.

Coded message from Madame
Briar
Recipient unknown

Chapter Forty-One

"Arthur, I didn't expect you. I thought you were going to be waiting at the stables." Ella opened the door of her lamp and saw who had come up behind her. Recognizing Arthur, her training kicked in as she fell back to keeping in character.

Ears straining, she heard the sound of creaking wood. The baroness must have heard them talking and returned. She would have to send Clementine to look into that.

"Why are you still here?"

"I got lost. Why are you making a young lady like myself go running around in a haunted dark cave?" Ella let her fear of being caught show on her face. Did the baroness recognize her voice? Or was she worried about getting caught herself?

He shuffled and pulled at his collar. "Sorry. I'm not used to dealing with ladies such as yourself. I just thought that you would want to see the horses without the prying eyes of the baroness. And I wouldn't send you someplace that wasn't safe. Look at this," he said, knocking on the wall. "This is solid stone. This isn't going to hurt you. Plus, you have your maid with you."

Ignoring those questions for now, Ella focused on her performance. Putting on a childish pout, Ella crossed her arms and turned away from him. "There were noises, and no, it wasn't from the rocks. There was someone here. You said that people didn't use passageway, so I wouldn't get caught. Then why was I hearing voices?"

His brows creased with concern in the dim lamplight. "Voices? There shouldn't be anyone who knows about the passageways."

Did he know that there would be people here? Things were odd around this man. With his personality, it was difficult to imagine him doing something bad, but odd things kept cropping up around him. But if he was telling the truth, then why were the baron and baroness down here?

Hoping to shake loose some information from him, Ella let slip a seed of truth, "Yes, and we were nearly caught by the baroness. I thought you said she wouldn't know about it. She is the whole reason I'm down here. To avoid her."

"The baroness was down here?" His eye widened with surprise, then quickly turned to his charming smile. Arthur tried backtracking his words, "I'm sorry, I just never expected someone like the baroness to traverse the passages."

"And yet you expected me to? I'm going back." It was time to keep his interest on her; too much more and he may run away. Ella started to turn away when he grabbed her hand.

"Unhand my lady," Clementine spoke up, and Arthur released her arm. Clementine quickly stepped between them.

He raised his hands innocently. "I'm sorry, but do you at least want to see the horses? We are almost to the stables. And this time, I will escort you back to protect you instead of having you walk by yourself. I don't want things to end up poorly between us. We still have to dance together tomorrow. It would be ill-advised of me to make my lady upset when she is in a position to step on my toes."

He was really good at that charming act. Why did he want her to come with him so badly? Did he truly like her, or was he wanting to be close to her for other more nefarious reasons?

Ella hesitated in answering, making it seem like it was a difficult choice for her.

She let out a sigh, as if relenting. "I really do want to see the horses. Only if you promise that you would take me back. And if we meet anyone, you are going to take the blame."

Arthur smiled with a twinkle in his eyes. "It will be as your lady wishes. Shall we?"

Acting the gentleman, he held out his arm for her, and Ella took it. With her fingers behind her back, Ella signaled Clementine to pay close attention to their surroundings. Arthur was all hers.

Ella didn't get any more information out of him; the rest of the trip was uneventful. William, on the other hand, stared at them the entire time they were there. Ella managed to head back to her room on account of still being shaken up by the incident in the tunnels.

"What do you think?" Ella asked when they made it back to their rooms.

"That Arthur is a snake," Clementine tutted as she helped Ella into her nightclothes.

Ella pulled her hair in front of her as Clementine undid the laces. "I thought he was rather charming."

Snorting, Clementine said, "So is a snake. That doesn't mean I want to keep it as a pet. That man has an agenda, and he is using you."

"Why do you say that?"

"You don't say you like a person or go hunting about for information on a person before they even arrive." Clementine rolled her eyes. "That just screams that the situation is fishy. He heard about you coming and wanted to get information on you."

Ella laughed, "And so am I. We just need to get information from him. That was the plan. And if he is using me for an agenda, it will be easier to keep him close. I just need to make sure to keep my real identity a secret."

Clicking her tongue, Clementine didn't reply. Instead, she pulled Ella's hair out of the red-haired wig so she could get some sleep and hid the wig in a false bottom of one of her suitcases.

"But you are right. I do need to figure out what his agenda is before I get pulled in. What does he have to do with the tunnels, and is he involved with whatever the baroness is involved in?"

"Looks like the baron is involved in some sort of illegal trading. No one does legitimate business in the middle of the night at a secret harbor that you get to through a hidden passage with iffy men. Do you think that the baroness knows about it?" Clementine asked before braiding Ella's frazzled hair.

"Maybe. We don't know what she doing other than that she was there. But what is he selling? He was speaking of chains. Could it be exotic animals? I wonder if those servants got injured by them, and that is why they go missing."

Ella sat on the bed, mulling over the information.

There was a piece she was missing. She just didn't know what. And how was Arthur involved in this? Why was he interested in her? Was he there to keep her distracted from the odd things around the manor? Or was it something else? There had to be a connection.

"Either way, I still say something is off about Arthur. The baron and baroness are more understandable, but how does a stable boy know how to dance?"

Clementine was right. How did a stable boy know how to dance? And what about his odd reactions to her questions? And why was the baroness allowing a stable boy to teach her? Did she know something about him?

"I see you are in thinking mode. I'm going to head out. Make sure you get some sleep as well," Clementine said with a sigh and a wave of her hand.

Ella barely noticed Clementine turning down the lights and leaving the room. Her mind was so full of questions that sleep was out of the question.

"How is everyone connected?"

Motivations are key to learning why and what. Why are they doing what they are doing? What are they trying to accomplish? How they go about it is based on personality and what is needed for their goal. The more information you have, the more you can read your opponent.

Book with a fan on cover
Chapter 30

Chapter Forty-Two

The next few weeks were spent with Clementine keeping a careful watch on the hidden passage and Ella keeping watch on Baroness Smith and Arthur. During this time, she learned a few things.

One, Arthur was right, and only a few people knew of the secret passage. Clementine had only seen the baroness and two employees go through the passage. Both of those had been at the manor for six months. Some of the longest employed.

Two, the baron was rarely seen. According to Baroness Smith, the baron spent most of his days locked in his study. He was even more of an eccentric than his wife. He hadn't left his territory in over twenty years.

Three, Arthur had a connection to the missing servants. Every time that was brought up, he flinched. He also possessed an odd skillset. He knew proper manners, how to dance, and also about horses. Arthur was charming, and considering Ella's training, he did a very good job with gaining information, but he felt untrained, and after her dance classes, she had seen him watching the baron's study door.

Four, Baroness Smith didn't hide anything in her quarters. If she had suspicious things going on, she didn't hide it there. Though, every now and again, she did go into the baron's study.

The last thing learned was that the servants who were near the study door were the ones who tended to disappear.

That study held the key, but it would be difficult to get in there. Ella just had to find the opportune moment.

The opportunity came around sooner than she expected. Now that winter had hit in full force, the baroness had begun inviting other ladies to her house for tea. Ella was expected to join them in preparation for when she would have to do such on her own.

They settled in the tea room, a cozy space with a warm fireplace and a few ornate paintings similar to those plastered all over the manor. Seated at the table were the baroness and her three friends.

Refraining from itching her red wig—it was the one thing she still couldn't get used to—Ella sipped her tea and tried to listen to the conversation.

"I can't wait until the ball. It is always my favorite time of year." The one speaking was Lady Robinson, who was the resident busybody. It took all of her training to answer her questions about her family when they first met. And Ella still had to keep a watch on her when she threw out a question.

"It is the biggest event out this far. It's nice not having to drive all the way out to the city. Those carriages make me sick. I can't believe that anyone would make their way out to the city every year," Lady Pitt remarked in return. She liked to look down on other people. But she did it with all the poise of a lady who had been in society for many years. Even Luella would have trouble with her.

"That is because we don't need to get a match. The young ones need to see more men than the ones we have out here," Lady Manners replied. She was soft-spoken and a great mediator for the group.

"That's right. When are we going to see your husband? Is he going to be at the ball? He usually comes," Lady Robinson asked the baroness. Her short, thick fingers were delicately poised as she sipped her tea.

Ella's interest piqued at her questions.

The baroness offered a tight smile. "Of course. It would be bad if he never showed his face to the people."

Jumping into the conversation for the first time, Ella asked, "Is he really going to leave his study?"

"Yes, he should. I know he hasn't been out, but the baron is very busy." Baroness Smith eyed her over the rim of her cup, brow raised. It reminded Ella of her conversations with the head-mistress.

Ella tilted her head. "After all this time, I haven't seen him. I was hoping to meet him at least once before I head home."

"Well, my dear," Lady Manners said, a warm smile on her home-ly face, "he will be out preparing for the ball, and about a week before the ball, you can see him them. Though you won't be able to talk to him until the ball though since he will be busy."

"You mean when Lady Smith forces him to play host with her," Lady Pitt chimed in, with a comment as sharp as her features. "I can't understand why you have to force your husband out."

After calmly taking a swig of her tea, the baroness answered, "He has his reasons."

And that was the end of that conversation. Ella had hoped to glean more information, but the other conversations delved into more innocuous topics. Her thoughts tumbled around as plans settled into place. The ball was the best chance she would have of checking out the baron's office since Baroness Smith would force him to play host.

Over the next few weeks, Baroness Smith pushed Ella hard in dance class. Due to wanting her to be ready for the upcoming ball, they had two dance classes a day. That meant seeing Arthur more often.

When he was walking her back to her room, Ella commented, "I don't know if I will ever get used to the weather here. It feels colder. Maybe it's because there are so few buildings here to block the wind."

"My sister always hated winter, but she always reminded herself that it was just what needed to happen before spring could come."

"Sister? I didn't know you had a sister."

At that question, Arthur stopped walking. Sadness and anger warred over his features until he finally managed to take a breath and plaster on a smile. It didn't quite meet his eyes.

"Did something happen to her?" Maybe this was the reason for his odd avoidance of questions.

Arthur struggled with his expression. "No, she is just somewhere far away. I hope that you stay warm this winter, my lady. If you would please excuse me, I forgot some work I had to do."

He fled.

Every time she met him after that, he avoided her questions. Though he couldn't necessarily avoid her due to him being her dance partner, he did pull back.

Ella spent the next few weeks checking the hidden passageways for any other nighttime meetings in the secret cove, but all she ended up with was frozen fingers. Nothing happened, which only made her more eager for the ball.

I have found tunnels under the manor. It will be through those that I will be passing my reports from now on.

Encoded message to Madame Briar
Sent from North Sea Manor

Chapter Forty-Three

T he week before the ball was a flurry of activity. It was then that Ella caught glimpses of the baron. His tubby frame from his long hours spent behind a desk was now being dressed in various pieces of clothing, foisted upon him by the baroness. Ella had already gone through such ministrations before arriving, and her dress had already been made. It wouldn't have been wise to have a tailor measure her and find out she was wearing a wig.

Ella spent her days avoiding the servants who were hurrying to get things ready and trying to avoid bumping into them. One such time, she was backed into a side hallway and was startled by a person at the end. What she had first thought was another person was actually her reflection in a mirror that had been hanging there.

Walking forward, Ella placed her hand on the mirror. Now that she was older and some of her gangly features had filled out, with the red hair, she looked like her mother. Not up close, but from a distance. Ella had always thought she didn't look anything like her mother. But now, standing here, she could see what Madame Briar had seen.

This was where she was supposed to be, and her mother would have been proud. She would soon enact her plan to go into the study and would discover the secrets behind the manor.

She was startled out of her thoughts a deep voice whispered beside her. Something that hasn't happened since had some training from the Fan Society.

"You frightened me, dear girl. I could have sworn Lady Nora was coming to haunt me. I forgot my wife said her relative was here."

Ella froze in shock at the baron's words. The joy she had been feeling fizzled out. And fear replaced it. Did he recognize her as Lady Nora's daughter? He couldn't have. The baron hadn't left the territory for years. Then how did know what her mother looked like?

"Who's Lady Nora?" The question spilled from her lips before she could catch it and shove it back in.

He looked at her with a brow raised, but Ella held her features as a curious young girl empty-headed and dull.

"She is no one of importance. Now, I don't want to get roped into the party, so can we keep this a secret between us? Whatever you do, don't tell my wife I was here. Good girl."

Ella watched as he disappeared around the corner, and as he did, she couldn't help but notice the sand on his boots and the smell of salt that dissipated when he left.

The breath she had been holding released after he was well out of earshot. Thankfully, her cover held. He must have disregarded the resemblance to her mother as a passing thought. More mysteries than ever surrounded the manor, and the want to get into the study became a need.

Ella had to keep herself from running to the study. She had to stick to her plan.

The ball would be tomorrow night, many guests would be here, and the baron would be out of his study. That would be when Ella would find out the dark underside of this manor.

The next evening the ball started at 9 p.m., and people had already begun to trickle in. This was a private ball, but it was the biggest event for this area. And since Ella was not a hostess, there would not be much needed from her, but for one of the hosts, namely the baron, there would be plenty of distractions. Though Ella was eager to enter the study now, she knew that she would be missed if she left. The baron and baroness had Ella follow them while they did their introductions. Ella itched to leave, and it looked as if the baron did as well.

Since his comment a few days previously, Ella had watched him like a hawk. He didn't look dangerous, but considering her innocent-looking stepsister was willing to throw herself down the stairs to place the blame on Ella, she knew that looks weren't everything.

It had now been an hour since the festivities had started, and eager to leave, Ella knew there was one last thing she needed to do: She needed to dance.

Ella eyed the servants on the fringes of the dance floor, ready to assist in any way. Catching the eye of Clementine, Ella tapped her nose with her fan, letting her know that the plan to escape the ball was ready to be set into motion. As the song that was playing came to an end, Ella made her way toward a gentleman who had signed her dance card.

He was a grandson of Lady Manners named Ralph. He had just entered into society and was close in age to Ella. He was just as affable as Lady Manners and had a calming presence. Baroness Smith had introduced her to him and asked if he would be willing to dance with her. He had accepted.

When he saw Ella approaching him, he smiled and asked, "May I have this dance?"

Giving him a small bow of her head, she returned the gesture. "I would be honored."

Ralph led her to the dance floor, and they joined a group nearby and stood in a square. As she waited for her turn to start, she saw Arthur sneaking around the edges of the dance floor. Ella wondered why the stable boy would be here, but it was too late to do anything about it. The upbeat song had started playing, all of the dance lessons she took fell into place.

Ella followed the complicated steps of the song, weaving in and out of the other dancers. It was much easier when she was in the moment. Sweat dribbled down her neck as the final note was played.

Being ever the proper gentleman, Ralph led her to the side of the dance floor. Ella fiddled with her bracelet, releasing the catch and causing it to drop to the floor. Then she stepped on it, making herself fall.

Ralph caught her. "Are you alright?" he said, concern in his voice.

"Yes, I think so," Ella replied hesitantly, making her voice shake. Then, taking a step, she winced and pretended to stumble.

"You must have injured yourself. Let me help you move to the edge. We wouldn't want you more injured. What did you trip on?"

Clementine came rushing up and bowed. "My lady, are you alright?"

"I seemed to have tripped on something and lost my balance. I don't believe that I will be able to dance."

Ralph bent down upon catching sight of Ella's bracelet. Picking it up, he handed it to her, "I think I've found the culprit."

"My bracelet! Thank you for returning it to me," Ella beamed.

He held out his arm. "Can you move?"

Ella smiled; he really was a kind person. "Thank you for your help, but I don't want to interrupt your festivities. My maid can take me to my rooms, but would you be ever so kind as to let Baroness Smith know what happened? I would be very grateful."

"As you wish, my lady." He bowed and headed toward the baroness.

Leaning on Clementine, Ella continued her performance of having an injured foot. She continued to limp until they were out of the dance hall and down to the private quarters. The escape plan worked wonderfully since Ralph would verify her injury, and no one would be looking for her since her maid was taking care of her.

"Did you see Arthur?" Ella asked when they were out of sight.

"No. But things were busy, so I could have missed him. But why would he be at the party?" Clementine retorted as they headed toward the baron's study.

"That is a good question." Ella could have been mistaken, but she had to trust her instincts. Arthur had been there. But why? She was missing something.

Those questions had to be placed on hold. Heading to the study, Ella slipped out her lockpicks from her hair that had been hidden among the feathers that had been placed there.

Clementine kept watch while Ella tried to pick the lock, but it wasn't needed. The door was already unlocked. Ella tapped her on her shoulder and signaled a warning. Clementine moved Ella aside. It would be easier to explain why a maid was here than why Ella was.

And then Clementine opened the door.

There will be times when you get caught in the act of espionage. Be aware of who is finding you. They could also have been caught in the act, and you both were there for the same reason. The best way is to bluff or to catch the intruder in their own bluff.

Book with fan on cover
Chapter 35

Chapter Forty-Four

E lla peeked into the darkened room as Clementine opened the door. There, hovering over the baron's desk, was Arthur. Taking the lead and shielding Ella from view, Clementine asked, "What are you doing here?"

Dropping the papers that were in his hands and nearly knocking over a lamp, he fumbled for an answer, "I was just checking to see if there were any new horses that were coming in."

Poor excuse, Arthur, Ella thought. She prodded Clementine, letting her know to push.

"Why didn't you ask the stable master then?" Clementine continued her questioning. "You aren't even supposed to be in the main house unless specifically asked. I should call the baron to see if this is true."

Clementine had pushed a little too far. Arthur was too smart for that. He turned the questions on Clementine, "Are you not Lady Eden's personal maid? What are you doing in here?"

Clementine was too calm and collected to react the way he was expecting. Instead, she turned around. "There is—"

Her words were cut off when Arthur came from behind, pulling her into the room. "Shh, all right? No, I'm not supposed to be here. But you should be happy that I am."

"What do you mean?" Clementine demanded.

This was what Ella was looking for. Arthurs's motivation for his suspicious activities.

Sighing, Arthur shuffled around, agitated. "Have you not noticed the servants who go missing? Have you never questioned where they go? Why they are constantly disappearing?"

"Then why don't you leave?" Clementine retorted. "If you are so scared, why haven't you left?"

"Because he's trying to find his sister." Ella came into the room then. The piece of information that had been nagging at her finally clicked into place. His odd reactions to Ella joking about missing servants, and also to him gathering information started to make sense. "Your sister isn't away. She went missing."

When she entered the room Arthur had frozen in surprise but was now hanging his head. "Yes. Just let me search his study, and then I will be on my way. Please don't say anything."

"Only if you answer my questions." Even though Ella figured out that he was trying to find his sister, some things still didn't add up. "Why did you act as if you liked me?"

"I do like you," he quickly piped up, but with a look from Ella, he glanced sheepishly at the floor. "Because I figured that if I got close to you, you might let some things slip. I hadn't really been getting anywhere with the baron and baroness."

"How do you know how to dance and read?"

Arthur sighed. He looked at Ella's determined expression in the lamplight and hesitated.

"I'm waiting," Ella said, impatiently tapping her foot.

Opening his mouth, words tumbled out, "I come from a fallen noble house, alright? And since my family earned their nobility, they still had some practicality that made it easier to survive after we lost the lands."

Ahh, and there was her answer. He had an odd sense of street smarts, yet had the proper manners of a nobleman.

"Why are you here?" Arthur asked.

"I should be asking you that question, but since you answered my question, I will reply in kind." This question Ella had been expecting. Answering easily, she said, "I am the second once removed cousin of Baroness Smith, and my mother sent me here because she has no idea how to function in society. So, she decided to send me here to the only person she knows who can teach me. It was actually the best decision she has ever made."

Confusion was still on his face as he asked another question, "Why are you here, in this room?"

Ella laughed, "Because things are odd, and I want to find out what's going on. And a study is a lot less creepy than being in an underground tunnel."

"Are you going to tell the baron?" His shoulders were tense, but he had managed to put on his charming smile.

"No, as long as I join you." It was an easy way to keep an eye on him, as well as look for some clues.

The tension eased away from his shoulders, and he started acting as he did during dance classes. "A lady such as yourself shouldn't be doing such things."

Raising a brow as she had seen Madame Briar do often, Ella replied, "Then you shouldn't have asked me to go down a dark underground tunnel. I learned a lot about making bad decisions from my mother. And you do realize we are not supposed to be here, right? We should be quiet."

An easy grin rose on his face. "As you wish, my lady."

Now that that was settled, Ella started to search the room. When Arthur started to as well, Ella signaled for Clementine to keep an eye on him. Clementine acknowledged this with a nod.

As they scoured the area, Ella felt like this room was odd. For a room that the baron spent so much time in, it seemed like no one came in. There was even some dust on pieces of furniture. It didn't even look like the bookshelves were used at all. They were only ornamental books. There weren't even that many papers. The few that were on the desk didn't have anything important on them and appeared to only be there for show.

"There's nothing here," Arthur growled, slamming his fists on the wall. They had been looking for a while, and it seemed he was right. But he couldn't be. Ella had watched the baron come into this room, for hours on end, not leaving. There must be something here.

In the shadows of the lamplight, Ella saw it. The panel that Arthur had hit had shifted. Ella might not have seen it except the lamp cast an uneven shadow, revealing it.

"Check that panel," Ella said, pointing behind Arthur.

He furrowed his brows, but then widened his eyes in realization. Hurriedly, he turned around and pushed on the panel, causing it to shift open.

"Seems we found something." Ella grinned.

"Indeed, we did." He headed forward, then turned back to look at Ella. "You should stay here with your maid. It could be dangerous."

Holding back a snort, she replied, "Did you not hear me when I said I tend to make trouble? Besides, I'm the one who found the hidden passageway."

Though his smiled his usual charming smile, he still hesitated to allow her through.

Sighing, Ella pushed him aside. "It's not like you didn't put me in a dangerous situation before. And you aren't going to leave me down here by myself, are you?"

Instant guilt filled his face, and he stepped aside. Ella walked through, with Clementine following closely behind. Ella stepped down the path that turned to cut stone walls that smelled of the sea.

During the time spent as observers, you can find horrifying things. Mistakes can be made and end with destruction. As a member of the Fan Society, your job is to protect as many people as possible. Since it is hard to maintain discipline in a disastrous situation, here are ways to help maintain your composure. The first thing you can do is take a deep breath . . .

Book with a fan on cover
Chapter 37

Chapter Forty-Five

The path sloped down and then took a turn. It was wide enough that two people could walk side by side. As they made their way through the tunnels, it was difficult for Ella to know where they were without any landmark to guide her; she only knew that with salty air, it would end at the sea.

When the floor leveled out, they had reached a door; it was then that Arthur stopped her.

"I may have put you in danger in the past, but let me make up for it and go through first."

Ella nodded and watched. The door was thick enough that with the moisture in the air it hadn't warped much, though the metal was showing signs of rust. The only metal that didn't have rust was the lock that shined in the lamplight. Arthur pulled out a hairpin and started to pick the lock.

"Where did you learn that skill?" Ella whispered.

"I didn't. I was just hoping it would work," Arthur said as he continued his futile attempts.

Ella had to keep from pushing him out of the way and picking the lock herself. But a lady wouldn't know how to pick a lock, and she had no desire to show him that particular skill. Still, time was moving ahead without them, and they needed in.

Watching him try to pick the lock, and failing miserably, Ella noticed that though the lock itself was new, the metal that it was attached to was not. Thinking fast, she asked, "Why don't you try just breaking it? The metal is rusted. I'm sure a strong groomsman like you would be able to break it."

Arthur turned to look at her, his lips slowly spreading into a sly grin. "Well, my lady, I do believe you are right. But please stand back. I wouldn't want to kick you."

Complying, Ella and Clementine backed away. Arthur rolled his shoulders and lifted his leg so he knew where to kick. His flirtatious smile didn't sway her; she knew that he was nervous. His smile still didn't reach his eyes, and his hands were shaky. Taking a deep breath, he kicked the door.

It didn't budge. Holding her breath to keep from laughing, Ella watched his chagrin expression as he did it again. It took three hits to get it open.

With the clank of metal and thunk of wood, the entire piece of metal clattered to the floor, lock and all. He cleared his throat and turned to speak to Ella, "I would say after you, but I would rather you not be put into a dangerous situation, since we don't know what is on the other side of the door."

Ella nodded; it would be better to allow him through first, though she could tell he was just eager to find his sister.

The room they entered was smaller than the baron's study, and it was filled with books and papers, all of whose pages were warped by the dampness that came from the sea. On the opposite wall was a heavy metal door, its age scored on its surface by the accumulated rust. Beside the door was a key on a ring next to it.

Ignoring the door for now, Ella headed to the shelves while Clementine watched the door to make sure that no one would sneak up on them. Grabbing a book at random, Ella flipped through the pages. There were names and dates with amounts of money listed on each page. It was difficult to tell what they were exchanging, only that money was changing hands. She put the book back, then grabbed another one. It had information along the same lines as the previous one. She was about to close it when a name jumped out at her.

Nora Cooper.

Even the noise of the key turning in the metal door and it clanking open behind her didn't stop Ella as she looked through everything that could give her information.

Haste at the need for more information, and annoyance at Arthurs's impatience, pushed her to skim through the book faster. The only thing that she could glean was that the exchange happened in 1819 in the spring with Viscount Edmund. The very time that her mother went missing. The odd comment about her mother by the baron made sense.

He knew what had happened to her mother.

Once the door opened, cries of help came from behind Ella that she couldn't ignore. Understanding at what the baron had been doing came to her, along with a sickly feeling. She needed to go and help, but Ella hesitated, holding the book. She wanted to take it with her, but for now, it would be safer here. She would just have to make sure that it was in her possession when she left.

Ella signaled to Clementine to continue keeping watch while she went to check out the noise and what horror she might find behind the rusted door. Most of the sobs and pleading shouts had been blocked out by the thick stone and heavy door, but as she entered the room, she could see the atrocity of what lay beyond its threshold.

Lining the room were cages with people inside. Most were weak as they reached through the bars crying for them to help. They all were dressed as servants. A familiar face watched from behind the bars. The server from her first dinner.

"The missing servants," Ella gasped. Disgust filled her at the thought of what had been going on, but she needed to get these people out of here. Since the door was broken, the next time the baron was down here, he would know others had infiltrated the cells. And if he knew that, the evidence of his crimes would disappear, as well as his prisoners.

Ella's eyes fell on Arthur, who was crouched next to a cage holding a young woman. Though it was difficult to tell with her tear-streaked face. Arthur was clasping her hand as he called her name, "Theresa. Open your eyes. Talk to me."

The desire to let him reconnect with his sister and the urgency of the situation warred with Ella. Most of these people were too weak to stand, let alone walk. She would need his help.

Ella knelt down next to Arthur. Shaking his shoulder, she said, "We need to get these people out of here."

"My sister. Yes, we need to get her out," Arthurs said as he stood on shaky legs. No longer did he have his charming smile. The vacant gaze showed that he was in shock. He was not going to be able to help.

"Clementine," Ella called.

A look of horror overcame Clementine's face when she walked in the room. She breathed deeply until she regained control of herself. "What do you need me to do?"

"We need to get these people out of here. I think for now the best place would be the stables. I think that William should be able to help."

"How are we going to get all the people out of here without anyone finding them? Though spring has come, it's still freezing outside. I don't know if they can make it outside."

"You can go below."

These words came from the server who had mistakenly dumped a berry off her plate. No longer did he have his nervousness that he had when she first met him. Instead, he looked like a withered old man, hunched over without a care of the world around him.

Ella moved closer to him above the cries of the other captives. "What do you mean?"

His dark hair had gone limp with the salty air, caked to his face. His once crisp uniform was now covered in sand and encrusted with salt. Lips cracked, he said while pointing, "There is a tunnel that runs below us."

Ella's eyes followed his hand and saw a hatch in the floor. It had been hard to see in the dark room, and she had missed it in the horror that she had encountered. The hatch was big enough that a fully grown man could easily fit in. Luckily, this wasn't locked.

Hefting it up, Ella looked down into the depths. With the faint light, she could see the slimy algae covering the bottom.

"Alright, this will be our exit." Ella looked behind her and already, Clementine was using the key she had taken from Arthur's limp fingers to unlock the cells. Ella turned to Arthur, who was holding his sister in his arms. She touched his shoulder to get his attention, "Arthur, you need to get her out of here before people find out. You need to help Theresa."

It was when she said his sister's name that he looked up and started moving.

Tides can be dangerous. If you aren't paying attention, they can be higher than you realize. People have
gotten caught in high tide, and the path that they had
taken was then under the water.

Tides and Other Dangers of the
Sea
Chapter 3

Chapter Forty-Six

It was difficult getting everyone down the hole. The servants had little energy, and it was difficult to help them down. And what she didn't see from above was that water was slowly filling the corridor. Thankfully, it did slope gently upwards, leading everyone out of the water, but the initial shock was sometimes too much for them. The water was freezing, and though Ella and Clementine were strong, lifting people several times, their size heavy with water and no energy was difficult for them.

Arthur wasn't much help at the beginning. Though his shock had begun to wear off, he wouldn't help the others until his sister was safe.

But Ella couldn't worry about that now. The most important thing was getting these people out. She didn't know how much longer they had until they were found. Judging by how much time the baron spent locked in his office, it wouldn't be long.

It had been slow, grueling work, and by the time the last few people needed to be helped down, Clementine was having difficulties. She slipped and was about to fall into the freezing water when a pair of hands caught her.

Arthur had returned. He called up to Ella. "The path leads to the stables. Your groom, William, is helping them get warm. I believe we can trust him. He really doesn't have anything on his mind other than horses. I don't think he will betray us."

His charming smile was back on his face, though his expression still twinged with worry. The water had risen higher, and Ella's worries had risen with the tide. Having him here helped. And Clementine, whose lips had turned blue by the time he arrived, could help lead the weaker ones out.

"I concur. Clementine, lead the others to safety while I help the ones up here down. Use the stable blankets to keep get them warm and keep the baron and baroness away from them."

Clementine shot Ella a worried look but couldn't say much from the chattering of her teeth. Giving her shoulder to the young maid who had been helped down, she headed up the incline.

"Thank you, Arthur."

He smiled and offered her a bow of his head. "Of course, my lady. Now, who is next?"

After the last person had been helped down, Arthur held his hands up to her.

Ella waved him away. "The water is too deep for a lady like me. I will be going another way. Head back and get warm."

"My lady?" His concern was evident from his next words. "I have already put you in some serious danger. And for now, it has turned out alright, but I cannot leave you here where you are going to be in danger."

This was not what was planned; she had wanted time to look through the baron's files to see if there was anything else she missed about her mother, and who knew if she would have another chance?

"Arthur, have I not said that you couldn't order me around? Besides, that water is freezing; it would do no good for a lady to be in ice-cold water. All I need to do is head back out the entrance and no one will be the wiser. I am a guest here."

He hesitated.

"Now, before you freeze. I will not have someone freeze to death because of pointless chivalry. Go."

Arthur looked back at her one last time to see if she would change her mind, and when she didn't, he headed back up the corridor.

Relief surged through her as Ella headed back to the study. Even as she was helping everyone get out, the book was in the back of her mind weighing on her. It was the first hint about her mother in years, and she wouldn't let it go.

Easily finding the book she had left behind, she pulled it free of the shelf and hunted through its pages. Now knowing that the baron was into slave trading, Ella used that information to decipher what the book was talking about. The only thing that she could glean was that her mother had been sold to the baron by the viscount, meaning he was fully involved in her disappearance.

As Ella was helping the others down the hatch, she remembered where she had heard that name before. That name was the one that Eleanor had used to fake a marriage with Lady Hill. A man who was involved in shady business.

Ella now had a name, and it was more than she had had before. The book didn't say where she was sold, but Viscount Edmund may know.

Footsteps echoed down the corridor, stopping her yet again from the information. This was not the place for her to be found. If she had been in the office, Ella could have bluffed, but here in his secret room with all of his documents, Ella would be killed or become the replacement product. She had to hide, but the only place she could find would be the hatch.

Did she dare risk destroying the book in the water, or should she leave it behind and hope she could retrieve it later?

Ella took the middle ground. She would hide the book. Striding to the prison, Ella tucked the book into one of the cells in the back, hiding it under the moldy straw that had been placed on the stone.

The voices appeared with the footsteps as they saw the broken door. They moved faster toward her, and Ella barely had time to make it to the hatch and jump.

Water in the ocean is much colder than one expects. The weather can be warm, but depending on the time of year, the water can still be freezing. Unexpected drowning can occur from the shock of cold water. Do not get caught in it.

Tides and Other Dangers of the
Sea
Chapter 4

Chapter Forty-Seven

B lackness overcame Ella as she landed in the frigid water. Her skirts pulled her down, and the motion of the water and the depth made it difficult to stand. She was able to grasp a breath as the tide shifted right before it pulled her back under again. It was difficult for her to breathe as the cold ripped through her. Already, she was losing feeling in her fingers and face. As the tide pulled back, Ella slammed into the edge of the stone wall, knocking the wind out of her and causing her to choke as she inhaled water.

The hit actually did her good, as it cleared away some of her shock and her thoughts started to move sluggishly. She could hear the shouts come louder above her before she slipped back under the water. This time, when the water shoved her forward, she kicked against the wall, pushing her farther up the incline. Her feet scraped the bottom as she hauled herself further up the corridor.

And none too soon. Two men peered down at her from above and reached down the hole to grab her. Ella fell forward, avoiding the men as she splashed through the water, her numb feet making it difficult to walk.

Ella could hear the baron shouting at the men to go get her, and a splash came from behind her. She would only have a few seconds before the shock wore off and they would come after her.

Hitching up her sodden skirts, she made her way forward until she was out of the water. Ella lurched up the incline as fast as her numb legs could carry her as the splashing grew louder. She had hoped it would take him longer to deal with the shock, but she couldn't mind that now. Flexing her fingers, Ella tried to warm them up, but they still felt numb. The soaked gloves didn't help matters.

Ella fumbled for one of her hidden weapons but between running for her life, being frozen to the bone, and her heavy, wet skirts, it was difficult to grab the dagger that had been strapped there.

The darkness was the one thing that played to her advantage, but as she went further up, the lamps lit the walls staining the stone with soot. Clementine must have lit them to help lead the prisoners out.

If Ella could only get out, Clementine could help her. The only problem was she didn't know what or who was by the entrance.

The footsteps closed in on her just as she managed to grab the handle. Turning her head, Ella could see a massive hand reach for her. A flash of fear ran through her as she ducked, but it turned into a fall as her body refused to move the way she wanted it to. Her numb fingers released the dagger that she had managed to grab, and it skittered across the floor away from her. The drenched man cursed under his breath as he missed.

"Come here, missy. Don't make this harder on yourself. A dame like you shouldn't be in these halls."

As if Ella would listen to the man who was reaching for his own knife at his belt. Pain was shooting through Ella as the adrenaline started to warm her. It felt as if she was being stabbed over and over by thousands of needles. But if she didn't get moving, she would be stabbed and be very dead or captured if she didn't get her weapon or an upper hand soon.

Forcing out a shuttering breath from her chattering teeth, Ella smacked away the cobwebs in her head as she used her fear to propel herself into action. She rolled towards her dagger just as the man lunged for her. He missed, grabbing her sash and pulling it free. Ella pounced on the dagger and stood, facing him.

"Come now. See here? That knife is too dangerous for a little thing like you to hold. Just come closer and I'll make sure I take you nicely to the boss," the man said, tossing aside her sash. The man was one of the few servants who had been at the manor the longest. Now Ella knew why.

Ella didn't reply. It was obvious that he thought her a lady who spent her days chatting about tea. But Ella was a member of the Fan Society, and this was where her strength lies. If only her body would cooperate. Her mind worked franticly as she tried to figure out a way out of this.

The man had managed to pull his own knife free and lunged at her again, slashing at her. Ella parried the blow, skidding to the side. The shock of the parry rang through her hand, causing her still-numb fingers to drop the knife.

Laughing, the man called to her again, "I told you ladies shouldn't hold a knife. That is what us men are for. And I would rather not damage you too much."

Anger and determination filled her as the blade gleamed in the flickering light. Ella hunted for something to help her; she would not end here. Her gloves were out of the question, as it would be too difficult to pull them off wet. Any of her other weapons would take too long for her to pull out. Her bracelet had disappeared sometime during her escape, as well as most of her hairpins. Ella's eyes landed on her sash that had been tossed to the ground. Diving for it, Ella avoided the man's slash as she grabbed the fallen fabric.

"What are you going to do with a scrap of fabric? Sew?" The man laughed again.

Ella furrowed her brow. What did that man know of the things ladies of society had to do? It was hard work. Everything they had to remember and the dexterity needed to sew and dance. But Ella clamped down on those emotions. It was time to focus.

Wrapping the end of the sash around both hands, Ella watched for the man to make his move. He eased his way towards her, a lazy smile on his face. When he reached for her arm, it was then that she attacked.

When his knife came forward, Ella stepped to the side and wrapped the sash around his wrist. Then, twisting his hand backward, she bent his arm behind his back. With a pull, she forced the man to bend forward, bringing him in the perfect position for her to smash him in the face. Releasing her anger, she bashed him with her knee until the hand holding the knife relaxed and fell to the ground.

Ella dropped the man to the ground with a thud. Kicking the knife away, she knelt down and pulled the man's other hand behind him, using her sash to tie him. Should he wake up, she wouldn't want him chasing after her.

When Ella stood, she nearly collapsed back to the ground. All of the things that fear and adrenaline had been hiding came back in full force. Wobbling, she headed towards the light as the world blurred around her. Up ahead, the sound of stomping hooves and the whinny of horses greeted her. Voices blurred together as they made their way toward Ella.

Ella could only stand in a stupor as a shadowed figure approached her.

A familiar voice said, "This wasn't supposed to happen this way."

With the information revealed this year, I found that it only motivated me to find my mother more. And I will find her. I will not let go of this piece of information until my mother has come back.

Journal of Arabella Cooper
Year 1830

Chapter Forty-Eight

Ella felt as if she had been used as a training bag for class and it had gotten way out of hand. It took her a few seconds to even want to test out how badly she had been injured. Keeping her eyes closed from what she assumed would be an onslaught of pain from her abuse, she was surprised when, instead of protesting muscles, she just felt tired.

With heavy limbs, Ella let out a groan as she opened her bleary eyes, revealing the oddly furnished room she had been staying in. Blinking away her tiredness, she nearly jumped out of her skin as she realized she was not alone.

Lady Pitt, Lady Manners, and Lady Robinson were looking down at her.

"Oh, look, you startled the girl." Lady Robinson said to Lady Pitt, who had been hovering very close to Ella's face.

"Are you sure it wasn't just you she was startled by?" Lady Pitt retorted.

"Well, I'll be—"

Calling out in a calming manner, Lady Manners said, "Ladies, the patient had just woken up. Can you please not make things worse for her?"

Confused by the situation, Ella merely laid there in stunned silence as they spoke above her. She had no idea why the ladies she had talked to during winter at tea time were here. Her mind struggle to catch up to the quick conversations as she tried to sit up, and Lady Manners helped her into a sitting position.

At the mention of her name, her brain started to function again, and Ella asked, "What happened?"

"You have been sick for a while with pneumonia. It has been difficult taking care of all your wet clothes. I'm sorry to say that your wig is ruined," Lady Pitt said.

Panicking, she raised her hands to her head, feeling her unruly curls instead of the wiry hair of her wig.

"Now look at what you have done," Lady Robinson interjected. "You startled her. Don't worry, dear, we are on your side."

She lifted a hand, and Ella noticed a ring that was on her finger that she had never worn before. A gold ring, just like the ones on all the portraits in the Hall of Legacies. The same one her mother wore. The same one the headmistress wore. It was a gold ring with the Fan Society symbol on it.

These ladies were part of the Fan Society.

Baroness Smith opened the door. Nodding to the ladies, she made her way toward Ella. The others in the room walked out, leaving Ella and the baroness alone.

Baroness Smith sat on the chair that Lady Manners had vacated, putting her close to Ella. Looking at her finger, Ella saw that she also had on the membership ring on her finger. If she hadn't been feeling so poorly, she would have felt more ashamed that she didn't notice right away.

"I would like to apologize."

Ella looked up at the baroness's words, meeting her gaze. "What?"

"After learning more things, it was getting dangerous to keep you here, and the headmistress ordered me to keep you safe and I failed. I apologize."

The oddities that surrounded the baroness started to make sense. Ella spoke out loud as her mind put the pieces together. "There is a reason this was called an internship. I was under your tutelage while you were also judging me to see how I did. And since my mission was to watch you, you could keep an eye on me and keep me out of danger should I get caught. As well as train me in the things I need to know when I get my own mission. You are a Guardian. You were sent here to keep an eye on the baron."

Baroness Smith bowed her head in acknowledgment. "That is correct. We knew that something was wrong with the baron, and I was sent here to become his wife to discover it and keep it under control. Though I managed to marry him, it had been rather difficult to get any information. That man was paranoid about everything."

Another thought occurred to Ella. "You haven't been having any luck with getting a Ghost in here. Since the baron is paranoid and the servants are constantly changing, you were having a hard time getting information."

"You are as clever as the headmistress says, though you still have a blind spot in some areas such as your extreme focus. It is wonderful to have focus, but you need to still be aware of everything else," the baroness said, eyeing her.

Ella blushed and fiddled with the sheets. The baroness's gaze reminded her too much of the headmistress's.

The baroness's admonishing look changed to a smile as she continued, "But yes, it had been rather difficult. I needed something to change in the household, and you needed to do your finals in an out-of-the-way place that was safe. It was a perfect situation."

"Until I got too deep."

The baroness nodded. "You were supposed to be observing me, as per your mission, but you went above and beyond what was asked. You got involved with Arthur. But I didn't know much about Arthur and had only just received information on him not that long ago."

It made sense Arthur had arrived not long before her and because she was a baroness, she couldn't really interrogate him without seeming suspicious or alerting the paranoid baron. "That must have been why you pushed the two of us together."

"Yes," she said. "I had hoped that you could figure out what he wanted. It would have been less suspicious if you became closer to him. And he truly did know how to dance, and you are doing so much better, dear."

That cleared up some of the oddities surrounding the baroness allowing a stable boy to teach her how to dance. But another question came to Ella.

"What about the prisoners?"

The baroness smiled. "They will be returned to their families after they are treated. Some money, as well as gratitude, will keep them from talking. But the baron did manage to escape during your tussle."

"What?" Anger flashed through Ella. That man knew more than what those books had told her. He knew what had happened to her mother. And now he had escaped. How could she have let him go? Could she catch him?

She seethed, "How did that happen?"

The baroness replied, "He has been using that party every year to sell people. He had left the party to start the sale when he found that they had all escaped. After realizing that he wasn't getting them back, he bargained for passage on the pirate ship he sells to and escaped."

Ella could see her hand clenching. The baroness was just as angry as Ella was, if not more so since it was on her watch. Releasing the fire, Ella felt deflated. Bone-weary, and still feeling chilled, Ella couldn't help but pity herself for the loss of information.

"We will be looking over all of his records to see if we can find any information. After finding out that I had nothing to do with the baron's black dealing, Arthur came forward. Because of his guilt for pushing you into the tunnels which put you in danger, he offered his help and has become a Ghost for the society. And the boy had been very helpful. After all, he has the desire to help rid England of any slave traders. He has the talent to be a wonderful Ghost. Just as you have the talent to be one of the best Guardians."

The baroness's words touched Ella and rekindled a measure of hope within her. Ella had found one piece of information, and with the power of the society, she would find her answers. Nothing would stop her from finding her mother.

Chapter Forty-Nine

After sufficiently recuperating, Ella was sent back to the academy. She was already seated in the headmistress's secret office waiting for her to arrive.

Staring at the wall with the Fan Society emblem, happiness filled Ella at finally being able to bring back information on her mother. The simple stone room had become familiar to her after taking so many lessons in here with Madame Blair. It was within these walls that she found out about her heritage. It was in this room that Ella had made her choice to follow in her mother's footsteps. Her musings were interpreted by the door opening.

"I do apologize for making you wait. There was some trouble with some of the first years," Madame Briar said as she entered the room and sat in her chair.

"It is alright. I still don't know how you manage being the headmistress of the most prestigious school of England as well as running a secret society." Ella smiled at her teacher.

With a warm chuckle, Madame Briar answered, "With many years of practice. Now, we are here to discuss the results of your final grade. Baroness Smith gave you glowing praise. Though, she did mention that you tend to fixate on one thing and thus at times miss other things. This is a tendency that happens frightfully often around you. If you don't fix that soon, it will cause problems for those around you. You will also miss things that would have been obvious had you been paying attention."

Flushing at the deserved admonishment, Ella bowed her head.

Madame Briar smiled, releasing Ella from her embarrassment, and said, "It happens. But you must be congratulated on your work at stopping the baron. Well done."

At the mention of the baron, the question that she had been holding back bubbled forth, "What about the information about my mother?"

At that, Madame Briar sighed. "We still need to look through all the books. We won't know much until we scan through every book. But for now, you need to rest and recuperate so that way you will be ready for the debut ball."

Deflated at the answer but unsurprised, Ella nodded. Thinking that this was the end of the conversation, Ella readied herself to go when Madame Briar spoke one last time.

"You will be getting your mission so you can be put in place as a Guardian. Do not lose yourself when the time comes. It could be dangerous for all those around you, and innocents can lose their lives."

Madame Briar gave her a look of one lost in memories, but Ella didn't comment on it. Instead, she bowed and left the room.

Her mission would be starting soon. After these four years, she had learned so many things. Now would be the chance for her to show her newly learned skills and, should all prove well, her chance to find out about her mother. And if she did, she could prove to all the others that her feeling that her mother had been alive would have been right. After no information for so long, it felt as if something big was going to happen.

She only hoped that in the end, things would turn out in her favor.

Dasha Tryon Wallace is a mother of a very active son, and newborn daughter. With her husband, they live in the middle of nowhere with their dog in a small town. She loves practicing martial arts, which may have had an influence in the fighting style in the book.

Dasha is an avid reader and librarians have had a hard time keeping her well-stocked with new material. Her friends at school always wondered why she was reading more than one book at a time and how she could tell where she was at in each book.

With so many interests, she is more than capable of engaging in conversation with everyone, much to the dismay of her untalkative husband. This is the compellation of a series of novellas that she has written, and she has plans for many more. You can find out more about her and her upcoming books at www.dashawallace.com.

www.ingramcontent.com/pod-product-compliance
Lightning Source LLC
Chambersburg PA
CBHW051951240626
47153CB00005B/1715